Once he seduces you, there's no turning back…

D0032174

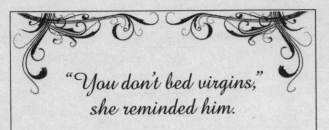

"You don't bed virgins," she reminded him.

"I've decided to make an exception. God help me. I've not been able to stop thinking about you." Then his mouth came down on hers again, hard and demanding, as though he were intent on devouring every inch of her.

Fool that she was, she gloried in being wanted. It didn't matter that everything he yearned for, all that he knew of her, was the surface, her body and limbs. At long last, a man wanted to take her to his bed. Desired her. Was mad to possess her.

It wasn't complete or perfect, deep or binding. But it was all heat and fire, urgency and need. She'd take it.

She wanted to wrap her arms around him, but he still held them in place, maintaining control, taking without quarter. When next he broke off the kiss, he was breathing as harshly as she.

"Remove the mask. Reveal yourself," he commanded.

LORRAINE HEATH

FALLING INTO BED WITH A DUKE

AVONBOOKS

An Imprint of HarperCollinsPublishers

This is a work of fiction. Names, characters, places, and incidents are products of the author's imagination or are used fictitiously and are not to be construed as real. Any resemblance to actual events, locales, organizations, or persons, living or dead, is entirely coincidental.

AVON BOOKS
An Imprint of HarperCollins*Publishers*
195 Broadway
New York, New York 10007

Copyright © 2015 by Jan Nowasky
ISBN 978-0-06-239101-8
www.avonromance.com

First Avon Books mass market printing: November 2015

Avon Trademark Reg. U.S. Pat. Off. and in Other Countries, Marca Registrada, Hecho en U.S.A.
HarperCollins® is a registered trademark of HarperCollins Publishers.

Printed in the U.S.A.

10 9 8 7 6 5 4 3 2 1

For the Cover Girls
Who share their love of good books,
robust laughter, excellent wine,
and amazing friendship.
To Kathy and Becky for getting us started.
To Wendy, Jenn, and Felicia
for keeping us together.
Book clubs rule!

FALLING INTO BED
WITH A
DUKE

Prologue

On the night of November 15, one of the most horrific disasters in British railway history occurred when a passenger train collided head-on with a train transporting flammable goods. Several cars were instantly engulfed in a fireball of orange flames. It is impossible to adequately describe the horrendous carnage of mangled bodies, impaled and dismembered travelers, and blackened corpses. Twenty-seven souls were lost . . .

Reported in the Times, *1858*

As the coach rattled over the rough, uneven road, Nicholson Lambert, the recently anointed Duke of Ashebury, stared at the passing landscape that was as bleak and dreary as his soul. He felt hollow, empty, as though, at any moment, his body would simply crumple in on itself and cease to exist. He didn't know how much longer he could continue to breathe, to carry on, to—

"Don't touch me," the Earl of Greyling, sitting across from him, demanded.

Nicky glanced over in time to see the earl's twin, Edward, shove on his brother's shoulder. The earl pushed back. Edward slapped at him. The earl scrambled onto the seat, resting on his knees, his new position giving him height as he made a fist, brought his arm back—

"That's enough now, lads," Mr. Beckwith said, quickly setting aside the book he'd been reading and lurching forward to put out an arm to shield Edward from his brother's attack. Still, the earl let his balled fist fly. It landed with an undamaging thud on Mr. Beckwith's forearm.

Any other time, Nicky might have laughed at the younger boy's ineffectual fighting technique. Only a few months before, shortly after Nicky turned eight, his father had taken him to view a boxing match, so he was quite familiar with the sound of a punch that carried power behind it as flesh met flesh. The earl's fist could have been a rose petal floating to the ground for all the impact it had made.

"That is not the sort of behavior that a lord of the realm displays," Mr. Beckwith admonished.

"He started it," Greyling grumbled, not for the first time since they'd begun this arduous and horrendous journey from London.

"Yes, and I'm finishing it. Your Grace, please trade places with the earl." The order was spoken easily as though Nicky—he was having a difficult time thinking of himself as Ashebury, wondered if he ever would—had the ability to move at will, as though he didn't have to dredge up the strength from some hidden reservoir buried deep inside him.

Glancing back over his shoulder, Mr. Beckwith arched a brow over blue eyes that seemed to see far too much. "Your Grace?"

Taking a deep breath, Nicky summoned up the fortitude to push off the bench until his booted feet thudded to the floor. With a great deal of effort, he maintained his balance and swapped places with the Earl of Greyling. Once they were all situated to Beckwith's satisfaction, the solicitor adjusted his spectacles and returned his attention to reading his book. Edward stuck his tongue out at his brother. Lord Greyling crossed his eyes and pushed up the end of his nose until he resembled a pig. Nicky looked back out the window to the passing scenery, wishing Mr. Beckwith would read aloud so his voice might drown out the screeching of the wind over the moors. He wished—

"I'm not staying," Edward announced. "I'm going to run off. You can't make me stay."

Nicky looked over at Edward. He appeared so confident, so assured, his chin held high, his dark brown eyes penetrating as he glared at the solicitor. Was that all it took to end this nightmarish journey to Dartmoor? To simply make a proclamation that it wasn't going to be so?

Slowly, Beckwith lowered his book, his eyes filling with understanding, compassion, and sorrow. "That would not please your father."

"My father's dead."

The earl gasped. For Nicky, the words were a physical blow to his chest. He could hardly breathe at the stark truth that he'd not dared whisper even to himself. He kept thinking if he never thought the words, they wouldn't be true, his father wouldn't be gone, and he wouldn't be the Duke of Ashebury. But he was struggling to hold on to the illusion that his world hadn't shattered.

"Still, he would expect you to behave in a manner befitting your station," Mr. Beckwith assured him kindly.

"I don't want to be here," Edward said with vehemence. "I want to go home."

"And you shall . . . in time. Your father"—he looked at Nicky—"both your fathers knew the Marquess of Marsden quite well. They went to school together, were mates. They trust him with your upbringing. As I've explained before, they left instructions that in the event of their deaths, the marquess was to serve as your guardian. And so it shall be."

His lower lip beginning to quiver, Edward looked at his brother. "Albert, you're the earl now. Tell him we don't have to go. Make him take us home."

With a quiet sigh of surrender, the new Earl of Greyling rubbed his right earlobe. "We have to do it. It's what Father wanted."

"It's stupid. I hate you. I hate you all!" Edward

brought his feet up to the bench seat and, turning his back on them, buried his face in the corner of the coach.

Nicky could see his shoulders shaking, knew he was trying hard not to let on that he was weeping. He wished he could cry but knew it would disappoint his father to show such weakness. He was the duke now and had to be strong. It didn't matter that his mother and father were dead. His nanny had assured him that they could still watch him, would know if he were misbehaving. If he were a bad boy, he'd go to hell when he died and never see them again.

"There it is, lads. Havisham Hall. It'll be your home for a while," Mr. Beckwith said solemnly.

Pressing his face to the glass and looking back, Nicky could see the behemoth silhouette standing ominously against the darkening gray skies. The manor house in which he'd been growing up had been as large, but it didn't appear as foreboding. He swallowed hard. Perhaps Edward had the right of it, and they could run away.

The coach came to a shuddering halt. No one came out of the house to greet them. It was as though they weren't expected. A footman climbed down and opened the carriage door. Mr. Beckwith stepped out.

"Come with me, lads." His voice carried no doubts that they were supposed to be here, that this was the correct place, and that they would be welcomed.

Nicky darted his gaze between the earl and his brother. They'd both gone pale, their brown eyes too huge and round. They waited. He was the oldest, the higher rank, so it fell to him to go first. While everything within him screamed to stay where he was, he gathered up his resolve not to be cowardly and clambered out. He sucked in his breath as the cold winds buffeted against him. The brothers fell into place behind him. In silence, they followed Mr. Beckwith up the steps. At the stoop, the solicitor lifted the heavy iron knocker and let it fall. A clang echoed eerily around them. Again, Beckwith knocked. And again, and again—

The door swung open, and a decrepit old man stood there, his black jacket and waistcoat faded and threadbare. "May I be of service?"

"Charles Beckwith to see the Marquess of Marsden. I'm expected." With a practiced flick of his wrist, Mr. Beckwith produced his card.

Taking it, the white-haired butler opened the door farther. "Come in, and I'll alert his lordship to your arrival."

As grateful as Nicky was to get out of the wind, he wished he'd stayed where he was. The entryway was shadowed and just as chilly as outside. The butler wandered away into a darkened hallway that Nicky feared led into the very bowels of hell about which his nanny had warned him. He could see no end to it. A quick glance at the twins did not reassure him. They looked as though their wariness had increased tenfold. As for his own, it was at least double that. He wanted to be strong, brave, and courageous. He wanted to be the good son, to please his father, but staying here would kill him. He was sure of it.

They waited in the oppressive quiet. Even the tall clock in the hallway wasn't ticking, its hands weren't moving. The silent sentry caused a shiver to race up Nicky's spine.

A tall, thin man stepped out of the sinister-looking hallway. His clothes hung on his frame as though they had been fitted for a man twice his size. Although his cheeks and eyes were sunken, and his hair was more white than black, he didn't really appear particularly old.

Beckwith snapped to attention. "My lord, I'm Charles Beckwith, solicitor—"

"So your card said. Why are you here?" The rasp of his voice hinted that it wasn't accustomed to being used.

"I brought the lads."

"What use have I for lads?"

Beckwith pulled back his shoulders. "I sent you a missive, my lord. The Duke of Ashebury, the Earl of Greyling, and their wives were tragically killed in a railway accident."

"Railway. If God meant for us to travel in such contraptions, He'd have not given us horses."

Nicky blinked. Where was the man's sympathy and sorrow at the news? Why was he not offering comfort?

"Be that as it may," Beckwith said evenly, "I had expected to see you at the funeral."

"I don't attend funerals. They're ghastly depressing."

Nicky didn't think truer words could have been spoken. He'd hated the one for his parents. During the wake, he'd wanted to open the casket to be sure they were there, but his nanny had told him that he wouldn't recognize them. His parents had been burned to cinders. They knew which body was his father's because of his signet ring, a ring that Nicky now wore on a chain about his neck, but how did they know that the woman they'd buried with his father was really his mother? What if she wasn't? What if she wasn't with him now?

"Which is the reason that I've brought the lads to you—since you didn't retrieve them yourself," Beckwith said.

"Why bring them to me?"

"As I stated in my missive—"

"I don't recall a missive."

"Then I offer my apologies, my lord, for its being lost in the post. However, both the duke and earl named you as guardian of their sons."

As though only just becoming aware of their presence, Marsden homed his dark green eyes in on them. Nicky felt as though his heart had been stabbed with a poker. He didn't want to be left in the care of this man, who didn't seem to possess an ounce of kindness or compassion.

Furrowing his brow, the marquess gave his attention back to Beckwith. "Why would they be foolish enough to do that?"

"They obviously trusted you, my lord."

Marsden cackled as though it was the funniest thing anyone had ever said about him. Nicky couldn't bear it. Rushing forward, he balled up his fist and punched the marquess in the gut, again and again.

"Don't you laugh," Nicky cried, mortified that tears were burning his eyes. "Don't you dare laugh at my father!"

"Easy, lad," Beckwith said, pulling him back. "Nothing is accomplished with fisticuffs."

Only that wasn't true because the marquess had stopped laughing. Breathing heavily, Nicky was prepared to go at him again if he had to.

"Sorry, boy," the marquess said. "I wasn't laughing at your father, merely the absurdity of my seeing to your care."

Ashamed by his outburst, Nicky turned away, taken aback when he spotted the scraggly boy—wearing only breeches that looked to be too small and a white linen shirt—crouched behind a large potted frond. His long black hair fell into his eyes.

"But you will honor their request," Beckwith stated emphatically.

Shifting his eyes back to the marquess, Nicky saw him give one quick nod.

"I will. For friendship's sake."

"Very good, my lord. If you could send some footmen out to retrieve the lads' trunks—"

"Have your driver and footman bring them in. Then be on your way."

Beckwith seemed to hesitate, but eventually he knelt before Nicky and the twins. "Keep your chins up, be good lads, and make your parents proud." He curled his hand over Edward's shoulder and squeezed. Then Greyling's. Finally, Nicky's.

Nicky wanted to beg not to be left behind. *Please, please, take me with you!* But he held his tongue. He'd already shamed himself once. He wouldn't do it again.

Beckwith stood, eyed the marquess. "I shall be checking on them."

"No need. They're in my care now. Be off with you as quickly as possible." He looked toward the windows. "Before it's too late."

With a slow nod, Beckwith turned on his heel and walked out. No one moved. No one spoke. The trunks were brought in. Shortly afterward, Nicky heard the creaking of the coach's wheels, the pounding of the horses' hooves as though Beckwith had ordered the driver to hurry, as though he couldn't escape fast enough.

"Locksley!" the marquess shouted, making Ashe jump.

The boy behind the frond rushed forward. "Yes, Father?"

"Show them upstairs. Let them select the bed-chamber they want."

"Yes, sir."

"It'll be dark soon," the marquess said, a faraway look coming into his eyes. "Don't go out at night."

As though no longer aware of their presence, he wandered back into the dark and foreboding hallway from which he'd originally emerged.

"Come on," the boy said, turning for the stairs.

"We're not staying," Nicky suddenly announced, deciding it was time he took charge, time for him to be as dukish as possible.

"Why not? I'd like to have someone to play with. And you'll like it here. You can do anything you want. No one cares."

"Why isn't your clock working?" Edward asked, stepping nearer to it as though suddenly intrigued by the craftsmanship.

Locksley scrunched his brow. "What do you mean?"

Lifting his hand, Edward drew a circle in the air. "It's supposed to be ticking. The hands are supposed to move around the numbers." He reached up—

"Don't touch it!" Locksley shouted as he darted in front of the clock. "You're not supposed to touch it. Ever."

"Why not?"

Looking confused, Locksley shook his head. "You're just not."

"Where's your mother?" Greyling asked, stepping nearer to Edward, as though he needed the comfort of a familiar presence in this dreary, ominous place.

"Dead," Locksley said flatly. "That's her ghost

shrieking over the moors. If you go out at night, she'll snatch you up and take you away with her."

A cold, icy shiver skittered down Nicky's spine. He looked toward the door, the windows on either side of it revealing the darkness descending, and he feared it would claim him as well, that when he could finally leave this place—like his parents— little of him would remain except ash.

Chapter 1

*E*TIQUETTE dictated that a gentleman caller did not extend his visit beyond fifteen minutes, so it was that Miss Minerva Dodger knew that her time in the company of Lord Sheridan would be drawing to a close within the next one hundred and eighty interminable seconds. Sooner, if luck was on her side, but the gentleman sitting to her left on the sofa in the front parlor was apparently determined to eke out his maximum stay. Since she had handed him a cup of tea shortly after his arrival, he seemed to have forgotten his purpose in coming here. The fine bone china with the red roses hadn't once left the saucer that he balanced so expertly on his thigh.

This visit was his third within the past seven days, and all she'd really garnered from their time together was that he used a little too much bergamot cologne, kept his fingernails well manicured, and periodically released sighs for ostensibly no reason whatsoever. And that he cleared his throat to signal the end of his calling upon her.

She now welcomed the harsh gurgle as he set aside his cup before standing. Placing her own cup and saucer on the low table in front of her, she pushed to her feet and fought not to look too pleased that the ordeal was finally over. "Thank you so much for coming, Lord Sheridan."

"I hope I may call on you tomorrow." The earnestness in his brown eyes alerted her that he was not truly asking for permission but was merely stating his intent.

"If I may be so bold, my lord, allow me to ask if this is truly how you want to spend the remainder of your life—sitting about in heavy silences with only the ticking of the clock to remind us of the passing of time?"

He blinked. "Pardon?"

Now she was the one to sigh, hating that she was forced to be blunt because he refused to acknowledge the truth of the situation. "We are not suited, my lord."

"I'm not certain how you've reached that conclusion."

"We don't converse. I have tried to engage you in several topics of conversation—"

"On the wisdom of England's expansion in Africa. It is not a subject that should concern a lady."

"It is going to concern a great many ladies if war erupts, and they find themselves catapulted into widowhood. Not to mention the financial toll on the country—" She held up a hand. The man looked positively horrified. "My apologies. You didn't want to discuss it earlier, and I'm quite certain you don't wish to now as you are preparing to leave. It's simply that I have opinions and believe I have the right to voice them. You seem to have no interest in hearing my view on anything other than the weather."

"You will be a countess."

Now it was her turn to blink. "What has that to do with anything?"

"You will be Lady Sheridan. As such, you shall be too busy overseeing your duties and your charitable endeavors to be sitting about in the parlor with me during the afternoon."

"And in the evening?"

"I have an extensive library that will be at your disposal. Although surely you do needlework."

"I don't, actually. I find it tedious. I much prefer a rousing debate on social reform."

"I will not tolerate a wife who engages in *rousing debates*. It's unseemly."

"Which is why, my lord, we are not suited." She said it kindly when she yearned to ask him why he thought any woman would want to be his wife.

"I have a very large estate, Miss Dodger. Granted, it does need some upkeep, but your dowry will set it to rights."

And there it was, spoken at long last: the reason for his presence in her parlor.

"But you see, Sheridan, I come with my dowry. Furthermore, I come as I am. With my own ideas, not necessarily my husband's, with my own interests, again, not necessarily my husband's. But I want him to respect my opinions and interests. I want to be able to discuss them with him and know that he is listening."

"I'll give you children."

What did that have to do with his listening, which he obviously was failing to do. She felt rather like a mule being tossed carrots in hopes that one would get the beast to move along. And while she desperately wanted children, she wasn't willing to pay any price in order to obtain them. If she wasn't happy, how could they be? "Will you give me love?"

He tapped his front teeth together. "It is possible that, with time, my affections would grow."

She gave him a tolerant smile. "I think you would find living with me to be quite challenging."

"I have two estates. Once I have my heir, I see no reason that we must live at the same residence."

It took everything within her not to laugh hysterically. The man refused to heed what she was saying—which had been the problem from the beginning. "Call on me if you wish, my lord, but know that under no circumstances will I ever marry you."

"You won't get a better offer."

"That may well be true, but I seriously doubt that I shall receive a worse one."

Jerking his head around, he glared at her mother, sitting in the corner with her needlework as though she were responsible for the words spewing from Minerva's mouth. "Your Grace—"

"Mrs. Dodger," her mother interrupted succinctly.

Sheridan released a frustrated sigh. "You are the widow of a duke."

"I am the wife of Jack Dodger and prefer to be addressed as such."

He tapped his front teeth together several times before clearing his throat. "Very well, if you insist."

She smiled sweetly. "I have from the moment I married him a good many years ago, but I don't believe you're here to discuss the choices I've made in my life."

"You are quite right, madam, I am not. Will you be so kind as to explain to your daughter why she should not be so quick to dismiss my suit?"

Her face serene, she bestowed upon him an indulgent smile. "To be quite honest, Lord Sheridan, I think your afternoons would be better spent elsewhere."

Harrumphing, he pinned Minerva with his glower. "I intend to have a wife by the end of the Season. I shall not wait for you to come to your senses, Miss Dodger. I shall move on."

"I think that would be most wise."

"You're foolish to give up what I can provide."

"With the help of my dowry."

The tapping of his teeth again. In time, the habit would no doubt drive her mad.

"Good day, Madam, Miss Dodger." With that, he spun on his heel and strode from the parlor without so much as a backward glance.

With a deep sigh releasing much of the tension that had accompanied Minerva with his visit, she rolled her shoulders before wandering across the room and dropping unceremoniously into the chair beside her mother's. "Strange, but I'd have felt more foolish if I'd married him."

Reaching across, her mother squeezed her hand. "You're not foolish at all. You know your own mind. Somewhere, there is a man who will relish that aspect of you and view you as more than an ornament."

While Minerva wasn't prone to pessimism, on this particular subject she couldn't dredge up her mother's optimism.

"I just passed Lord Sheridan going out as I was coming in," Grace Stanford, the Duchess of Lovingdon, and Minerva's dearest friend, said as she walked into the parlor, her two-year-old son perched on her hip. "I daresay, he bore the look of a storm cloud."

"What a marvelous surprise to have you drop by," Minerva's mother said, her smile brighter than anything the sun could produce as she rose and crossed over to their newest arrivals. "How is my grandson?"

The boy reached for her, and she took him into her arms. "I swear, you have grown so much since last I saw you."

"You saw him a few days ago," Grace reminded her mother-by-marriage.

"Too long."

Approaching, Minerva tried to read her friend's expression, but Grace was known for never giving anything away. It made her an extremely skilled opponent at cards.

"So, Lord Sheridan?" Grace prompted.

With a sigh, Minerva shrugged her shoulders. "He thought we were well suited. I didn't."

"He has considerable debt," Grace said.

"Precisely."

"He is rather nice-looking and can be quite charming."

"He sat here for fifteen minutes staring at his teacup as though hoping to catch a glimpse of his tea evaporating."

"Oh dear." Her eyes held sympathy and understanding. Before her marriage to Minerva's half brother, the Duke of Lovingdon, Grace had been navigating the sea of fortune hunters as well.

"So what brings you to our door?" Minerva asked.

"I simply wanted to visit with you for a bit."

"I'll leave you girls to it," her mother said distractedly, pinching the child's chubby red cheek. "Come along. Let's find your grandfather. He'll be delighted to see you." She looked at Grace. "That's all right, isn't it? If I take him off for a bit?"

"Of course. I'll find you when I'm ready to leave."

"Take your time," Minerva's mother said, before wandering from the room in search of her husband. If Society ever saw Jack Dodger playing peekaboo with his stepgrandson, his fierce reputation would be shattered.

"She does love him," Minerva said, ignoring the ache in her chest because she might never give her parents a grandchild.

"I know. Furthermore, I knew his presence would ensure we had some time alone when we wouldn't be disturbed."

A mixture of anticipation and dread coursed through Minerva. "You acquired the address?"

"Let's have a seat, shall we?" As though she could outrun the conversation, Grace moved swiftly to the sofa and sat.

Minerva joined her there, the excitement over the possibilities drowning out any of her initial trepidation. "Do you have it?" she prodded impatiently.

Grace shifted uncomfortably. "Are you certain about this, Minerva? Once it's lost—"

"I'm well aware how virginity works, Grace." She snapped her fingers impatiently. "Give over the address."

She didn't dare say aloud the name of the establishment. No one did. Rumors of the existence of the secretive Nightingale Club had been floating through

London for years, but its location was a closely guarded secret because its owners were supposedly ladies of the aristocracy—married ladies who had established a place for others such as themselves to bring their paramours for discreet rendezvouses, their husbands none the wiser regarding their illicit affairs. Its purpose had evolved over the years so that even those who had no lover might secure one for a night. That was all she wanted. One night.

"Your brother will kill me if he learns that I assisted you with this endeavor."

"He won't do any such thing. He adores you to distraction. Besides, he isn't going to find out. It's not as though I'm going to announce it, but you know full well the sort of life he led before he married you. Why is it acceptable for men to be naughty but not for women to partake in the same liberties?"

"It's simply the way of it. What if you fall in love—"

Minerva couldn't help it. She laughed out loud at that. "I've seen six Seasons, Grace. I'm on the shelf gathering dust, except for the occasional fortune hunter. I have no interest in a marriage that is a business arrangement. I want to be loved for who I am. My immense dowry doesn't aid me in finding love. I'm not particularly pretty."

Grace opened her mouth to protest, and Minerva cut in before she could speak. "You know it's true." Based upon the dowry her father—one of the wealthiest men in London—had bestowed upon her, she had not wanted for men's professed affections, but not a single one had carried an ounce of truth. She wasn't particularly beautiful, couldn't even classify herself as pretty or endearing in the looks department. "I have too much of my father in me. His dark eyes, his common features. And I've his head for business. I'm smart, and I speak my mind. I'm not demure or biddable. I want passion and fire, not the coldness of silence and sighs as we wait for the minutes to pass until we're no longer in each other's company. Do you have any idea how often I have sat in this very parlor with a gentleman who did little more than hold a teacup on his lap and comment on the biscuits and cakes as though they are the sum of my life? I'm intimidating. I know that. I consider holding my tongue, but I don't want to give a gentleman a false impression of whom he is courting. I'm not shy about spouting my opinions, and men find such behavior intolerable."

"You simply haven't met the right man yet."

"It's not as though I've taken to hiding behind fronds. I've been visible, seen by everyone. My dowry is attractive; I am not. Men do not seek me out with passion in mind, but rather purse strings. It's grown wearisome."

Grace studied her quietly for a few moments. "What if you should get with child?" she finally asked, and Minerva nearly groaned at the tedious questioning, but she appreciated that her dear friend meant well.

"I've researched. I'll take precautions."

Grace slumped back, nibbling on her lower lip. "The act itself is incredibly intimate, Minerva. I can't imagine engaging in such actions with someone I didn't love."

"I'm well aware that it won't be perfect, Grace, but at this point in my life, I want to feel desired. I've heard that most of the men who frequent the place are of the aristocracy. So it's quite possible it will be someone I know, possibly someone I favor. I fancy many of the gents; they simply don't fancy me."

"But after all that you'll share, won't it be awkward when you see him in the future?"

"He's not going to know it's me. I'll be masked." The mask she'd purchased in anticipation of acquiring the location of the infamous club covered two-thirds of her face, leaving only her eyes, lips, and chin visible.

"But *you'll* know. Everything he did. Everywhere he touched. Everywhere you touched."

Warmth and a bit of discomfiture coursed through Minerva as she imagined being caressed with large, strong hands. She took the images to bed with her every night even though they did little except leave her aching for what she'd never experienced. Her greatest fear was that she might actually weep if a man ever fondled her with bare hands. She'd been touched by men before, but always with cloth—gloves at the very least—serving as a barrier. "I've thought about the ramifications long and hard, Grace. It's not something I decided on a whim.

Do you have any idea how lonely it is to have never felt so much as the stroke of a man's finger along forbidden flesh? During dinners, no one sneaks in an errant touch beneath the tablecloth, out of sight of others, when my gloves are resting on my lap and my hands are uncovered. No one does anything untoward where I'm concerned."

"If I might be honest, this recourse seems rather tawdry. Perhaps you should seek out a lover."

"You don't understand, Grace. Men don't find me appealing in that way. They don't have improper thoughts or consider me alluring. If a man even hinted that he fancied me, I'd marry him."

"You've had marriage proposals."

"From impoverished gents, and it became quite clear, quite quickly that they yearned to hold near my dowry, not me. Your advice helped me identify the fortune hunters, and thus far—to my everlasting disappointment—they've all been fortune hunters."

"Perhaps you took my words too much to heart."

"No one looks at me the way my brother looks at you. Even before he professed his love, it was obvious that he wanted you in the worst sort of way."

Unable to deny the words, Grace blushed. Minerva stood and began to pace. She was striving so hard not to show how nervous she was about this decision. It was the correct one for her. She wanted to know what it was to be with a man, and she'd grown weary of waiting. "The anonymity appeals to me. If I botch it all up, no one is going to know."

"You won't botch it. But I do worry that you'll be hurt."

Kneeling before her dear friend, Minerva took her hands, squeezed. "How can I be hurt when, for a little while, I shall feel as though I am desired? Grace, I have never once in my life felt as though a man desired me. And while I know that he won't know it is me, that all he truly wants is my body, it will be *my* body that he touches, *my* body in which he takes pleasure, *my* body that receives pleasure in return. It's not perfect, but it's something."

"It's rather rash when there are alternatives. You could proposition a man to be your lover."

"And how do I deal with the embarrassment when he says no?"

"He might say yes."

"Six Seasons, Grace, and I've never been kissed. Never been ushered into a shadowy garden. My dance partners are becoming fewer and farther between. I am recognized for what I am: a spinster. It is time for me to acknowledge that I shall never experience a grand love, and I won't saddle myself with a man who can't love me as deeply as my father loves my mother. Or my brother loves you. If I'm going to be with him for the remainder of my life, I want a gentleman who is besotted. And if I can't have that, I want to know at least once what it is to be with a man without the barriers of societal mores. Maybe then, I can move on and find happiness elsewhere."

With a sigh, Grace worked her hands free of Minerva's clasp, reached into the pocket of her skirt, and withdrew a folded slip of paper. Minerva wanted to snatch it up, but she feared she would tear it because Grace's fingers were turning white with her death grip on the frail parchment.

"Along with the address," Grace began, "I have included a list of gentlemen to avoid should they cross your path. Lovingdon assures me that they are selfish lovers—not that he knew why I was asking, but it seems that in the privacy of their clubs, men are prone to boasting about their conquests." Pursing her lips together, she extended the paper. "Please be very careful."

Minerva closed her steady fingers around the answer to her dreams. The time for being careful was long past. She yearned for a night to remember. "Don't suppose you have a list of whom I should consider?"

Grace released a forced laugh. "Afraid not. I just wished a gentleman could see you for your true worth, something that has nothing at all to do with your dowry."

"Not every gentleman can be as wise as my half brother."

"Pity that."

Pity indeed. But then, Minerva wasn't one to languish on the negative. She'd had no luck with the marriage market. It was time to move into the realm of pleasure.

*T*HE Duke of Ashebury was on the hunt for a pair of long, shapely legs. Standing casually with a shoulder pressed to a wall in the front parlor of the Nightingale Club, he observed with a jaundiced eye those who entered. The ladies wore flowing silk that caressed their skin as a lover might before the night was done. The shimmering fabric seductively outlined the body, hinted at dips and swells. Arms were bared. Necklines were low, the silk gathering just below a tasteful showing of cleavage designed to entice. People murmured and sipped their champagne, while exchanging heavy-lidded gazes and come-hither smiles.

The flirtation that occurred within these walls was very different from that found in a ballroom. No one here was searching for a dance partner. Rather, they wanted a bedding partner. He appreciated the honesty on display, which was the reason that he often stopped by when he was in London. No pretense, no ruses, no duplicity.

He had already claimed a bedchamber, the key nestled in his jacket pocket, as he wanted no one to disturb what he had so painstakingly set up. His needs were unique, and he knew that within these walls, they would be kept secret. People did not discuss what occurred at the Nightingale Club. For most of London, its existence was something spoken about in longing whispers by those who knew it only as myth. But for those familiar with it, it served as a sanctuary, liberator, confidant. It was whatever one needed it to be.

For him, it was salvation, bringing him back from the brink of darkness. Twenty years had gone by since his parents' deaths, yet still he dreamed of mangled and charred remains. Still, he heard his mother's terrorized screams and his father's fruitless cries. Still, his behavior when he'd last seen them taunted him. Had he known that he'd never look upon them again—

With resolve, he shook off the haunting musings that sent a chill down his spine. Here, he could forget, at least for a few hours. Here, the regrets didn't gnaw unmercifully at him. Here, he could become lost striving for perfection, for the ultimate in pleasure.

He had merely to determine which lady would best suit his purposes, which would be willing to concede to his unusual request without protest. It bothered him not at all that the ladies wore domino masks. He cared little for their faces, understood their need for anonymity. Their concealment worked to his advantage as he'd discovered that ladies were more comfortable with his request when they were assured it would remain their secret—and his not knowing their identity made them bolder than they might have been otherwise. They liked being a little naughty as long as they weren't caught. He couldn't catch them if he didn't know who they were.

Still, he had one cardinal rule he always observed: never the same lady twice.

The ladies brought their own masks, seldom

changed them, as the façade became their calling cards, as effective at identifying them as the ones handed over to butlers in the early afternoon when they were making proper visits. The woman in the black mask decorated with peacock feathers had a scar just above her left knee from a tumble she'd taken from a pony as a child. The blue mask, black feathers had two delightful dimples in the small of her back. The green mask outlined in yellow lace possessed bony hips that had proven a challenge, but he'd been pleased with the results when their time together was finished. But then he'd always embraced the challenge of discovering the perfection in imperfection.

The three glasses of scotch that he'd enjoyed were thrumming through his veins. The din of intimacy was calming. The muscles that had been so tense earlier were relaxed. He was in his element here, or he would be in short order. As soon as he found that for which he was searching. He wouldn't settle for less than what he wanted; he never did. If one sure thing could be said about the Duke of Ashebury, it was that he knew his own mind. That he was stubborn when it came to acquiring what he needed—or wanted. Tonight's endeavors straddled the line of both what he needed and what he wanted. All needs would be met before dawn. Then, perhaps, he could be glad to be back in London.

Lifting his glass for another sip, he watched a woman wearing draping white silk and a white mask with short white feathers walk hesitantly into the room as though she expected the floor to drop out from beneath her at any moment. She wasn't particularly tall, but based on the way the silk moved over her flesh with each graceful step, it was obvious that she possessed long, slender legs. He wondered if she was meeting someone, already had an arranged assignation. Some ladies did—it was one of the reasons that the men didn't wear masks. So they were easily identifiable if their paramours wanted to meet them here. Another reason was that men simply didn't bloody well care if anyone knew that they were in the mood for a good tupping. Even the married ones were brazen with their presence.

The woman in white appeared to have dark hair, gathered up in an elaborate style that no doubt required an abundance of pins. He couldn't be absolutely certain of the exact shade because the lighting in the room—only flickering candles—enhanced the mood of secrecy as well as creating an ambiance for intimacy while providing a gossamer disguise for some distinguishing characteristics that were easily identifiable by color: hair, eyes, even the fairness of skin. Perhaps she moved slowly because her eyes were adjusting to the dimness. Gentlemen not yet spoken for did not swarm to her side. But then that was the rule here. Seduction happened slowly. Ladies needed to hint at an interest.

But then, if this was her first time, she might not be aware of the subtle rules. He was fairly certain he'd never seen her before. A connoisseur of the body, he would have remembered the elegance of her movements, the way the cloth glided over her skin, outlining her form. Slender legs, but meat where it counted. No bony hips there.

With one long swallow, he finished off his scotch, relishing the realization that the hunt was over. He'd thought he wanted a tall woman. He'd been mistaken.

He wanted *her*.

Chapter 2

MINERVA had spent a little over three hours preparing for her first visit to the Nightingale Club, only to discover upon her arrival that she had to change into something that very much resembled a silk nightdress. Although no nightdress she'd ever worn revealed as much or caressed her skin as lovingly as this one did. After a maid had assisted her in changing, she'd caught sight of her reflection in a mirror. With no undergarments or petticoats between her and the silk, she almost changed her mind and quit this place. Grace no doubt had the right of it, and she should just return to her world, proposition someone she knew, someone she liked even if it was only a little bit—

But that seemed even more awkward and unsavory than her present course. What if he wasn't interested in the least or things between them were . . . awful? He would know who she was. What if he told people, his best mates, of their assignation? Grace said men boasted of their exploits. Minerva suspected they made sport of women who did not live up to their expectations. They certainly weren't likely to confess to any shortcomings of their own. No, coming here was the way to go. The anonymity assured it remained her secret. No one would ever discover what she had done or with whom she'd done it.

Not to mention there was a bit of titillation to the notion of his not knowing, to her being secretive. Surely men found it provocative as well when an air of mystery was involved.

Glancing around the dimly lit parlor, she was struck with both curiosity and a dash of irritation. The men were completely clothed in trousers, jackets, waistcoats, shirts, perfectly knotted neckcloths. Why weren't they forced to wear something that might make them feel as though they were standing about almost naked? Perhaps because a gent's clothing didn't leave as much to the imagination as a lady's might. Still, it seemed rather unfair. Surely, if given the chance, ladies could appreciate muscled arms and bared chests. She fancied wide shoulders. And eyes that glinted with the ability to tease. Most of the men who had visited in her parlor had dull eyes or ones that revealed their thoughts drifting off to other places.

She recognized several lords. Lord Rexton was standing by the fireplace talking to a tall woman. How she longed for height. Not that she wanted Rexton's attention. With a blush no doubt creeping from her toes to her hairline, she turned away, knowing it was ridiculous to fear he might recognize her or to be embarrassed by the sight of Grace's brother wooing someone. He was young, virile. Ladies were no doubt thrilled to have an opportunity to be in his company. He was heir to a storied and powerful dukedom.

Dear God, she hoped she didn't run into her brothers. But even if she did, it wasn't likely that they would recognize her by the sight of her chin and mouth. The rest of her face was covered. She couldn't do much about her hair, but then the dark russet strands weren't that memorable anyway. Her dark eyes weren't the sort to incite poetry. Men weren't going to drown in them. They were as boring as the rest of her physical appearance.

Many couples were talking. That was no doubt part of the ritual. Silly of her to think that some man was simply going to toss her over his shoulder like some medieval pillager and haul her upstairs to a bed. She wouldn't have allowed it anyway. She wanted a bit of wooing.

A footman approached, carrying a tray of glasses filled with amber liquid and flutes of champagne. Going for the amber, she snatched it up and tossed it back, relishing the burn and the heat cascading through her center. In their youth, she and Grace had never shied away from sneaking into liquor cabinets. She supposed, however, to be attractive to a man, she should at least pretend to have a preference for champagne. It was more refined and lady-like, but just as she hadn't pretended in ballrooms to be other than what she was, she wasn't going to pretend here. A man might not see her face, might not know who she was, but she intended to own her behavior. If they shied away from a woman who drank scotch, she wanted nothing to do with them. As much as possible, tonight would be on her terms.

The footman took the empty glass from her. Before he could walk off, she snatched another one, probably should have taken two, then settled for taking merely a healthy swallow. There would be other footmen, other opportunities, and apparently she would have ample time to imbibe. All seemed to go at a snail's pace. That was good. It gave her a chance to decide.

As her gaze swept over the crowd, she realized that she had spoken with most of these lords at one time or another. If they hadn't appealed to her in a ballroom, what made her think they would appeal to her here?

You're not going to marry him. You don't have to really like him. You simply need to determine if he has the physical qualities to be a good lover.

This was to be a night for fantasy. For broad shoulders and narrow hips. Kind eyes, full lips. A thick head of hair. Shade unimportant. She scoffed. Maybe hair itself was unimportant. A bald man might make a wonderful lover. Having been judged by her too-large nose, strong brow, and round cheekbones, she wasn't hypocrite enough to judge a man based on his looks. She wanted someone with a bit of intelligence, a dash of humor, and an interest in the different.

She considered her options. Lord Gant was dashing, but he tended to spit when he spoke. Lord Bentley was a dull conversationalist. Would he be dull in bed?

She hated that she was beginning to agree with Grace. This lover business was more than height, strength, and good looks. She needed someone she didn't know. A complete stranger, not someone who had taken her on a turn about the dance floor or spoken to her during a dinner. No preconceived notions.

Or she could select someone whom she had fancied but hadn't fancied her—at least not enough to ask for her hand. The problem was that she hadn't really fancied anyone, which was one of the reasons she was here. Truth be told, she'd yet to meet a man whom she *wanted* to pursue her. Perhaps she was too particular. Was it really so awful if a man wanted only her coins? Could he fake passion and caring? Would he? She deserved better than that. Every woman did.

Starting to take another sip of the scotch, she realized that she'd finished it off at some point. Another should chase away the last of her nerves. Before she could begin to look around for a footman, a deep voice asked, "Let's switch glasses, shall we?"

Jerking around, she found herself staring up into the Duke of Ashebury's incredible blue eyes. She could count on one hand the number of times she'd been this close to him. They might have exchanged half a dozen words in passing. Handsome as sin with a devil-may-care attitude, he usually had a bevy of ladies circling about him, vying for his attentions. His tragic past, orphaned at eight to become the ward of a madman—not that anyone had realized the state of the Marquess of Marsden's mind at the time—caused some ladies to find him even more appealing. They wanted to provide a safe haven and ply him with the love that he'd not had for years.

And well he knew it. He wasn't above taking advantage of generous hearts. She didn't know how many ladies he'd ruined although no ladies had ever confessed to ruination at his hands. But still, the rumors abounded. Yet in spite of his questionable reputation, there wasn't a mother in all of England who didn't yearn to see her daughter standing at the altar beside this man. And Minerva, drat her feminine heart, would have been content to have had a dance with him, to have spent a few minutes in the circle of his arms. He was, quite literally, the most beautiful creature she'd ever had the good fortune to lay eyes on. The irony of her thoughts did not escape her. Her looks held men at bay while his drew attention as though they were magnets—and she, drat it all, had turned into metal shavings.

With a smile designed to melt hearts and cause a

woman not to care that he had no interest in permanence, he took her tumbler, set it aside, then, with his long, warm fingers covering hers, he folded her hand around his glass. She'd never had a man's bare hand touch hers or any other part of her for that matter. It should have been unsettling. Instead, the touch seemed to spread along her skin—

Because it was. Without taking his gaze from hers, he slowly, ever so slowly, glided his large, roughened hand along her forearm, over her elbow, up to her shoulder before letting his fingers linger lightly in one place, toying with the thin strap of her gown, as though he longed to ease it aside and watch the silk flutter to the floor. She could hardly breathe, and yet it was rude not to acknowledge him.

"Your Grace," she managed, with the rough throaty voice she'd been recently perfecting, adding another layer to her disguise. "I didn't realize you'd returned from the safari."

Those gorgeous blue eyes widened slightly, his smile diminished a fraction as he angled his head to study her more closely. "Have we been introduced?"

She had barely parted her lips to speak when he pressed one of his long, thick fingers against them. "Don't answer that. Here, for the ladies, anonymity is sacred. I'd be cast out if anyone thought I'd deliberately tried to determine who you were."

She doubted anyone would cast him out. His was a powerful family—or it had been before his father died. From rumors she'd heard, he'd yet to take his responsibilities seriously, not that anyone blamed him. Rather, Society seemed to take delight in his adventures. He spent more time out of England than in, traveling the world with those with whom he'd grown up. Raising hell wherever they went if the stories were to be believed. Certainly they were known for the trouble they created. But they were indulged, sought after, encouraged. The timid lived vicariously through them, and, compared to them, most of London was timid.

"What shall I call you?" he asked, his finger still against her lips, causing little tingles to play over the sensitive flesh. "And don't use your real name."

Even without the admonishment, she wouldn't have. She wasn't so befuddled by his nearness that she couldn't think clearly. Her lungs might have ceased to work properly, but her mind was still agile. "Lady V."

A dark eyebrow arched. "Victoria?"

Virgin. Not that she was going to admit that to a man who'd probably deflowered half of Christendom.

His eyebrow lowered, his dazzling smile returned, his eyes glittered with a hint of wickedness. "No," he murmured in a provocative way that caused warmth to bloom in the pit of her stomach and spread throughout her entire being. "Something more exotic. Venus, perhaps."

"Perhaps." It was unconscionable that she could be so enamored of a man with his reputation, and yet for a lady seeking adventures in a boudoir, this man could deliver. Of that she had no doubt. Sensuality radiated from every pore of his being, from his immense height—he had to be well over six feet—to his well-shod toes.

She moved her head back slightly so his finger was no longer on her lips although his other hand had yet to leave her shoulder. Taking a sip of the scotch, she was grateful her own hands weren't quaking with her nervousness. When she had considered her plans for this night, she'd certainly never contemplated falling into bed with a duke, especially with one known for his sexual exploits. Women spoke of him in whispers, his prowess legendary. He would no doubt laugh at her fumbling, her inexperience. She wanted her first, possibly her only, time to be with a mortal, not a god.

Another swallow, more gulp than sip. She wasn't certain how to extricate herself from this situation. Did she simply walk away? Or did she confess that he was too close to fantasy—

But then wasn't fantasy what she yearned for? If she craved memories that could carry her through to her dotage, wouldn't it be best to seek out a man with vast experience, a man who knew his way around a woman's body, a man who would take charge, would ensure the coupling was unforgettable? Based on his reputation, he was the perfect man for her needs. If she was honest, he reigned at the top of her list of desired lovers . . . not a difficult status to obtain when he was the only one on it. But she'd always known that he could barely be bothered to give her the time of day, much less consider her as a bed partner. He didn't need her dowry. He didn't need anything from her.

"Is this your first time—" he began, making her wonder if she wore her inexperience on her sleeve. Only she didn't have sleeves. She had only the bare arm that he was slowly drawing tiny circles along.

"—here," he finished.

Probably no harm in admitting that. She nodded. "It's not quite what I expected."

"You thought it would be an orgy?"

"Something like that. People are standing around talking, when I suppose I thought they'd be doing naughty things."

His blue eyes darkened. "Oh, make no mistake, they're doing very naughty things. You see Lord Wilton speaking to the lady in the red mask?"

"Yes."

"I suspect he is telling her how he plans to nibble on her earlobe, her neck, her shoulder, how he will take his mouth on a journey over every inch of her body."

"Why doesn't he simply get on with it?"

"The pleasure is heightened with anticipation, with a slow stoking of the fires that will eventually consume."

Yes, she could see that. Ashebury's words alone had set kindling alight within her. Imagining him nibbling on her, she grew so warm, it was a wonder she didn't melt into a puddle of molten desire at his feet. "Is that what you do? Build the anticipation with words?"

"No, I'm more a man of action. I simply do it."

"And if the lady objects?"

"I suppose I'd stop. But I've yet to have a lady object."

"You're certainly not lacking in confidence."

He captured her gaze, held it with a challenge in his own. "Would you want a man who was?"

He had the right of it there. She wanted a man who knew exactly what he was doing and how to do it remarkably well. With a quick shake of her head, she turned her attention to her scotch, finishing it off, grateful that it was finally kicking in, helping her to relax.

Taking the glass from her, he passed it off to a footman, never shifting his eyes from her. She found herself wishing a man would look at her with that intensity if she weren't masked. She considered tossing it off, but then he would walk away and she would never again have the opportunity for the attentions of one such as he. Or worse, he would laugh at her audacity to come here. She had confidence in all things save her ability to lure a man into wanting her.

"I must beg your forgiveness," he said. "Gentlemen aren't supposed to approach the ladies but rather are to wait until they've made their selection."

"But then you're not one to follow the rules."

His eyes narrowed again. "We *are* acquainted."

"Your reputation as a hellion is quite well-known and documented from what I read in the gossip papers."

"I suppose I have my moments."

An abundance of them based on the rumors and speculations. She'd never much cared for the gossip sheets. It wasn't real journalism, and yet it did provide information that was serving her now.

"I am at a disadvantage," he said, "for all I know about you is that you are adventurous."

Her heart gave a little kick. Had he realized who she was? "How would you know that?"

"You're here. This is not a place for the timid but rather the bold. Although the question remains, exactly how bold are you?" He skimmed his finger along the side of her neck. She'd never before noticed how sensitive the skin was there. Or perhaps it was simply his flesh carrying some magical properties that heightened awareness. She imagined his touch over her entire body, the gratification it would bring. "Bold enough to retire to the bedchamber that I've already reserved, to adhere to my wishes, to find pleasure in my arms?"

She had never shied away from anything: drinking spirits, smoking her father's cigars, using profanity. She was quite certain it was her bold behavior, her unwillingness to be perceived as a simpering female, that was largely responsible for her never having had a suitor fall head over heels in love with her. Yet here was a man who seemed to admire boldness in a woman, at least in a woman he wanted to bed, not necessarily in one he wished to wed.

Squaring her shoulders, she met and held his gaze. For tonight, she could give but one answer and come away satisfied. "Yes."

His eyes darkened with triumph, his smile one of pure maleness that set her heart to thundering. She wanted him to give her that smile when they were finished. She wanted to be far more than he'd ever known, to give him something better than he'd ever had. Her competitive streak—which more than one gentleman told her was unattractive—was rising to the fore. But wouldn't every woman want to be un-forgettable?

With a slight bow, he indicated the doorway through which she'd entered earlier. As she turned for it, his hand came to rest possessively against her lower back, the heat of his flesh seeping through the thin fabric to warm her from head to toe. He so easily ignited her passions. Her nerves thrummed, yearning for a heavier, more sure touch.

Confidently, he guided her into the hallway and up the stairs. With each step, her knees seemed to weaken. Grabbing onto the banister, she refused to swoon or give any indication that, as much as she wanted this, she was also quite unnerved by it and where their journey would lead. The landing branched out into three hallways. They took the one to the right. Their feet were eerily quiet on the thick carpeting. Apparently, no one wished to be disturbed. Moans, high-pitched squeals, grunts drifted from rooms they passed.

"Thicker doors would be nice." She didn't realize she'd spoken until he chuckled.

"Your cries of pleasure will eclipse all of theirs."

She snapped her head around to look at him. No arrogance, simply knowledge and confidence. He knew what he was about. That was what she wanted: a man of experience and skill. It seemed silly to hesitate now that she had it. She'd come here to shed her virginity in a manner that left no regrets. Being with the Duke of Ashebury was certain to be memorable.

When they reached the very last door, from inside his jacket he withdrew a key and inserted it into a lock. With a turn of the brass, a twist of the knob, the door swung open only a fraction, only enough to reveal the bed laced with shadows that danced as candles flickered.

It was incredibly large, roomy enough for two, perhaps even three. A canopy of heavy velvet was tied back to reveal the thick counterpane, one corner neatly folded to expose red satin sheets. She would lie between them with him.

He didn't push her forward, urge her to go in. He merely waited as though they had all the time in the world, as though minutes weren't ticking by, as though no one would stumble upon them and know the sort of mischief into which they were getting.

"If you've changed your mind . . ." he said quietly. Perhaps not all the time in the world although his tone reflected no impatience.

He would let her go was left unspoken, and yet she heard the words as though he'd shouted them. Nothing he could have said, nothing he could have done would have reassured her more that he would take care with her. That he was the one with whom she should spend this night.

She walked into the room. The few flickering candles placed at strategic points and a low fire burning in the hearth were all that held complete darkness at bay. A table to the side housed a bottle of champagne, decanters, tumblers, and crystal flutes. A sofa rested before the fireplace, a fainting couch waited near the window.

He stepped in. The door clicked closed. The lock *snicked* into place.

She jerked her gaze back to the satin sheets, then turned her attention to a box perched on three legs that rested near the foot of the bed. With two steps she neared it, studied it, tried to make sense of why it would be here. "Is this your camera?" she asked.

"Yes."

She swung around to face him. "Surely you don't intend to take a photograph of us . . . copulating."

He chuckled low. "That would be quite the trick. No. I want to take a photograph of only you—lying on the bed,"

Chapter 3

*A*SHE didn't know who was more shocked: her at his request or him for her use of the word *copulating*. Ladies tended to fancy the act up with genteel words like "make love" when he had never in his life made love to a woman. He bedded, he fornicated, he . . . copulated. It was refreshing to be with a woman who was realistic about their purpose in being here.

Still, based on the sudden widening of her eyes, she might very well be prepared to copulate, but pose for him was another matter entirely. Not uncommon. His request generally caused hesitation. "Before you say no, allow me the opportunity to explain."

"It's perverted. No explanation is necessary."

Perhaps her forthrightness was not to be welcomed after all. "I assure you that what I have in mind falls well outside the realm of perversion. Please, have a seat before the fire." Giving her no chance to decline his invitation, he marched over to the table and lifted a decanter. "I've never known a lady not to prefer champagne." He poured the scotch he'd reserved for himself into two tumblers, lifted them, and faced her.

She'd not moved.

The disadvantage to not knowing her identity was that he had no history of her with which to map out his strategy. It was also a challenge that he embraced. Most ladies wanted to be with him badly enough that they were willing to do anything he asked. But not her. He was taken off guard by the thrill of being in the presence of one who wasn't so quick to fall into his arms.

Since she knew who he was, she had to run about in his posh circle, which meant that in all likelihood she was an aristocrat. Possibly married. Insufficient light prevented him from determining if there was a fading indention on her finger from the recent removal of a wedding band. Not that it mattered. Her presence indicated that she was either unhappy or curious or bored. Women came here for all sorts of reasons. Men for only one: They wanted a willing partner who was unlikely to be infected with the French disease. Men paid a membership; ladies did not.

With a slight tilting of his head, he indicated the sofa. "Please."

He watched the delicate muscles of her throat work as she swallowed before gliding over to the sofa and tucking herself into a corner. Every movement was poised and elegant. Her deportment had not been left to chance. She'd been trained. Definitely nobility.

Settling into the opposite corner, he extended the glass, grateful when she took it. He stretched his arm over the back of the sofa. An unfurling of his fingers would have him touching her skin, and he was tempted to do exactly that, but he feared his boldness would make her more skittish, and his desire for the photograph came first. She didn't flinch or retreat, but her eyes were alert, watchful. He liked that she wasn't afraid, but neither was she stupid.

"I'm not one to hurt women," he felt compelled to say.

"I should hope not. My father would kill you. Extremely painfully and very slowly."

No husband then, or perhaps a bastard who didn't care. He arched a brow. "You would confess to being here?"

She lifted a pale, delicate shoulder. "I could suffer through his disappointment much more easily than I could suffer through not gaining retribution for being wronged." A corner of her mouth hitched up. "On the other hand, I might just kill you myself." She gave a quick nod. "Probably would. I'd find immense satisfaction in it, come to think of it."

She took a sip of the scotch, a glittering in her dark eyes as though the notion of doing him in pleased her, and for a moment he almost forgot about the photograph, as desire stronger than any he'd felt in a good long while pierced him. He almost asked her to remove the damned mask, to reveal herself. To tell him why she'd chosen to come here tonight. Instead, he honored the purpose of this place to hold secrets sacred.

"You certainly don't seem to lack confidence," he mused.

"No, I've never been accused of that."

But he heard in her voice that she had been accused of something, been found lacking in some regard. He almost followed that trail of inquiry, but this place was not a confessional, and he wasn't here to lighten anyone else's burdens. Merely his own. To that end, he swallowed a good portion of his scotch, welcomed its fire, allowed it to work its heat through his chest. "There is beauty in the human form," he said quietly.

Her gaze came to rest on him, and he thought there was beauty in the eyes as well. He cursed the mask that shadowed hers. Brown perhaps. But intelligent. He'd like to see them in the sunlight. He'd like to see them smoldering when she was lost in a vortex of passion, when her body was reaching for the peak, when it flung her off it. "Yet we hide it beneath layers of clothing as though it's something of which we should be ashamed."

"Our bodies are personal, private."

"I won't take that from you. All I want is your legs."

As though he were a schoolboy in need of having

his knuckles rapped with a ruler, she narrowed her eyes. "A lady's ankles are not to be shown."

"And yet at this very moment you're barefoot."

"I was told it's the way it's done here. Yet you're not."

"Would you like for me to be, to even things up a bit?" Before she could respond, he tugged off his boots and stockings, stretched out his legs. "As for your ankles, it's silly for Society to believe that a little showing of the leg is going to turn a man into an uncontrollable savage, unable to tame his baser instincts." He leaned toward her, grateful when she didn't recoil. But then something told him that she wasn't one to retreat. "The body should be celebrated. Every line, every dip, every curve. Everything comes together so perfectly. It's a marvel really. I take great pleasure in the beauty of it. There are nude statues considered great works of art. Nude paintings that people can appreciate, that very nearly bring them to their knees because they are so remarkable. Photography can be just as artistic, just as enthralling when done properly. I don't know who you are. No one will ever know that you posed for me. No one will ever see the resulting image, except for me. It's for my private collection. You won't remove the silk. I'll simply slip it up a bit past your knees. I'll work with the shadow and the light. Then you'll be captured in art."

"That's not really why I came here."

"You came here for sex."

She opened her mouth, closed it. Sighed. "Well, yes, to be perfectly blunt about it."

"You shall have that as well. A photograph before, perhaps one after if you're up for it. One in silk, one in sheets. We'll be telling a story."

She shook her head. "It seems wrong."

Not to him. He got up, went to the fire, and stared into the writhing flames. How could he explain to her what it was like to constantly dream of mangled bodies? After twenty years, there were still nights when he awoke in a cold sweat, nights when he heard the screaming winds racing over the moors and imagined that they were his parents' cries. He hadn't slept through the night since he was eight years old. He thought if he could just replace the ghastly images of severed and contorted limbs with beautiful perfection, that eventually the nightmares would lessen. Perhaps they would even go away entirely. "What is wrong with appreciating the beauty of a shapely leg, a well-turned ankle, the arch of a foot, the curl of small toes?"

He wouldn't photograph anything that would make a woman feel awkward or taken advantage of. He just wanted peace.

"I'm sorry, but I'm simply not prepared to be on display in that manner—for eternity."

He heard the absolute conviction in her voice and was torn between admiring her for standing by her convictions and cursing her for her stubbornness. Turning, he took a step toward her and held out his hand. "All right, then, if you're not comfortable being photographed, let's get on with what you came here for. I'll make do with that."

Without taking his hand, she stood swiftly and he could fairly see the anger shimmering off her. Why the devil did he find it so damned attractive? Women never expressed displeasure with him, no matter how badly he behaved.

"Make do?" she asked tartly. "I'd always heard you were a charmer. Now I have to wonder what other rumors regarding you are false."

"A good many of them, I suspect."

"Well, I'm certainly not going to climb into bed with a man who doesn't desire me, who is simply *making do*."

She spun on her heel. He grabbed her arm to stay her actions. The heated look she directed his way could have felled a lesser man. Damnation, it only made him want her all the more. There was fire in her, smoldering, never before banked. She was here for something that was as important to her as the photographs were for him. He'd bet his life on it.

"A poor choice of wording on my part. I'm disappointed that you won't pose for me, but trust me, I am not disappointed that we are going to . . . copulate."

He cursed the blasted mask that prevented him from seeing if she was blushing, cursed the shadows that prevented him from seeing the flush of her skin.

"You don't desire me," she announced.

"Not desire you? Are you mad? I've never desired anyone as much. I have an artist's eye, and while the silk may cover you, it still manages to reveal everything about you. That's why I knew you would be perfect for the photograph."

"Perfect?"

She spoke the word as though she wasn't quite familiar with it, as though it had never been applied to her. "Yes, perfect. You are not tall, but you have a good deal of leg. Based on the way the silk folds around them when you walk, I believe I would find your calves to be quite fetching."

"Fetching?"

Again doubt. He was beginning to wonder if a troll existed beneath the mask. But then, as much as he loved lines, angles, and curves, he'd never judged by appearance alone. She was more than a face or legs or body. Her presence here was testament to that. Shy misses didn't wander these halls, step into bedchambers. She was a woman who knew her own mind, knew what she wanted, and went after it. In truth, he found that aspect to her more alluring than anything that he might discover beneath the silk, or even the mask.

"I don't photograph just anyone," he told her. "Only those I find pleasing."

"And how many is that, Your Grace? Based on your reputation, I suspect at least a hundred."

"Not even a dozen."

She seemed surprised by that declaration. "Did you not think you were special?" he asked.

She didn't answer, didn't so much as nod, yet he saw the truth in her eyes. She thought herself lacking. Was that the reason behind her coming here tonight? Because she wished to feel appreciated? Again, he wondered if she was married, if some man failed to give her the attention she deserved.

"Is it possible you might change your mind about posing for me?" he asked.

"I couldn't do anything so lewd."

"It's very tastefully done, I promise you. The most intimate aspects of you will remain covered. Shadows will hide a good deal as well. The focus will be your legs."

"What do you do with the photographs?"

"I don't use them for any sort of erotic stimulation, if that's what you're thinking. I simply appreciate beauty."

"Beauty? In my legs?"

Going to one knee, he wrapped a hand around her ankle. "Allow me to show you."

MINERVA thought she must be mad to still be here, to not have removed herself from this room, this man, as soon as she realized that he wanted more from her than a romp between the sheets. On the other hand, was he truly asking for something so awful when she was willing to give him her innocence, her naïveté? An incredible intimacy was going to pass between them, and she was going to balk at a photograph? And yet to think of herself captured for all eternity . . . He might claim no one else would see it, but how could she be sure? How had the past six years managed to turn her into such a doubting Thomas, to not trust a man's word?

His hand was so large, so warm, so incredibly gentle as though he feared crushing her bones. No one ever made her feel delicate. She'd been raised to stand up for herself, to know that she was beneath no one. Yet she wanted to be beneath him.

His passion for the human body was evident when he spoke of its beauty. She'd never in her life been made to feel beautiful. At least not by anyone outside the family. She was her father's precious daughter, could do no wrong. But it wasn't the same as being looked upon with appreciation by someone who was no relation at all.

She gave a nod, not much of one, but still he saw it, and his mouth formed a slow smile that seemed to target the very core of her womanhood. He patted his knee to alert her that he was going to place her foot there. Of its own accord to balance her, her hand went to his shoulder, to his strong, broad, sturdy shoulder. She shouldn't have been surprised. He was an adventurer. He'd climbed mountains, explored pyramids, danced among natives. His skin was darkened by the sun.

That became apparent when his hand rested next to her pale foot. Earth beside snow, good soil beside white sands. Her toes wiggled and curled against his rock-solid thigh. Was there any aspect of this man that wasn't firm? She imagined how it might feel to run her hands over him, to test every muscle, to find no part of him that wasn't toned to perfection.

"Your foot is flawless," he said in a reverent voice.

"Not certain that's something to brag about."

He looked up at her, and she found herself wishing for more light so she could see the blue of his eyes. "You have a fine arch, exquisite toes. The lines are good, giving you a most attractive ankle."

"Which you wish to photograph."

"Yes." His hand moved up, his other joined it, to circle her ankle and to ease up toward her calf.

If she allowed him to bed her, his hand would be traveling much higher, would travel all over her. Whatever had possessed her to think she could be comfortable with a man in a situation such as this? Grace had been correct, blast her. The intimacy was too much.

She jerked her foot free, stepped back. "I'm sorry. I can't do this. I'm not so bold after all."

He unfolded his body in a way that was at once predatory, yet unthreatening. "Is this your first time alone with a man?"

She released a small scoff. "It's that obvious, is it?"

He chuckled low, but there was no joy in the sound. Rather, it seemed to echo with disappointment. "I should have guessed." Then his gaze homed in on her, sharp and demanding. "Why?"

"Why is it obvious?"

"No, why are you looking to be deflowered in a place of sinners by a man you—" He scoffed. "I was going to say hardly know, but I don't know if that's true or not. Who are you, Lady V, that this would be your recourse?"

Confessing to Grace was one thing. To bare her soul, her frustrations to this man who could have any woman he wanted, was beyond the pale. "Because I wanted to know what all the fuss was about. No one faults men for exploring their desires. Why should women not have the same consideration?"

"Because they are so much better than us."

"Yet the carnal act equalizes us, don't you think?"

"You are a woman of remarkable notions."

She released a quick breath of air in frustration. "You talk about how beautiful the body is and how we shouldn't hide it away. Why should what passes between a man and a woman be shrouded in whispers and only talked about in dark corners? Why must women repress their natural urges?"

Oh, she should be quiet now. He was studying her like she'd said something both profound and stupid.

"Do you have *urges*?" he asked quietly.

"Of course I do. And I don't believe it's wrong to have them. It's why I'm here."

He trailed the knuckle of his forefinger along her chin, and she almost removed the mask so he could outline the curve of her cheek.

"If I were any other man, I'd assuage your nervousness and have you on your back in a trice. Unfortunately for us both, I don't bed virgins."

Profound disappointment slammed into her. She should have taken comfort from the regret in his voice. Instead, she was somewhat cross. Was even her virginity to be held against her? "Why?"

"Because I prefer it hard and rough. I want women screaming from pleasure, not pain. A woman experiences discomfort the first time. You deserve someone who has a bit more patience. As a matter of fact, it should be someone who has a care for you, someone who would place your pleasures above his own. It should be someone you love; even if that love doesn't last past the coupling, it should exist beforehand."

"Your first time, did you love her?" She held up her hand to stay whatever response he might offer. "My apologies. It's not my business."

His eyes grew warm, his smile became one of fond remembrance. "I was madly in love with her, for an entire fortnight. A farmer's daughter, with hair the color of wheat and eyes the shade of a new leaf in spring. There was nothing I wouldn't do to please her. Nothing she wouldn't do to please me. The moon was full the night she introduced me to the pleasures of a woman's body. There was a new moon the night I discovered her in the hayloft doing the same for another fellow. But still, I can't look at a full moon without thinking of long limbs, warm flesh, and the fragrance of raw sex. The first time happens only once, Lady V. Be a little in love with him."

Dear God, she thought she might have fallen a bit in love right then. Just a little. She couldn't help looking over at the bed with a touch of longing.

"Gra—" She stopped. No real names, nothing to give away her identity. "My friend tried to explain to me why coming here was such an awful idea. She wasn't nearly as eloquent as you."

"Hardly eloquent." He returned to the sofa and begun tugging on his boots. "I'll escort you to your carriage."

"I took a hansom. Less chance of my adventures being discovered that way."

He stood. "I'll have my driver give you a lift home."

"That's not necessary."

"I'm not going to have you wandering the streets searching for a cab this time of night, and I'm too indolent to go searching with you."

"My anonymity will be compromised."

"I'll have my driver swear an oath not to tell me where he took you." He approached her. "I may be a rogue, but I respect the purpose of this place. Your secrets are safe with me."

It was probably foolish, but she believed him. "What about your camera equipment?"

"I'll return for it after I've seen you safely delivered from here."

She strolled to the door, very much aware of his footsteps echoing behind her. She turned the key in the lock, wrapped her hand around the knob, stared at the dark wood—

"I don't suppose you would at least kiss me?" She despised that she'd been reduced to pleading but to leave with nothing at all after all the planning, preparation, and risk seemed doubly unfair.

"Have you never been kissed?"

Mortification swamped her, but it was easier knowing that he had no idea who she was or how old or how unappealing. "Never."

She was aware of him moving nearer, the heat of his body radiating from him, enveloping her. Swallowing hard, she was on the verge of turning around when his mouth came to rest at the nape of her neck. She barely recalled that she'd wanted his lips on hers, as she became aware of dewy moisture gathering in a small circle on her skin, warmth seeping into her muscles and bones, traveling slowly yet ever so intensely through her, a delicious shiver passing in its wake. If he could create such sensations with only his mouth—

What a fool she was to have changed her mind. How ridiculous she would appear if she changed it once again. But even if she did alter her course, he wouldn't be the one to satisfy the cravings he was stirring to life. She was still a virgin, not at all his preference.

His hand came around, his fingers brushing over her chin but settling in to turn her face back slightly, then his mouth blanketed hers with unerring accuracy. His other hand cradled the back of her head while his tongue outlined her lips, before urging them to part. He took the kiss deep, so deep, exploring her mouth as she imagined he'd explored a good deal of the world, slowly, thoroughly, giving his undivided attention to every minute detail. He savored. He worshipped.

His guttural groan echoed between them, and she felt it rumbling through his chest, pressed against her back. Moaning, she was astounded by the intimacy of this prelude to something far more primitive. This man took; he gave no quarter. In bed, he would have conquered her, and yet she could not help but believe that she would have come away the conqueror.

She almost wept with longing when he drew back and lightly stroked his thumb over her tingling, swollen, and damp lips. Too many shadows prevented her from reading his eyes, his expression.

"You make me regret that I have an aversion to virgins," he said, his voice a low thrum that skittered through her.

"You make me regret that I turned cowardly."

"Not cowardly. You ensured you don't awaken in the morning with misgivings."

She questioned if it were possible for a woman to awaken with anything other than triumph after being with him. Reaching past her, he opened the door. "Let's get a move on, shall we, before we both change our minds?"

She wasn't convinced that would be such a bad thing. He escorted her to the changing room. When a maid finished helping her dress, Minerva found him waiting in the hallway, his back to the wall, his gaze distant, and she wondered where his thoughts had taken him. Still wearing her mask, she was grateful that he would never know the identity of the woman who had made a fool of herself this evening.

Offering his arm, he led her out to the street where carriages were lined up. They reached the coach bearing his ducal crest. A footman and a driver were standing near the horses. They both came to attention.

"Wilkins, you'll be taking the lady home. She's going to give you her address. Should either of you gentlemen ever tell me or anyone where you delivered her, I shall cut out your tongue." With an ironic twist of his lips, he looked at Minerva. "Sufficient to guard your identity?"

Even knowing it was no doubt an idle threat, and he'd simply sack the man, she said, "Yes, thank you." She whispered her address to the driver. The footman opened the door. Ashebury handed her up.

"Good night, my lady."

She paused in settling onto the seat. "How do you know I'm a lady?" Although she wasn't one who should be addressed as such. Her mother was the daughter of a duke, but her father was a commoner.

"The way you hold yourself, the way you move, the way you speak. And the fact that you came here, hoping for something more than a common tupping. I hope at some point you find what you're searching for."

Strange how she was no longer certain that she knew precisely what it was. "I hope you get your photograph. I suppose you'll go inside and find a willing lady."

Slowly he shook his head. "No. You were what I wanted tonight. I never settle for substitutes."

He slammed the door shut. With a jerk, the coach took off. Minerva removed her mask, set it on her lap, and leaned back into the plush padding of the carriage.

You were what I wanted tonight.

She wondered if he would have said the same if he'd known who she was.

Chapter 4

*S*HE smelled of verbena.

Lounging in a chair before the fireplace in his library long past midnight, sipping his scotch, Ashe was aware of her fragrance lingering on his fingers, her taste haunting his palate. He couldn't determine why he'd let her go so easily, why'd he'd not worked harder to convince her to pose for him, why he'd turned away the opportunity to bed her. Granted, he'd never taken a woman's virginity. He'd spoken true regarding his aversion to deflowering a woman, but going against his preferences seemed a small price to pay in order to uncover the secrets of such an intriguing woman.

She'd been at the Nightingale Club for more than simply determining what all the fuss was about. Something more compelling had driven her there, just as he was driven by the ghosts of his past. While he'd not been on the railway car, he might as well have been, because he felt as though he'd died alongside his parents in the fiery aftermath of the trains colliding. When they were departing for the railway station, he'd been so angry with them for leaving him yet again, that he'd shouted at their retreating backs that he hated them. His nanny had scolded him, rapped his knuckles with her ruler, and when he was still moping about by nightfall, had sent him to bed without his supper.

It was one of the last punishments he ever received.

The Marquess of Marsden seldom punished. Wandering the hallways like a wraith, he'd barely known they were there. The boys had been allowed to roam around as they pleased. The butler was too old to be much of a disciplinarian. The cook prepared meals, often containing more sweets than nourishment because they were "poor orphaned lads." If they hadn't spent so much time running over the moors, they'd have probably become little tubby lads who could do no more than roll over the grounds. But they had run wild, climbing trees, scrambling over ruins, and breaking more than one bone each. Ashe had once walked with a broken ankle to the nearby village to have a physician patch him up. No one could claim that they weren't hardy although a good many had declared them uncivilized. They had a series of schoolmasters who attempted to reform them, but they were beyond reforming.

Being familiar with how easily and swiftly death could come to call, they wanted to get as much out of life as they could. So they did as they pleased.

And it would have pleased him to have bedded tonight's mysterious woman. To have captured more than a glimpse of ankle and calf. To have focused his lens on her—

He heard a thud and rattle in the hallway as though someone had knocked into a table, followed quickly by a deep-voiced apology, probably to the object itself as there were no servants wandering the residence this time of night. Looking toward the door, he watched as Edward Alcott stumbled into the room.

"There you are," Edward announced. "I've been looking for you. I'm in need of lodgings. My brother's blasted wife has kicked me out."

He staggered to the table housing spirits, and, with an awkward clumsiness that threatened to upend more than one decanter, poured himself a drink. "She claims I smell like a distillery, doesn't approve of the hours I keep, and thinks I'm a bad influence."

"Julia seems to have pegged you quite accurately."

With a scowl, Edward dropped into the chair opposite Ashe's. "That may be, but still I don't know what Grey sees in that beastly woman. She's an utter nag, no fun whatsoever. She won't even let him go on adventures with us."

"Why would you want him to? The two of you only argue when you're together." They were constantly at each other. Ashe and Locksley had learned to ignore them, not to interfere in all their little spats. Eventually, the brothers would resolve whatever the issue was and move on to another.

"Because he's my brother."

The simple statement seemed to carry a wealth of power and truth behind it. Ashe had no siblings, although Edward, Grey, and Locke were as close to being his brothers as anyone could be and not be related by blood.

"Anyway," Edward murmured, "I was hoping you could spare a bed for a few nights. If not, I'll make do at the club."

"You can stay here as long as you need. I've no plans for the guest rooms."

"You're a sport." He settled back in the chair, sipped his scotch, then lifted his glass. "It's good to be back in London. Plenty of scotch here, gaming hells, and women. Tonight, I indulged in all three. Think I shall do the same tomorrow."

"You're not going to Julia's soiree?" The countess had wanted to host a celebration of their return.

"Of course I'll be there, but it's not going to go on all night now, is it? She'll leave us with plenty of hours for mischief after. So what did you do this evening?"

"I went to the Nightingale."

Edward grinned. "You do like your women classy."

"I don't know how classy a woman is if she's married and searching for a lover."

"They're not all married. I've deflowered a couple."

Ashe's stomach clenched with the thought that maybe Lady V had returned—

"Not tonight." He was surprised that he sounded as though he were growling.

Edward scoffed. "No, not tonight. Too many games have to be played there, ladies protected. This evening I wanted a woman with no reputation to defend. Had two of them actually. Sweet girls."

"And you wonder why Julia finds you offensive?"

"The woman has no spirit of adventure. She is no doubt as boring in bed as she is out of it. I'm surprised Grey hasn't taken on a mistress."

Although they'd been married for a little over two years, it was unlikely the length of time would matter. "He loves her. Besides, he was never quite as wild as the rest of us."

"He thought he had to be responsible, set an example for me." Edward shrugged. "I'm glad to be the second son and not have responsibilities. Besides, as the younger brother, I'm to be indulged."

"You're younger by all of two minutes."

"More like an hour, I think. I seem to recall Nanny telling us that at some point—before the world went topsy-turvy." The night their parents died. None of them liked to talk about it although Ashe was more likely to refer to it as the night all went to hell.

"Did you meet anyone of interest tonight?" Edward asked.

Ashe wasn't surprised that Edward was shifting the conversation away from himself. In spite of Edward's need for attention, he didn't like to divulge much about his personal matters. It was a trait they had in common.

"No." Ashe couldn't explain his reasoning, but he didn't want Edward heading to the Nightingale with the purpose of deflowering Lady V. He expected she would return at some point. Based on the kiss they shared, she was an extremely passionate woman with untapped desires. He'd been so incredibly tempted to remove the mask, to discover her identity.

Damn his obsession with capturing the perfection of the human form. Damn his aversion to taking a woman's innocence. She had wanted to be bedded. He should have obliged, instead of spouting all the drivel about love and the farmer's daughter who had broken his heart with her callous betrayal. It hadn't helped that it had been Edward in the blasted hayloft with her. But that was long ago, and with distance, he came to realize his heart had been barely bruised. Still, he did have fond memories of the girl. Might have had fond memories of Lady V if he'd truly thought she understood exactly what she was getting into. There had been moments when she'd seemed a woman of the world, strong and tough. And others when she had seemed almost naive. Innocent. Too trusting.

The women who usually visited the Nightingale had been hardened by something in life: an uncaring husband, a cruel one, an indifferent one. A disappointing lover. They'd given up on dreams, love, and happy-ever-afters. Lady V didn't fit the mold of those who usually frequented the place. He nearly scoffed aloud. What did he truly know about her?

Perhaps she didn't deserve love. Perhaps she was a termagant. Or unlikeable. Maybe she was dying. Maybe she was merely young and foolish.

Why hadn't he questioned her? Why hadn't he cared about her reasons for being there? Because, like Edward, he was accustomed to merely caring about his own needs and desires. She wasn't the fool. He was. For missing an opportunity simply because something about her had struck him as fanciful, had made him believe she deserved more than an anonymous coupling.

But it had been what she'd wanted. It had been her choice to go there. Who was he to question it?

Who the devil was she? Lady V. No doubt, for her, the V stood for virgin. For him, it was verbena. He brought his glass to his lips, and her scent wafted around him, caused a tightening in his gut. If he seduced her properly, she would pose for him. But to seduce her properly, he needed to know more about her. He needed to know who she was.

He shot to his feet. "I'm going out. Take whichever bedchamber suits you."

Edward shoved himself out of the chair, then leaned on it for support. "I'll go with you."

"No, it's a personal matter."

"Has she a name?"

The problem with growing up with someone was that he tended to know him too well. "I'm sure she does. Unfortunately, I've yet to learn it."

Leaving Edward to ponder the cryptic statement,

Ashe went in search of his coachman to have his vehicle readied. It was after midnight, but his man was accustomed to his keeping odd hours. Ashe felt no degree of remorse when Wilkins, dressed in his nightclothes, answered the door to his bedchamber.

"What address did she give you?" Ashe demanded.

Wilkins blinked, clearly flummoxed by the question.

"The woman at the Nightingale, the one I had you take home," Ashe explained.

"I rather fancy keeping my tongue, Your Grace."

Ashe sighed. "Right." He had a good many faults, but lying to women wasn't one of them. He'd given her his word that neither his driver nor footman would tell him the address. To gain what he wanted from her, he required her trust. If his driver told him—

"You can't tell me the address but you can take me there." He could see the discomfiture cross Wilkins's face. "Look, man, I told her that you wouldn't *tell* me. I didn't promise you wouldn't divulge it in some other manner. I realize it's semantics, but it works. Now come on, get dressed. I want to see where she lives."

Hopefully, he would recognize the house, would know who resided there. If he didn't, he would find someone who knew, or he'd send Wilkins to the servants' door to make discreet inquiries among the staff. Determining her family was the first step to figuring out who she was.

Nearly an hour later, Ashe was staring at the building, one with which he was far too familiar. As he hadn't bothered to awaken the footman, Wilkins had opened the coach door for him and was now standing beside him.

"She had you bring her to the Twin Dragons?" Ashe asked, incredulously. A few years earlier, Drake Darling had extended membership in his exclusive gaming hell to women.

"Yes, Your Grace."

"Did she go in?"

"Marched right up the steps. Footman opened the door before she got there. Didn't appear that she had to show her membership card."

That Lady V would come here rather than being returned home indicated she didn't trust him, was extremely clever, and had a reputation to protect. Or perhaps she had a gambling addiction. She'd certainly been playing the odds tonight at the Nightingale.

"So she comes here on a regular basis. She's known," Ashe murmured.

"It would appear so."

It was unlikely that she was still there, but on the off chance . . . he bounded up the steps. Unlike her, he did have to present his membership card. He'd not been to the place since he returned to London. Once inside, he stopped by the counter, where a woman was only too happy to take coats and keep track of them. She smiled at him.

"Have you seen—" he began, not certain where to go from there. When Lady V had emerged from the dressing room at the Nightingale, she'd been wearing a dark green cape over her pale green gown. How could he describe her? Her hair was some shade of brown, which he couldn't properly identify because of the dimness at the Nightingale. Dark eyes that could belong to any woman although the shade could have been an illusion caused by the absence of any significant light. Not terribly tall. That was a certainty. Not heavyset but not particularly slender, either. She was the sort a man could hold on to, and dammit all if he wasn't suddenly desperate to do just that.

The clerk was waiting expectantly, leaving Ashe to feel completely idiotic. He was accustomed to being in charge of a situation. He didn't like that she had such control over him, could make him lose sight of all rational thought. "Never mind."

He strode into the gaming area. This time of night, there were gents aplenty, only about a half dozen ladies. But not a single female garbed in pale green. She could be in the area restricted to women. He wasn't going to send someone in to search for her. That wouldn't gain her trust. And again, he couldn't provide an accurate description. He might know her if he saw her, but then again, he might merely make a fool of himself.

Still, he walked the perimeter of the room, searching. He meandered between the gaming tables, wandered into other areas that were open to both genders. Surely, if she spotted him, a measure of surprise would cross her features. But then there were so few women, and while they acknowledged him—a couple even seemed quite pleased to discover he'd returned to London—none of them seemed taken aback, embarrassed, or nervous by his presence. She was either a damned fine actress, or she wasn't here.

Disappointed, he acknowledged it was most likely the latter.

However, knowing she frequented this establishment increased his chances of finding her at some point. He'd return here tomorrow night after Julia's blasted affair.

MINERVA was curled on a sofa in the morning room reading Brontë when Grace walked in. Considered family, she didn't require a butler announce her arrival. Her eyes filled with worry, she quickly crossed the room, sat on the sofa, and searched Minerva's face. "How are you this morning?"

Minerva smiled. "Quite fine."

With a huge sigh, Grace slumped back against the cushions. "Thank God. I hardly slept a wink last night thinking of you going to that decadent place. I'm so glad you didn't."

"But I did."

Grace sprang forward. "So it's done?"

The heat rushed to Minerva's face, nearly scalding her with its intensity. "Not exactly. Seems I didn't have the nerve for it after all."

"But you went." Grace glanced around as though she expected to see spies hidden behind the plants. She lowered her voice to a whisper. "What was it like?"

Minerva laughed. "After all your warnings, you have the audacity to ask?"

"I'm curious. I would never go there, but now I have an opportunity to hear all about it."

"That's really why you're here, isn't it? Curiosity, not concern that I might be suffering through misgivings."

"I'm here first and foremost for you. I've been so worried that you'd select someone who wasn't kind or someone who cared only about his own needs. I didn't want you to have a selfish lover."

She didn't think Ashebury would have been selfish. If his kiss were any indication, he would give far more than he received.

"So come on, Minnie, don't be cruel. Satisfy my curiosity. Tell me about this wicked, wicked place."

She almost suggested Grace ask her brother, but she was obligated not to reveal who all she'd seen there even if it was someone she considered family. "It wasn't what I expected. It was all very proper. People stood around talking. Ladies masked for secrecy. Men not caring who knew they were there."

"Who was there?"

"I can't say."

"Because you didn't know them?"

"I took a vow not to reveal any identities. The woman in charge wears an emerald green gown and matching mask. Very flashy. You have to reveal yourself to her so she knows who everyone is. She'll come after you if she learns you've spoken the name of anyone there. I don't know how she would manage to find out, but I believed her."

"But you can tell me. I won't tell."

"I really can't."

"Well, you're no fun."

"So more than one gentleman has told me."

"Minerva, I didn't—"

She squeezed Grace's hand. "I know. I'm just being difficult. And the truth is that I'm not bothered by the myriad of ways that gentlemen find me lacking. It doesn't matter what everyone else thinks as long as I'm true to myself—as my mother, bless her, constantly reminds me. Last night, for the first time, I actually believed it. It was quite liberating." While everything that happened there was not to be spoken of, this was Grace, her dearest friend. "I caught a very fine gentleman's attention."

Grace's eyes widened as she leaned forward. "Who?"

Minerva scowled.

"Right then. You can't tell me. Was he handsome?"

"Why does everyone care about looks? But, yes, exceedingly so."

"Charming?"

"Very."

"Nobility?"

"Yes."

"Dark hair?"

Laughing at her friend's blatant attempt to deduce who he might have been, she shook her head. "Enough, Grace. I'm not going to play your little game. You'd never guess anyway. But I will tell you that he was immensely intriguing. He spoke about the beauty of the human form, in particular my legs."

"He saw your legs?"

"Well, not the entire leg. Just up to my calf. But when I arrived, I had to change into this silky bit of nothing, very similar to what is depicted in paintings that reflect the women of Rome. It's extremely easy to get into and, I suppose, exceedingly easy for a gent to get you out of. While I was almost completely covered except for my arms and décolletage, it didn't leave a lot to the imagination. No corset, no petticoats. I rather liked it, actually. It was light as a feather. But I suppose its purpose is to provide a more accurate assessment of one's figure."

"What did the men wear?"

Minerva scoffed. "That was the irritating part—they wore everything. I shall never understand why men and women must have different rules." She smiled. "But he removed his boots, so I would be more comfortable. Still, I just couldn't get comfortable enough to climb into bed with him."

"So what did you do?"

"It's going to sound silly, but we talked." She moved closer. "Here's the thing—he looked into my eyes when we conversed. So intensely as though he was truly interested. I have sat in the front parlor with gentlemen who were mesmerized by the design of their teacups. I ask a question, they answer with a solitary word. I attempt to start a discourse, and they can't be bothered to keep it going. I'm irrelevant. They seek to impress me by merely making an appearance. My man last night was attentive. He asked me questions. He told me a story from his past." She sighed. "It was bittersweet, Grace. To experience what it is to have the attention of a man who was intrigued by me. After I arrived home, I rather wished I hadn't left the Nightingale."

"It wasn't real, Minnie."

"Trust you to be so honest and blunt. Still it felt real. I'm rather convinced that not everyone is there for what goes on between the sheets."

"Why are they there?"

"I'm not sure. I expected to see people hungrily kissing or maybe even fornicating on a table or a chair—but there was none of that." She gave her head a slight shake, lifted a shoulder. "Oh, people sat closely together, and I saw a hand on a thigh here or a hip there, but they weren't ashamed of what they were doing."

"How could you tell? They were wearing masks."

"Not the men."

"But men are never ashamed."

Minerva smiled. "I suppose you have a point. Still, it would be nice if we were a bit more open about things."

"So you were open with your parents and told them where you were going?"

"Absolutely not!" She shoved playfully on Grace's shoulder. "I didn't mean we should be that open about things. No, I waited until they'd gone to bed. I slipped out, found a cab. Then my gentleman insisted his driver bring me home—only I had him take me to the Twin Dragons. I couldn't risk his discovering who my parents are. I don't think he's the blackmail sort, but you know my father. He would protect me and my reputation at any cost."

"Well, jolly good for your man, not letting you roam the streets searching for a cab at all hours of the night. If you should ever decide to go there again, you're to let me know, and I'll have one of our carriages waiting for you at the end of the street. I should have thought of that before. I was just so muddled with the notion of your actually doing it that I wasn't thinking."

"And how will you explain the carriage to my brother?"

Grace smiled slyly. "Not to worry. I can handle Lovingdon."

"You're the dearest of friends, but I doubt I'll go

back. Although I can't seem to stop thinking about what might have been."

"It can still be, just not there," Grace assured her. "My mother was on the shelf when she fell in love with my father."

"I'm not certain she could be considered on the shelf when she didn't have a Season. She was a commoner, a bookkeeper. I don't think commoners worry about getting married as much as we do."

"I suppose you have a point, there."

"I've also been a terrible hostess. Shall I ring for tea?"

"I can't stay. I'm meeting my mother in a bit, and we're going on a round of the orphanages. You should come with us."

"You're kind to invite me, but it was a rather late night, so I shall probably take a nap. By the by, did you receive an invitation to Lady Greyling's soiree this evening?"

"The one welcoming the hellions back to London?" She rolled her eyes. "I don't know why their return is given such fanfare."

"They went on safari. I think everyone wants to hear about it."

"Are you going then?"

"I was thinking of it, yes." Especially as Ashebury was certain to be there. She knew it was silly to take an interest in him, to place herself in his path so soon after last night, but he intrigued her. Besides, it was unlikely he'd approach her, that he would realize she was Lady V, but she would still have the opportunity to gaze on him—and to imagine what might have been between them.

"Shall we go together?" Grace asked. "Lovingdon and I could pick you up at half past seven."

"That would be lovely."

"Jolly good. I'll see you tonight then." Standing, Grace leaned in and kissed Minerva's cheek. "I'm glad nothing untoward happened last night."

"As am I," she lied.

Chapter 5

THE Countess of Greyling's drawing room was packed to the gills with ladies sitting on sofas and chairs while gentlemen stood about wherever they could find a few spare inches of space. Minerva and Grace had managed to secure tight spots near the center of the room, sharing a sofa with Ladies Sarah and Honoria.

Leaning against the wall, near the fireplace, the Duke of Ashebury radiated confidence and openly flirted with the ladies nearest to him, while gifting others with a secretive look that made each think she had his unfettered devotion. Not that he directed any of his heavy-lidded gazes Minerva's way. Fighting not to let his inattention sting her pride, she was incredibly grateful that she hadn't allowed him to bed her. It would have hurt immeasurably to see him showering others with his attentiveness while she received not an ounce of interest from him—even though her purpose in going to the Nightingale had been to ensure her anonymity. She could hardly bemoan his not dashing over to greet her when his not even batting an eye at her arrival was reassurance that he didn't recognize her from the night before.

All the trouble she'd gone to in order to hide her identity had worked. Her success should be met with pleasure rather than disappointment.

Standing in front of the fireplace, Mr. Edward Alcott, for the better part of the last half hour, had been regaling his audience with tales of their adventures in Africa. He was animated, constantly using his hands to add excitement to the various accounts of their exploits.

Minerva had been so caught up observing Ashebury, hoping in vain that he might at least give her a passing glance, that she'd barely listened to Mr. Alcott, but Lady Honoria's pressing a hand to her throat with a startled gasp had Minerva redirecting her attention to their orator.

"So there we were on the African savanna standing around for the better part of half an hour while Ashe set up his photography equipment," Mr. Alcott continued in a mesmerizing cadence that had the ladies sharing the sofa with Minerva scooting to the edge of their seats.

"When all of sudden"—Mr. Alcott took a quick step forward and swept his arms in a dramatic gesture—"out of the blue, the lion pounced."

Ladies inhaled sharply, jerking back as though that very creature had leaped from his fingertips.

Gloved hands covered mouths. Eyes widened. Minerva took some satisfaction in not visibly reacting—she had little tolerance for women pretending they were far too delicate for the realities of life—although her heart was hammering madly.

"It was an incredibly spectacular sight. Muscles bunching, sinew stretching, a roar that echoed—"

"For God's sake, Edward, get on with it," Ashebury said from his far-too-relaxed stance, arms crossed over his chest. With gaslights rather than flickering candles illuminating the room, his black hair, unfashionably long, served to make the blue of his eyes that much more noticeable. He appeared bored. She wished she'd had a clearer view of him last night when he'd seemed more interested, wished she hadn't closed her eyes when he'd kissed her. Had he closed his?

Mr. Alcott straightened. "Weaving a tale that mesmerizes is my talent. If you will be so good as to indulge me—especially as you serve as the hero of the story." He turned back to his audience. "As I was saying, the lion sprung forth from the tall grasses so magnificently. Locksley and I were quite taken aback by the sight of nature at its most primitive, its most feral. I daresay, it took us a few seconds to actually register that *a lion* had indeed *attacked* Ashe, taken him to the ground. That the duke was the huge fellow's prey, that the creature was in fact intending to make a meal of him."

"Oh, my dear Lord, you might have been eaten,"

Lady Honoria exclaimed. "What a ghastly way to go!"

Ashebury lifted a shoulder laconically and tilted his head slightly in a manner that implied he'd never doubted he would be the victor. Arrogant man. Minerva didn't know why she found that so appealing.

"Its roar still echoing around us, we sprung into action and readied our rifles." Mr. Alcott lifted his arms, leaned forward slightly, lowered his hands and his voice. "Unexpectedly, the great beast went completely and absolutely still. A hush settled over the grasslands. Then we heard a muffled cry. 'For God's sake, get him off me!' Locksley and I rushed forward. Somehow Ashe had managed to pull his knife from its scabbard and kill the creature." He straightened. "Not before it got its teeth into his shoulder unfortunately."

As the ladies sitting near Ashebury fluttered their hands and looked on the verge of swooning, he slowly rubbed his hand over his left shoulder. Minerva wondered if he were even aware of the action. Then a corner of his mouth hitched up. "But I got my photograph."

"Indeed you did," Mr. Alcott admitted. "And a splendid one it is."

There was such pride reflected in Ashebury's tone, in his mien. Minerva couldn't help but wonder if he would have exhibited the same satisfaction if he'd had success in convincing her to pose last night. Had he wanted the photograph of her as badly as he'd wanted the one of the lion? Not that he'd come anywhere near to placing his life at risk, but he'd spoken so passionately about the human form. She had to wonder now if he'd been terribly disappointed by her refusal to give in to his request. Or was the evening simply one of many? Had he already forgotten Lady V? Although he'd claimed that he wouldn't seek a substitute, she couldn't help but believe that he would have found someone to replace her quite easily, someone more adventurous, less prudish. She'd always taken such pride in her willingness to explore opportunities, to engage in new experiences. In hindsight, she couldn't be more disappointed in herself.

"You must have been so terrified," Lady Sarah said, breathlessly, both hands pressed to her chest, drawing Ashebury's eyes to her cleavage. The duke, blast him, grinned wickedly at Lady Sarah and her heaving bosom, and Minerva fought back a spark of jealousy as she wondered if he might want to photograph those ample orbs.

"Petrified," he admitted cockily, "but then I realized that if I didn't take some action I'd never get back to England, and it became quite clear rather quickly that neither Edward nor Locke were going to be of much assistance."

"You had to be incredibly strong to kill the awful beast," Lady Angela said.

"Incredibly so. Perhaps you'd like to test my muscles later."

Lady Angela turned red as a beet, her face splotchy, looking as though she'd broken out in hives. She never had been one to blush becomingly.

"That will be quite enough of that bawdy talk," Lady Greyling admonished, coming to her feet. It had always amazed Minerva that she could so easily control the hellions. "Refreshments are waiting for us in the main salon, along with the displays of Ashe's photographs. Let's make our way there, shall we?"

Ladies began to rise and join the gentlemen. Ashebury sinuously shoved himself away from the wall, so very slowly as though he were mimicking the great cat that he had killed. Minerva had seen lions on display at the zoological gardens, knew their graceful movements. She couldn't imagine the terror of facing one in the wilds.

"I'm going to make my way to Lovingdon," Grace said, touching her arm, obviously wanting her attention.

"Yes, all right. I'll catch up with you in a bit."

Grace departed. Minerva considered making her way to Ashebury to commend him on his quick thinking, his strength, his ability to stare death in the face and come out the victor, but two ladies approached him, and he graciously offered each an arm, then began escorting them from the room. Last night for a few fleeting moments, he'd been hers.

"I wonder where Lord Locksley is?" Lady Sarah mused, holding Minerva back as though she had the answer.

"Is he the reason you're here?" Minerva asked.

With a little wobble of her head, Sarah sighed. "Well, yes, I have to admit to being somewhat curious about him. He always makes an appearance in Mr. Alcott's stories and yet he so seldom attends any social functions."

"Why the interest?"

"Because he's mysterious, and I'm fascinated by mysteries. Besides, aren't you fascinated by the lords of Havisham? They're so adventuresome and brave and—"

"They're indulged," Minerva cut in, as they wandered from the room and into the hallway. "People let them do whatever they want with no consequence. Other than Greyling, I don't think any of them are seeing to their duties. How can they when they're always traipsing about the world?"

"But their parents were killed in that awful railway accident."

"A lot of parents were killed." Sisters, brothers, sons, and daughters. Not that Minerva had any recollection of the event. She'd been a child, yet all these years later, people still spoke of the awfulness of it, especially when the hellions were about.

"They were left to fend for themselves," Lady Sarah said, as though they'd been abandoned on the streets with no means whatsoever.

"Hardly," Minerva stated. "They had a roof over their heads, food in their bellies, clothes on their backs."

"But they ran wild over the moors. No one cared about them."

Minerva had heard those stories as well. Mr. Alcott had an entire reservoir of mishaps to share at dinner parties. "I believe Mr. Alcott embellishes."

"You're no fun at all."

Worse things had been said of her. They walked into the parlor. "Why? Because I want the facts?"

"Precisely."

"They can ruin a good story," a deep voice announced.

Minerva spun around to find Mr. Alcott standing against the wall, arms crossed over his chest, his dark blond hair a riot of curls that seemed to mark him as untamable. The only reason she knew he wasn't Greyling was because the earl seldom left his wife's side. She wondered how much he might have heard, how much of their conversation might have echoed up the hallway. His eyes, the shade of hot cocoa, dark and somber, gave little away. Lady Sarah might have thought Locksley was the mysterious one, but Minerva couldn't help but believe that Mr. Alcott had secrets of his own.

"Well, we wouldn't want to have that now, would we, Mr. Alcott?" she asked, fighting not to have quite so much sarcasm dripping from her voice.

A corner of his mouth lifted into a seductive smile that, if rumors were to be believed, had ladies surrendering to his every whim. "Please, call me Edward. And stories should be designed to entertain."

"They should not be purported as the truth when they stray from the facts."

"Did Ashebury really kill the lion?" Lady Sarah asked, with hero worship fairly lending a dreamy-like quality to her voice.

"He did."

"With a knife?" Minerva asked, not bothering to disguise her disbelief.

"It had a wickedly long blade and was incredibly sharp." He lifted a broad shoulder in a casual half shrug. "Although he might have been assisted by some of our guides, who jumped into the fray. But where is the excitement in a story such as that?"

"There is beauty in facts."

"Miss Dodger is terribly practical," Lady Sarah said in the same tone that one might use when referring to an eccentric aging aunt who was boring people to death at a dinner party.

"So it would seem," Edward said. "But the question is: Did you enjoy the story?"

"I adored it," Lady Sarah responded enthusiastically.

But his gaze remained focused on Minerva. "No embellishment, Miss Dodger. Only the truth or if you prefer: only the facts. Did it hold you enthralled?"

Blast him. She relished the truth too much not to admit, "I found it rather fascinating."

"High praise indeed. I consider the night a success." With a laziness to his stride, he walked off.

Undoubtedly, she had somehow managed to insult him. Was it a fault to value honesty?

"Drat," Lady Sarah murmured. "I should have asked him about Lord Locksley."

"I'm sure you can catch up with him if you really want to know."

"Wish me luck." Then she was gone, leaving Minerva to wonder why luck was needed to receive an answer to a simple question.

Shaking her head in wonder at the girl's youthful exuberance—dear God but she suddenly felt old—she glanced around the salon. In its center, a table was adorned with food, another sported an assortment of spirits. Footmen meandered around offering tiny bits of pastry or glasses of wine. Along the outer edges of the room were the photographs, displayed on easels. Ashebury's work.

It called to her, enticed her to draw near. She approached the photograph of a crouched lion barely visible through the tall grasses, but his gaze was intense, that of a hunter. And she regretted with everything inside her that they'd killed such a proud beast.

𝒜SHE surmised that the guests weren't really interested in the photographs. Oh, they gave them a passing glance as they flirted, stuffed tiny pies into their mouth, or sipped fine wine. But they were here to have fun, to take delight in each other's company, to flirt. All except her.

Miss Minerva Dodger.

She took her time studying each photograph as though she appreciated what he had created with shadow and light, as though she understood it, as though it spoke to her. Once he even saw her lift her hand as though she wanted to pet the creature that he had captured with his lens. Photography was more than a pastime for him; it was a passion. Yet so few appreciated it. Not that he did it for public accolades. However, for some reason, he'd wanted these images to be admired. Perhaps because they'd nearly cost him his life.

So when Grey's wife had expressed a desire to host a small party so she could display them, he'd been only too happy to oblige her request. Except now he felt quite self-conscious and wished he'd merely lent her the photographs and avoided the tedious affair. Unlike Edward, he didn't crave attention, abhorred it, actually. He would do anything to escape the ladies presently fluttering their fans and cooing to him that he was remarkably brave and incredibly strong. One lady had even managed to discreetly squeeze his upper arm, testing his muscles, her eyes slumberous with invitation. He could no doubt find a secluded place to take her so she could squeeze to her heart's content any part of him that she wished—

Except now he was intrigued by Miss Dodger's perusal of his work. She lingered, perhaps because she despised the thing. He shouldn't intrude, shouldn't worry over her opinion. She'd no doubt give it bluntly if he asked. That was the thing about her—she was always so blasted blunt. Not that they'd spoken more than half a dozen times, if that, but sugar was certainly not going to melt in her mouth. Which was no doubt the reason she had yet to secure a husband. Money certainly wasn't a factor. Her father, a former gentlemen's club owner, had showered her in it, but her propensity to speak her mind made her troublesome and hardly wifely material. Not that he was in need of a wife or even desired one. He enjoyed his freedom too much for that. Grey had completely lost his when he married Julia.

Yes, Ashe should simply make his excuses and leave, go to the Nightingale and see if he had better fortune tonight in obtaining the photograph he wanted. Instead—

"Excuse me, but I have a matter to attend to," he told the three ladies vying for his attention. Before they could protest or distract him further, he slipped away from them and approached Miss Dodger, his shoes barely making a sound as he neared. Peering over her shoulder, he smiled. Ah, the chimpanzees. One of his favorites. He'd been quite pleased with the way it turned out. "Do you like it?" he asked, then wished he'd bitten off his tongue. He felt as though he were on display as much as the photographs.

She didn't so much as turn her head when she said,

"Quite. It's rather profound. I'm not certain I've seen photographs that managed to capture so much."

"It's the light and shadows, the way I use them. It's a relatively new technique, brings an artistic flair to the method, if you will, that elevates the work to something beyond a simple picture."

"They're in love," she said with utter conviction.

"The monkeys?"

"Yes." She looked at him. He didn't remember her eyes being so dark, so intense. And he was hit with the memory of other dark, intense eyes. On the cusp of that thought, he became aware of the scent of verbena drifting toward him. It took every ounce of control he could muster not to react, not to spin her completely around, not to peruse and catalog every inch of her. She could be the right height, depending on the heel of her shoe, her body the right shape if all the padding, petticoats, and corset were gone. He wished he could see her hair in flickering candlelight. He recalled its being darker, no hints of red. Here, in the brighter lighting, it was the incorrect shade. She was no doubt the wrong woman. He was just so desperate to find Lady V that he would imagine her in any woman he spoke with. But why hadn't he imagined her as any of the others who had given him attention thus far this evening?

"You're telling a story here," she said. "They're devoted to each other."

Her voice was wrong. It wasn't smoky and raspy,

resembling a whisper. Could she disguise it? Never slipping? But it was more than the timbre that gave him doubts. She spoke as though they were passing strangers, as though they hadn't spent an hour together, as though they'd never kissed. "They're animals, Miss Dodger."

"They're soul mates."

He might have laughed except that she was so blasted serious. And she could be Lady V. No, she was too practical for that. Then it occurred to him that perhaps she was exactly practical enough to want to know what all the fuss was about. Bold enough to go after it. While he'd not spent much time in her immediate company, knew her mostly by reputation, he had observed her from afar at balls, dancing with one gent or another, of late seeming to spend more time standing among the wallflowers yet separate from them. She would never be one to blend in. While most ladies would shrivel and shrink back if their dance cards weren't written on, she'd always left him with the impression of being someone who couldn't have cared less, someone waiting to throw down a gauntlet if the opportunity struck. "Tell me you don't believe in such nonsense."

"Unlike your storytelling cohort, I'm not one to lie, Your Grace."

"Edward? What lie do you speak of?"

She arched a finely shaped eyebrow. "He confessed that you didn't defeat the lion without assistance." She nodded toward another photograph. "Is that him, the one you killed?"

Censure didn't ring in her voice, but sadness thickened it. He wished he hadn't brought that particular photo. Almost hadn't. It saddened him as well, yet he was also remarkably proud of it. "Yes."

"He was measuring you up. Misjudged."

"Many often do." Grimacing, he wondered why in the blue blazes he'd revealed that tidbit, especially to her. He couldn't recall any of their previous conversations. Yet here he was blathering on as though his tongue had separated itself from his brain.

Tilting her head slightly, she studied him. "I find your work quite astonishing."

"It's my passion."

"Truly? Based on the rumors, I'd been led to believe that women were."

She didn't even blush. Most women would have. No, most wouldn't have voiced the words. She was no shy miss, but was she bold enough for the Nightingale? He was intrigued by the possibility. "One does not exclude the other, but you are correct. Women are first, and foremost, my most beloved passion."

"And yet, you have none here among your collection. You have men and children, but no women."

"A good many of the native women bared their breasts." He was hoping to make her blush with his candor, but she met his gaze head-on, no pinkening of her cheeks, no averting of her eyes. Lady V hadn't looked away either. "I fear our hostess was rather offended by their display and refused to allow me to share them. I had no luck convincing her that the beauty of the human body is not something to be hidden away. Perhaps you would like to see them sometime."

Now she was blushing, a deep lush hue that traveled high over her cheeks, and somehow managed to journey into his soul. Was she blushing at the possibility of viewing breasts or was his talk of the beauty of the human body causing her to recall images from last night?

"I'm not sure it would be appropriate," she said. "They sound rather risqué."

"They don't dress as they do to titillate. Rather, they have been raised in the glorifying freedom of not feeling shame with what God has bestowed. I envy their simpler dress. I assume, considering how much your clothing must weigh, that you would as well."

"You assume too much." She glanced around. "Where is Lord Locksley?"

Her interest in his friend struck him like a physical blow, which made no sense as he wasn't lusting after her, didn't want to carry her from this room and up the stairs to a bed—yet he couldn't deny that neither did he want to walk away. "Off fighting his demons."

She blinked, her lips parted slightly, and he wondered if he kissed her at that precise moment if he would be able to determine if he'd kissed her the night before. Perhaps lust was involved after all.

"Don't look so surprised. We all have our demons, even you, Miss Dodger. Perhaps that's the reason I saw you at the Twin Dragons shortly after midnight last night."

Chapter 6

OH dear Lord help her, he was onto her!

Minerva's heart slammed so hard against her ribs that she was certain she heard a bone crack. Her first instinct was to rail at him for breaking his promise not to demand her address of his driver. That had to be the reason he mentioned the Twin Dragons. He knew where she'd been dropped off—and he was forbidden from mentioning the Nightingale Club.

Having been raised by one who was brought up on the streets, she was schooled to consider all avenues before responding. That he'd gone to the Twin Dragons could have been coincidence, but she doubted it. His driver had informed him where she'd been dropped off. Or he'd followed her.

But even then, she'd whisked into the gaming hell and swiftly passed through to the back area of private rooms and offices. Accessing them had required a key, which she possessed. A dash through the inner workings of the establishment had brought her to another locked door, another key which had gained her access to the mews. She'd walked for a bit before turning onto a street where she hired a hansom to return her home.

Unless Ashebury were as quick as lightning, he couldn't have observed her at the Twin Dragons. He was fishing, suspected that she might be Lady V, and was searching for confirmation. But what had given her away? The shape of her mouth? Good God, was it that distinctive? Her chin? It was more square than she would have liked, but it wasn't particularly unusual. She had no moles or warts with hairs growing out of them for anyone to notice. He couldn't know with absolute certainty that she was the woman he'd met at the Nightingale. Maybe he was uttering the same words to every woman he spoke to in an attempt to find Lady V. She had to admit to being flattered that he wanted to find her, but she didn't quite trust the reason behind his effort. What did he want? What did he hope to accomplish? She toyed with the idea of playing his game, of following to see where he might lead— but she wasn't about to give him the satisfaction of having something to hold over her. Best to nip it in the bud before it got out of hand. She needed to manipulate her answers to deflect his suspicions, to ensure he doubted what he quite possibly suspected.

"I don't see how you could have," she said calmly. "I wasn't there last night."

"But you have a membership."

As did a good many women since it had opened its doors to the fairer sex. "My father owned the place before he sold it. Part of the condition of the sale was that he and all his descendants have membership for life. So, yes, I am a member, and I do frequent it on occasion. But not last night."

He angled his head thoughtfully. "I could have sworn it was you."

"The Duchess of Lovingdon will swear I was having dinner at her residence, should it come to pass that I'm required to prove my whereabouts. Although I must confess to feeling rather like a murder suspect in one of the cases dissected so blatantly in the newspapers." While she was bothered by Society's need for the minute details of gruesome killings, she couldn't seem to stop herself from poring over the accounts in fascination.

"My apologies, Miss Dodger, for putting you on the spot. In retrospect, I see I was mistaken. The woman I spied lacked your . . . shall we say, vivaciousness?"

"I did not mean to offend, Your Grace. It is simply that I know where I was and where I was not."

"An admirable quality, to be sure."

She bit her tongue to stop herself from reacting to his mocking tone, the scapegrace. He wasn't nearly as charming as he'd been the night before, but then, at the Nightingale, he'd been flirting with Lady V not Minerva Dodger. She was surprised he'd approached. Surely, he'd hoped for someone far more enticing, with more pleasing features. He would leave her now, she was rather sure of it. He'd come over here for mischief, to try to discern if she was Lady V. She'd deflected his inquiry.

She'd been a fool to come here, to put herself in his path. Although the journey of her thoughts didn't cross her face, his gaze bore into her as though he was desperate to know her contemplations. Other than last night, men never studied her with such intensity. She fought not to be flattered. He hadn't approached because he was attracted to her, but rather he thought he'd uncovered the mystery of her. Which made her wonder what he might have done with that information if she had confirmed his suspicions. Perhaps he simply wanted the satisfaction of solving a mystery. The rules of the Nightingale prohibited him from proclaiming she was there.

"We've never really talked, have we?" he asked quietly.

"No." Not in a perfectly acceptable social situation, anyway.

"An oversight that I should—"

"Duke?"

He turned at the squeaky intruding voice, one Minerva found particularly grating, although maybe it was only because the lady was able to snag his attention so easily. Minerva despised the sin of envy, constantly reining in the emotion when it reared its ugly head.

He smiled warmly, as though his fantasy woman

had suddenly materialized in front of him. "Lady Hyacinth. Aren't you a vision of loveliness?"

Minerva felt the need to pound her fist into his shoulder. There was the reason that they had never really talked. She was not a vision of loveliness. Yes, leaving him unsatisfied last night was the smartest decision she'd ever made. How silly of her to have regretted it earlier. She hadn't considered how difficult it would be to see a man she might have been intimate with flirting with other ladies. Somehow, she thought she could be immune to the petty jealousies, could spend a night with a man and move on. How did men manage to do it with such ease?

Lady Hyacinth blushed becomingly, batted her eyelashes, before acknowledging Minerva with the slightest tilting of her head, then returning her emerald gaze to Ashebury. "I was hoping you might take some refreshment with me if Miss Dodger is finished dominating your time."

Minerva held her tongue, refusing to be drawn into the cattiness that ladies often played. It was so unbecoming—at least to her. Men seemed to lap it up like milk.

"I fear it was I dominating hers," Ashebury said, much to Minerva's surprise. No wonder the ladies of London fell over themselves to have his attention. He managed to stand up for her so easily without offending Lady Hyacinth. "But you are quite right. We'll become the fodder for gossip if I linger much longer." He took Minerva's gloved hand, bowed over it slightly, and pressed a kiss to her knuckles. She felt the heat of his mouth clear down to her curling toes, toes that knew the feel of his thigh. "Thank you for appreciating my poor efforts, Miss Dodger. Should you ever like to see the photographs Lady Greyling found offensive, you need only send word."

Her voice had quite suddenly deserted her. His eyes took on a slumberous look as though he'd only just awoken. Something about them was decidedly carnal. "Then there is always my private collection," he said with a low purr that he had probably learned from some great cat in the wilds.

Then he was gone, escorting Lady Hyacinth into the midst of gaiety near the refreshment table. Minerva should have responded to his comment about his private collection, should have at least given an indication that she didn't know what the devil he was talking about even though she understood perfectly well to what he was referring. Did he know that she knew? Were his parting words a last valiant attempt to determine if she was the woman whose ankle he had held in his large hands? Or had he believed her lies?

"Dear God, it was Ashebury." At the familiar voice, Minerva spun around, wondering when Grace had approached, how long she had been observing her, and what she might have been able to read in Minerva's face that someone who didn't know her nearly as well would never be able to discern.

"What are you on about?" she asked as haughtily as possible.

"You were with Ashebury at the Nightingale Club. He was the one who gave you attention."

Minerva swallowed hard, not liking that she was lying to her dear friend, but there were some things a woman kept for herself because they were too delicious to share. Her moments with Ashebury, for example. "Don't be ridiculous. We were simply discussing his photographs. I find them quite exquisite."

"I saw the way you were looking at him. You're more than taken with him."

"Can you blame me? He's quite the handsome specimen, but that doesn't mean he was the one in my company last night. Don't jump to conclusions, Grace. It's vulgar."

"You're protesting too much." She moved up, and whispered, "If he was the one, you were wise not to let things go any further than they did. He'd have never done right by you."

"I wasn't searching for a man who would," she said sotto voce. She'd wanted a man who could provide lovely memories. "This is neither the time nor the place for this discussion. Appreciate the photographs, Grace."

With doubt mirrored in her eyes, Grace finally turned away from her and gave her attention to Ashebury's work. "Based on his reputation, I'm not surprised there is something very sensual about them."

Sensual, yes. Light and shadows that played off

each other. How might he have used them to capture her? Trying to deflect her thoughts, she said, "They're portraits of animals, men working, and children playing."

"But the lion," Grace said, her voice low, reverent. "It's like he's looking at a female he wants to possess. He's preparing to claim her, taking his time, waiting for the perfect moment to declare his intentions."

"I think he's considering having Ashebury for dinner."

"Oh, Minerva, don't be naive. I've seen that exact look in men's eyes on more than one occasion. Trust me, it's desire."

Minerva had seen that look only once: the night before in a bedchamber with Ashebury. And she'd walked away from it.

In spite of all her earlier arguments, she couldn't help but feel that in leaving, she'd been a fool.

*A*s lady after lady vied for his attention, Ashe didn't know why his gaze kept wandering back to Miss Dodger, would dart around the room searching for her if she'd moved away from where she'd last been. Gentlemen approached her, but it was obvious by their bored mien that it was only politeness or perhaps an interest in her dowry that prompted their hovering. It was equally obvious that she wasn't flattered by their attentions. No sparks ignited, no heated glances were exchanged.

He couldn't explain his sudden interest in her. If she'd been dining with the Duchess of Lovingdon, then she couldn't be Lady V. On the other hand, how late had the dinner run?

She had blushed when he'd spoken of the beauty of the human body, invited her to see what was forbidden in polite society. He'd thought then that she knew exactly the sort of photographs that interested him the most. Thought he had her, thought she'd provided a clue that they had indeed been together the night before.

He was desperate to discover Lady V's identity because he couldn't get her out of his mind. Not even when one of London's most beautiful debutantes, Lady Regina, gave him her undivided attention as she was doing now. He fought to pay attention to her nontitillating discourse on nightingales—

It dawned on him that she was striving to drop clues. He scrutinized her. The hair was wrong. The shade of her eyes, the too-slender shape of her torso, wrong. The way she carried on with her little innuendoes and gazed at him with obvious sexual awareness, he was fairly certain he could entice her into posing for him. But he simply couldn't work up any enthusiasm for the notion.

He wanted the one who had gotten away.

Because she'd gotten away? Or was there more to it? He didn't want to examine his motives. It was unlikely they would ever cross paths again. He'd blathered on about her not giving her virginity to just anyone. She wasn't likely to return to the Nightingale. His best hope for finding her resided with a visit to the Twin Dragons.

"Do you see what you missed out on?" Edward asked his brother as he perused the photographs.

"A near-death experience?"

The manner in which their parents passing had affected them was odd. It had made Grey more cautious as though he feared Death hovered around every corner. It had emboldened Edward, almost to the point that he dared the Grim Reaper to have a go at him. By God, if he was going to die young, he was going to make the most of the years given to him.

"Adventure," Edward stated succinctly.

"I seem to recall one of your letters filled with grumblings about the heat and insects and lack of good scotch."

"I believe I was fevered at the time." He remembered the chills, the sweltering heat, his aching body.

"While I was enjoying good scotch, modern conveniences, and an evening in the company of my wife."

Edward refrained from rolling his eyes in disgust at the absolute boredom of it all. "Don't you want to live life robustly? You once did."

"I assume you're implying until Julia. Love changes a man."

Edward growled low. "It's made you a milksop."

"But a happy one. She's with child again. I pray

she doesn't lose this one. I thought I would lose her as well the last time."

So maybe that was what had made him cautious. He feared upsetting the gods. In the span of two years, his wife had lost three babes. "I would simply like us to go somewhere, do something adventuresome together. Like old times."

"We're not children any longer, Edward. We have to grow up."

"Speak for yourself."

"I believe I'm doing exactly that."

"I've half a mind to punch you."

Grey grinned. "You have the oddest way of showing that you love me."

Edward scowled, but he didn't argue the point. He did love his brother more than he had ever loved anyone. At seven, he might have ceased to exist without Albert to hold him when word came that their parents were dead, if he'd been left completely alone. He couldn't imagine what it had been like for Ashe to have no siblings with whom he could have shared his sorrow and grief.

"By the by," Grey said, "I've not seen Locksley since you returned. Is he still in London?"

Edward shook his head slightly. "Off to visit his father."

"Bad business there. Do you recall when he rode a horse through the manor?"

Edward chuckled at the memory. "Up the bloody stairs in the middle of the night, chasing his wife's ghost. Total madness. When we left Havisham, it took me forever to get used to the ticking of clocks." The mad Marquess of Marsden had stopped every clock in the residence so it reflected the time of his wife's passing, as though all else had ceased to move forward as well.

"I didn't at the time, but now I understand the depth of his grief. I believe I would go mad as well if I lost Julia. I know the two of you don't get along, but she is a remarkable woman."

Remarkable at stifling fun. "I'll take your word for it."

"You should get to know her better."

"Bit hard to do when she cast me out."

"She had my blessings. You are an obnoxious drunkard."

"You wouldn't notice if you were into your cups as well. It's rather bad form not to join me in a glass or two."

"It's more than two, and you damned well know it. Besides, I have the estates to look after. I can't indulge to the extent that you can." He rubbed his right ear. "She wants me to reduce your allowance."

"Do it, if it will keep harmony in your marriage. Stop it completely."

"Don't be absurd. I'm not going to do that. This is neither the time nor the place to discuss it. I shouldn't have brought it up."

Edward disliked when they were at odds. Perhaps he should drink less, but there was a dark hole in him that needed filling and he didn't know what to fill it with. Still, he conceded, "I'm glad you have her, that you love her."

"I do. Very much. She's good for me."

But bad for Edward. Perhaps he never should have stolen a kiss from her while pretending to be Albert. It was only a harmless prank, but she'd taken such offense, one would have thought he'd lifted her skirts and caught sight of her ankles. Her only saving grace, as far as Edward was concerned, was that—as far as he could tell—she'd never told Albert about the incident.

"Gents," Ashe said as he joined them. "Lady Greyling is beginning to usher people toward the door, so I'm off to the Dragons. Come with?"

"Definitely," Edward replied quickly.

"Not I," Grey said.

"Big surprise there," Edward responded.

"One day you'll marry, and you'll welcome time alone with your wife."

"I'm not the earl. I don't need to provide an heir. I see no reason to take such drastic measures as to marry."

"Love is reason enough. Don't you agree, Ashe?"

"I find love to be quite fickle. I love a woman I'm with until I'm no longer with her. I've yet to meet one who draws me in enough not to leave."

"I'm not going to give up on either of you. Someday, you will both find a woman who will change your world."

Chapter 7

MINERVA couldn't say why she had decided to come to the Dragons tonight. Perhaps because she'd been contemplating returning to the Nightingale, but she feared if she encountered Ashebury there, his suspicions would be confirmed. Damn his keen observations. Having seen his photographs, she understood that he was the worst possible choice to take as a lover for a solitary night. He studied, scrutinized, and focused too intently on objects, too closely on her. Although after viewing the photographs, she did rather regret that she had walked away from him the evening before. He had attempted to explain what he was about, but until she saw the evidence of his skill, she'd failed to truly comprehend the level of his talents. She imagined lying across the bed with shadows and light playing over her body while he, looking through a lens, lay in wait for the perfect image to capture. Studying her with such intensity—

Just the thought of his blue gaze leveled on her caused her to grow warm.

Although had she gone to the Nightingale, she'd have not crossed paths with him, wouldn't have had the opportunity to be photographed, because he was here, at the Dragons. While she preferred private card games with higher stakes, after spying him, she had selected a table that wasn't quite full in hopes the duke might join her.

He, however, seemed to prefer roulette.

Minerva found the game boring as it required no skill, did not pit her against any opponent. She enjoyed games that involved more than chance. Perhaps that as much as anything had prompted her decision to go to the Nightingale. Being there had elicited a measure of excitement, a good deal of the unknown, and a bit of skill to ensure she wasn't found out.

But now that he was here, she was a fool to remain in the common gaming area, to risk his realizing that she was Lady V. He could blackmail her, threaten to destroy her reputation if she didn't pose for him, if she didn't do everything he demanded. As though she would ever give a man that much control over her. She would simply scoff—

"Pardon?" Lord Langdon asked.

Dear God, had she scoffed aloud? She smiled at the gentlemen circling the table. "The cards are not kind tonight. I believe I shall give roulette a go."

"You abhor roulette," Langdon said, demonstrating the disadvantage of doing things with childhood friends. They knew too much.

"I'm in the mood for something different." Something different, something far more challenging—an entirely different game that wasn't identified with cards, dice, or spinning wheels. One that relied on her cleverness. He might have had his suspicions that she was Lady V, but she'd managed to throw him off the scent. Where was the harm in putting herself back in his path, especially when he intrigued her so? "If you gentlemen will excuse me . . ."

Leaving her cards—two queens and two tens which she was ninety-eight percent certain would beat every other hand at the table even after the gents exchanged their unfavorable cards—she summoned a young lad in livery over to collect what remained of her chips. He would turn them in for her and bring her a voucher while she wandered over to the roulette wheel where Ashebury stood, seemingly remarkably bored, even though Lady Hyacinth was fairly draped over him.

She hadn't noticed the lady before, but now Minerva reconsidered her destination, was about to walk on by, when Ashebury's gaze landed on her, and he suddenly didn't seem at all bored. His blue eyes warmed with interest. Or was that merely wishful thinking on her part?

She sidled up to the table until she stood opposite Ashebury. After acknowledging him with a slight nod, she exchanged some money from her reticule for chips. Without hesitation, she placed half of them on black twenty-five. Waited while other bets were laid down. Waited as the croupier signaled an end to the wagering and, with a practiced flick of his wrist, sent the wheel spinning, the ball dropping, jumping, rattling around, settling . . .

All the while Ashebury's gaze remained on her, and she could only hope that he wasn't imagining her wearing a white domino mask with distracting feathers and sequins. Perhaps she'd been foolish after all to give him another opportunity to observe her. She wasn't so vain as to think she—Minerva Dodger—was enough to hold his interest for overly long although she certainly fantasized about doing so.

"Twenty-five black," the croupier announced.

The other people at the table grumbled. Ashebury narrowed his eyes. "I've been standing here for two hours, and not once have I picked correctly."

"I have extraordinary luck at the games," she said as humbly as possible.

"But not with men," Lady Hyacinth stated rather snidely.

The men standing around the table stiffened. One of the things Drake Darling had not considered when he had opened the doors of this establishment to women was that sometimes the catty ones bared their claws most unbecomingly.

"No," Minerva acknowledged, "not when it comes to men. So I suppose it's a rather good thing that I don't run about draping myself over them as though I'm an article of clothing."

Lady Hyacinth blinked repeatedly, opened her mouth, closed it as though having difficulty deciphering the words but suspecting that they were laced with insult. "I believe your words were an affront to my character."

"Merely an observation. Still, would you like to take this down to the boxing room?"

"Oh, I'd pay to see that," Edward Alcott said, grinning broadly.

"All my money goes on Miss Dodger," Ashebury announced.

With a sharp intake of breath, Lady Hyacinth shoved herself away from him, then glared at Minerva. "Ladies do not settle affairs in a boxing ring. You should have been born to wear trousers."

Was that the lady's attempt at offending? Minerva should cease taunting her. Instead, she said, "Who says I can't wear them now? I have two legs. Trousers do as well. Seems to me as though it would work. Perhaps I'll give it a go. Let you know."

"Is it any wonder you're a spinster, that no man would ever have you?"

While Minerva considered if there was anything to be gained by pointing out that gentlemen had in fact offered marriage, a large man approached and wrapped a beefy hand around Lady Hyacinth's arm. "My lady, your carriage is waiting."

"I didn't send for my carriage."

"Still, it awaits."

"That's all right, Greenaway," Minerva said, addressing the keeper of the peace. "I've grown bored with this game."

She signaled to the lad who had gathered her chips at the card table. He dashed over, handed to her the voucher he'd obtained earlier, and began placing her roulette chips in his bowl. Bending down, she whispered, "It's all yours."

His eyes widened. "Thank ye, Miss Dodger."

Straightening, she smiled at those circling the table. "Gentlemen. Lady. I hope your luck improves."

After taking a dozen steps away from the table, she lowered her defenses and felt Lady Hyacinth's barb striking deep. In spite of the offers for marriage, she knew the men had not wanted her. They'd wanted her money. Most had been polite. Some had feigned interest. Others had been blunt. She preferred the blunt ones, liked knowing where she stood, and it made it so much easier to decline without offending or worrying about hurting someone's pride.

Although her own was presently stung. Ashebury had shown interest last night, but he hadn't known who she was. She'd been mysterious, provocative, interesting. He might have been willing to place a bet on her tonight, and while her first thought had been that he'd done it out of support for her, her second thought sent the first straight to hell. He was placing the wager knowing the odds were in his favor that common Miss Dodger had a good right punch. Actually it was a left, but still. She'd once flattened her younger brother. Her father was a commoner, a former gambling-house owner, and she knew the ins and outs of that life like she knew the back of her own hand.

"Don't suppose you're headed to the ballroom?" a familiar voice asked behind her.

Staggering to a stop, she rebuilt her protective walls before facing Ashebury. "Your Grace, I hadn't decided on which game of chance to go with, but I'd not even considered going to the ballroom."

"I wish you would, and once there, I hope you'll honor me with a dance."

If he touched her with a feather, she'd fall over. "After the spectacle I just made of myself? I don't need your pity."

"It's not pity, but admiration. She had too much to drink, isn't very sharp to begin with. You, on the other hand are as sharp as a whip and could have sliced her to ribbons. Yet you didn't."

Dear Lord, what sort of spiteful women did he seduce? Although she was flattered that he saw her as intelligent. Her smarts intimidated most men, but then Ashebury wasn't most men. "There's nothing to be gained from inflicting that sort of hurt. It was beneath me to even taunt her."

"I daresay, she was the one doing the taunting."

"Be that as it may, she's only just been presented to the queen. She's young. I'm seasoned. I would have been better served keeping my mouth shut completely."

"I'm rather glad you didn't. I think every gent at the roulette wheel is now imagining ladies in trousers." He gave her skirts a long, leisurely perusal that caused her mouth to go dry. He made her feel as though he had the ability to see beneath the cloth and knew exactly what her legs looked like. Not just her feet and ankles, but all the way up to her hips. "Have you worn them?"

She shouldn't confess, and yet, where he was concerned, she seemed to find herself doing things she ought not. "At my half brother's estate."

His brow furrowed. "The Duke of Lovingdon?"

"Jolly good for you. Our family tree is a little confusing."

"You can sort it all out for me while we dance."

Her palms, which never grew damp, suddenly did. The thought of waltzing with this man brought forth images of doing other things with him, things she might have done had she not walked out last night. "I suppose I might find myself wandering to the ballroom."

"Allow me to escort you."

As he had last night, he offered her his arm, and she found it just as firm and muscled. Only now she thought of him trudging through jungles, battling a lion.

"Which shoulder?" she asked.

He shifted his gaze to her, and while he was considerably taller than she was, he didn't so much look down on her as much as he managed to look over at

her. He made her feel delicate when she was probably the least delicate lady in London. Yet, she appreciated the sensation he elicited, one no other man
ever had.

"Pardon?" he asked.

"The lion. Which shoulder did he sink his teeth
into?"

"Ah. The left. More a grazing than a sinking. Edward tends toward the dramatic. It makes him both
appealing and irritating, based on one's mood at the
time that he's waxing on."

"Yet he's your friend."

He gave her a self-deprecating smile. "Tragedy
makes for strange bedfellows."

So did reaching spinsterhood although she kept
that thought to herself.

"Is the roulette table rigged?" he asked.

"I beg your pardon?"

"As I mentioned, I spent two hours handing over
my money. You come to the table, set down a wager,
and win. Seems a bit fishy considering your associa-
tion to this place."

They entered the ballroom with its mirrored walls.
Minerva had always thought it a waste of space as
few people were here, and it brought in no money.
She had inherited her father's business acumen and
tendency to analyze every situation—every gentleman who showed interest. She took nothing at face
value, most of all flirtation and flattery.

"I'm not certain how they would rig it. Besides, it

makes no sense to deliberately let me win when this place made my father's fortune."

"Sentimentality perhaps?"

"No. Drake Darling has a head for business that wouldn't allow that. It's the reason my father sold the place to him. He trusted him with it, knew he would keep it profitable. Besides, the staff knows me well enough to know I'd be none too happy if they arranged it for me to win. I like a good challenge. There's no point in playing if things are rigged in your favor."

Having said that, it occurred to her that perhaps that was why she'd decided to forgo another Season. With her dowry, the chances of finding a husband were rigged in her favor. But it wasn't a husband she wanted. It was a man who loved her.

"You were simply so confident with your play," he said. "No hesitation at all in placing your wager."

"At the roulette wheel, I go with my instincts, don't give any thought as to where I place my bet. It's all chance."

"You stand toe to toe with the men then, not mewling or asking advice."

"I was practically raised within these walls. It would be quite insincere to pretend that I neither know how the games work or my own mind. I believe a person should take responsibility for his or her actions. I would have accepted a loss with grace."

"But it's always more fun to have the win. Ah, a waltz is starting up. Shall we?"

She'd barely given a nod before he swept her onto the dance area, holding her scandalously close, daring her with his intense gaze to object. They were in a place of vice and sin. She wasn't going to be a hypocrite about it. Besides, she liked being this close to him, taking in his sandalwood fragrance mingling with the aroma of scotch.

"I've never noticed you at the card tables, Your Grace."

"Cards are too much work. You have to think incessantly hard, constantly trying to outfox the other fellows. I like roulette because it's a simple game that gives me the freedom to focus on more *interesting* things."

His attention never strayed from her, and she was tempted to believe he found her interesting. "Like Lady Hyacinth?"

"No. Like you."

Miss Minerva Dodger had been on the periphery of Ashe's world for some time now, but not until Lady Hyacinth had referred to her as a spinster did he realize how long she might have been there. She saw herself as seasoned, and a seasoned woman with no prospects for marriage might very likely take it upon herself to visit the Nightingale.

If he asked her outright, she'd deny it. He was fairly certain of that. He was also quite certain that she *was* Lady V.

The ballroom here was not as well lit as Lady

Greyling's salon, and the flickering flames in the chandeliers highlighted Miss Dodger's hair in a way that made it appear very similar to Lady V's. With her in his arms, he was able to get a better sense of her figure. Although, damn, he wished for those trousers she'd alluded to at the roulette table. Then there would be no doubt at all. Although the doubt he now experienced was miniscule. He was once again hit with the fragrance of verbena.

He wondered if there was a chance in hell that she would return to the Nightingale, that she would allow someone else to escort her to a bedchamber—

He tensed with the thought, had to school his body not to react and crush her to him. If another man touched her, he might commit murder. He didn't know if he'd ever met a woman as bold, strong, sure of her own mind. She did not back down. He would have liked to watch her taking a turn in the boxing ring.

"You could have handled yourself downstairs, couldn't you?" he asked.

"In the boxing ring? Quite. My father was not one to allow me to grow up in innocence. He taught me early on how to handle myself. How to land a blow so it would be most effective. He gave me leave to practice on my brothers. I never had to deal with them teasing me as some brothers do. They rather fear me. To this day, even."

A woman with such talents wouldn't fear going to the Nightingale. And Lady V had indicated that she'd prefer to kill him rather than have her father do it if Ashe misbehaved. She was a warrior, not one to be taken lightly, to be overlooked, but it seemed a great many men had. He had.

"I'm imagining a photograph of you standing within the ropes, fists raised, skin glistening with sweat."

"I would not be so crass as to sweat. I might be lightly coated in dew."

"Even better. Hair askew, strands feathering out. Is there red in your hair?"

"Depends on the light. It might be the only thing I inherited from my mother. The rest of me, I fear, is pretty much my father, which makes me a handsome woman—according to one gentleman who wished to gain my favor. I didn't find the term particularly flattering, I suspect because his tone indicated that he didn't mean to imply it as such. His sentiments were along the lines of he hoped that God would be merciful when it came to the appearance of our children. And I'm not sure why I just told you that."

"He sounds like an arse."

Her smiled transformed her face into something quite extraordinary. He wanted to capture it in shadow and light.

"I daresay I thought he was," she said. "I may be plain of feature, but I'm not hideous."

"You're not plain."

"You're kind to say so."

But she didn't believe him. He found that interesting. "If you're discussing children with the arse, then I assume he was in serious pursuit."

"He was. However, when I declined his proposal of marriage, he warned me that I would live out my life as a spinster. To which I answered I'd rather be a spinster than his wife. Obviously, I've not mastered the genteel art of flirtation."

Maybe not, but still he was finding himself quite fascinated by her. He liked that there was no artifice to her. She was honest in a way he wasn't certain he'd ever before encountered in a woman. It was refreshing. Challenging. He didn't know what to expect from her. "You don't look old enough to be labeled a spinster."

"Well, I am. I doubt I'll go to many balls this Season."

"Then I'm grateful I had the opportunity to dance with you tonight."

"I imagine Lady Hyacinth was sorry you abandoned her."

"Her brother showed up two winks after you left, and he escorted her away." Which he realized, as the words left his mouth, was insulting to her, especially as he saw a flash of disappointment in her eyes before she glanced up at the orchestra in the balcony. "But I would have left her anyway," he added hastily, drawing her attention back to him. "I don't suffer the young gladly. Perhaps because I grew up so quickly."

"I know it's been years, but I'm sorry you lost

your parents. I can't imagine the devastation I will experience when mine are gone."

"I still mourn them. It's an odd thing to have been without them for all but eight years of my life. There are aspects to them that I barely remember, and some things are so sharp, so clear that it's as though I were with them yesterday. But it doesn't sadden me to speak of them, so you needn't worry there."

"Is it true what they say about the marquess?"

"That's he's mad?"

She nodded.

"Quite."

He said it so simply. Without prejudice or fear or condemnation.

"That must have been incredibly difficult," Minerva said.

"Not particularly. He wasn't cruel. We didn't always have his attention, but we had each other, so we didn't mind. I think he simply broke when his wife died."

"He loved her that much," she stated in awe although she suspected either of her parents might react in much the same way when one of them died. She didn't want to contemplate it.

"I believe he did," Ashebury said.

"Did it make you want to find a love such as that?"

"On the contrary. It has made me determined to avoid it."

Then why was he holding her close, gliding her

around the room so effortlessly? Lust perhaps. She nearly laughed out loud. When had any man lusted after her?

Last night perhaps, just a bit. His kiss had certainly implied a modicum of desire.

He lowered his gaze to her lips, and they tingled as though they had the power to recall the press of his mouth to hers, the silkiness of his tongue as he outlined them. He had such a lovely mouth. Wide and full, shaped for sin, skilled enough to make a woman lose her head. She suspected a countless number had. She'd almost been included in the group.

With a bit of alarm, she realized that his gaze had drifted lower, and he appeared to be studying the shape of her jawline. He was a man who appreciated strong, solid lines. Would he recognize hers? How mortifying if her square chin gave her away.

But then his eyes came back to hers and he seemed none the wiser although she could have sworn he wore the same expression of desire as the lion. What fanciful thoughts.

The music drifted into silence. They stopped moving, but he didn't release his hold on her.

"I can hardly countenance that I've never really spoken with you before today," he said.

"You've never lacked for fawning women."

"You don't fawn, do you, Miss Dodger?"

"I've never known a man worth fawning over." She released a light laugh. "Perhaps that's the reason I'm a spinster."

"Or perhaps it is simply that men are idiots."

"That goes without saying, doesn't it?"

He chuckled low. "I should be insulted."

"But you're not."

"No." He skimmed his gloved finger along her jaw, and she wished like the very devil that no cloth separated his skin from hers.

Oh, what a fool she was to be drawn to him as easily as every other lady in London. She cleared her throat. "Thank you for the dance, but I must take my leave. It's been a rather long evening."

"Will you be here tomorrow?"

Her heart fluttered at the question, at the possibility of his interest. "No, I have somewhere else to be."

"Perhaps you won't avoid all the balls this Season, and we'll have another dance sometime."

"Perhaps. Good night, Your Grace."

Bringing her hand to his lips, he held her gaze. "Good night, Miss Dodger."

Then, while her knees still had the strength to support her, she strolled away as calmly as possible, but all the while she seemed only capable of seeing herself spread out on a bed being photographed by him.

AFTER Miss Dodger left, the allure of the Dragons faded. Ashe meandered aimlessly around the gaming floor for the better part of a half hour before finally making his way to the gentlemen's private salon and settling in a chair near the fire. He'd

been there for less than a minute before Thomas
brought him two fingers of scotch. Ashe didn't recognize the footman, but in this room, they all went
by Thomas—saved the members having to bother
with learning names. And each member's drinking
preference was known, no doubt noted by the head
footman. Taking a leisurely swallow of extremely
fine spirit, Ashe gave his thoughts leave to drift back
to Miss Dodger.

Her verbena scent still wafted around him. If she
wasn't Lady V, he'd eat his hat in Trafalgar Square.
He knew her lines, had wrapped his fingers about
her delicate ankle, could still feel the impression of
her small foot on his thigh. But it was more than
what he knew of her from last night that held him
enthralled at that moment. It was what he'd learned
of her this evening.

Dancing with her had its charms. Talking with
her had even more. He found himself drawn to her
in ways he'd never been drawn to another.

"Miss Minerva Dodger has the most unattractive mouth in London." The somewhat slurred announcement was met with murmurs of agreement.
Ashe slowly turned his head to a grouping of chairs
occupied by several gents who, based on the flush
on the faces of the ones he could see, were well into
their cups. Unattractive mouth? He didn't know if
he'd seen one more attractive. Her perfect, bow-
shaped lips were plump, full. He envisioned them as
they'd been last night, outlined by the blasted mask,

the way they had greeted his when he'd settled his mouth over them, the manner in which they'd parted on a sigh—

"I told you that she wouldn't accept your suit, Sheridan," Lord Tottenham said. "Now pay up our wager."

"Bugger off, Tottenham. I'm good for it. But blast the woman for the impudent views that spew off her tongue."

So it wasn't the shape of those luscious lips that Sheridan found unattractive but the words she spoke. Ashe couldn't agree with him there either, couldn't think of another woman who carried on a more interesting conversation. He recalled her steadfast resolve that the chimpanzees were in love. For all her straightforwardness, she also possessed softness, small flights of fancy.

"Did you know the girl had the audacity to tell me we weren't suited?" Sheridan asked.

Ashe almost shouted, "Bravo for her!" He couldn't envision her with the arrogant toad. They'd have both been miserable. Then he thought of Sheridan crawling into bed with her, and he had to set his tumbler aside before he cracked the glass as a result of the distasteful image that caused everything within him to tighten.

The footman was suddenly at his side, refilling the tumbler. When the young man stepped back, Ashe called quietly to him. "Thomas?"

When he looked back, Ashe tapped the glass.

Thomas poured more. Ashe tapped it again. "All the way to the top, lad."

"She would have been a countess, much better than she deserves with her father being who he is."

Silence, thick and heavy, greeted that remark. People who wished to live long and healthy lives didn't disparage Jack Dodger, particularly in the gaming hell that had once belonged to him. Sheridan wasn't sharp enough for Miss Dodger. Ashe's respect for her went up a notch. Many women cared only for the title. It seemed Miss Dodger cared for more.

"Wouldn't have mattered who her father is," Sheridan mumbled into the silence. "She hasn't a docile bone in her body. No one will have her. She's practically on the shelf, should have been begging for my attention, the little chit."

"Don't take it personally, Sheridan," Lord Whittaker said. "She denied us all a chance at her dowry. She wants love."

"She's not going to find that now, is she, the little termagant? Why would any man want to be saddled with a woman who spouts her own view on matters rather than agreeing with his? Makes her deuced irritating."

"You have the right of it there," Tottenham said. "When I called on her, she dared to disagree with every opinion I uttered. Wed her, bed her, ship her off to the country. That's what I say. That's the only way a gentleman will have any peace if he takes her to wife."

Ashe stood—

"I've never known a more disagreeable wench," Sheridan said.

—grabbed his glass from the table—

"Will serve her right to find herself an old maid."

—took five long strides to reach the gathered men. "Her dowry be damned."

"It's an impressive dowry," Whittaker said.

"She, however, is not impressive in the least," Sheridan said. "Not a beauty. And as I said, when she opens that mouth—"

Ashe tossed his full glass of scotch onto Sheridan's ugly mug. The man came up out of his chair, sputtering and glaring. "What the devil, Ashebury?"

"Apologies, my lord. I seem to have stumbled." A footman discreetly removed the glass from Ashe's clutched fingers. "If you should disparage Miss Dodger any further, I fear you'll find me stumbling again, only this time I'll be leading with my fist."

"Why the bloody hell do you care? The little chit—"

His fist it was. Straight to Sheridan's jaw. The man's head snapped back, his body following as he staggered and dropped to the floor. Stepping forward, Ashe towered over him. "The *lady*."

His hand cradling his jaw, Sheridan glared at him. "She is no lady. Her father bears no title."

"Be that as it may, she comports herself as a lady while you cannot claim to comport yourself as a gentleman. Rather, you're acting like a gossipy washerwoman. Show some dignity, man, and keep your failures to yourself."

Ashe spun on his heel and strode from the room. He couldn't claim to know why he'd reacted as viscerally as he had. Although if Lady V were in fact Miss Dodger, he was gaining an understanding as to her reasons for visiting the Nightingale, especially if she was dealing with such pomposity. Perhaps he'd grown angry because he'd felt as though Sheridan were disparaging Ashe's judgment.

While dancing with Miss Dodger, he'd almost lured her into the shadows, drawn her into a kiss, but he wasn't certain he'd have the strength to stop there. On the other hand, if he was correct about her identity, she might not have wanted him to. She might have welcomed them going much further, might have gone home with him.

Some adventurer he was, not to have at least asked. But his gut told him that it wouldn't have gone as he fantasized. It was too soon. The lady wasn't ready for more.

But with a little coaxing, she would be. And he who had sworn that he would only ever have one virgin in his life—the woman he married—now conceded that perhaps he'd been a bit premature with that vow.

Chapter 8

"*Y*OU'RE quiet this morning."

Lowering her newspaper, Minerva looked at her father sitting near her, holding his own paper. From the moment his children had mastered reading, he'd insisted that the butler press an edition of the *Times* for each of them and set it at their place at the table, so it was readily available to them when they came down for breakfast. They needed to know what was happening in the world. Not the weather or the latest fashions. Rather, they were expected to discuss what would have an impact on business, the economy, and the nation. That endeavor required being informed to the fullest. He might have conquered the darker side of London, but he was determined his children would thrive and meet with success away from it.

"I'm reading the paper," she answered. His cardinal rule was no talking while reading.

"No, you're not."

Nothing escaped his notice. It was the reason Jack Dodger had survived the streets, built a successful business, and was rumored to be *the* wealthiest man in all of England. Not that he would confirm or deny the speculation. Her father was also a man who relished secrets, had a good many of his own, and excelled at holding them well.

Now she had one of her own that quite possibly rivaled the inappropriateness of his. Oh, she had others. Pilfering his cigars and liquor. Using profanity— but never in front of her parents. But those secrets seemed childish and silly compared with the latest one. The one that had kept her awake most of the night thinking about Ashebury, wondering what would happen if she dared show up at the Nightingale again. If she crossed paths with Ashebury there again, she couldn't back out a second time. Her pride more than anything wouldn't allow it.

Paper crinkled as her father folded up his newspaper and set it aside. "So what's troubling you?"

His dogged determination, which had resulted in his achievements, seldom allowed his children to escape his scrutiny when he suspected they were hiding something. While it was an admirable trait, when it was directed her way, she didn't much like it. Still, she knew he wouldn't give up until he had his answer. "I think it's time to admit I'm not the sort men marry."

His unwavering gaze on her, he sat still and silent for a moment. "Should I increase the amount of your dowry?"

She laughed lightly. "Dear God, no, Papa. Mine's

large enough to attract fortune hunters from across the pond. No, it's more to do with me. I'm not the type with whom men can fall madly in love. They don't find me very biddable."

"If they don't appreciate you, they can rot. Don't change for a single one of them."

He would defend his children to the death. She loved him for it. "I wasn't planning to. Here's an example, though. Last night at the Dragons, I challenged Lady Hyacinth to a bout in the boxing ring."

He arched a thick eyebrow, gave a curt nod of approval. "You'd draw a crowd. What were you going to charge for admittance into the room?"

Any other man might have been mocking her, but she knew him well enough to know he was serious. He never turned down an opportunity to add money to his coffers. Any other father might have been appalled. But he valued strength, courage, and fortitude. "I had no plans to charge anything. It was an empty dare that I wasn't going to see through. She said something unkind, and I reacted very poorly."

"I'll have a chat with her father this morning. She'll be apologizing this afternoon."

His influence was such that any confrontation yielded results. Terrified some when Jack Dodger showed up at their door. "That's not necessary. I handled it."

He studied her for a moment, no doubt trying to discern if it was handled to his satisfaction. "What did she say?"

"I don't remember exactly. Something about the reason I'm a spinster. It's not important. What matters is that ladies don't engage in fisticuffs, and yet I tossed the possibility out there as though it were perfectly normal and acceptable. I come across as being masculine, a hoyden, instead of dainty and feminine."

"You come across as a woman with the wherewithal to take care of herself."

"Not everyone values that in a lady."

"You don't want someone who doesn't."

"And therein lies the problem. I don't think a man who can accept me as I am exists. At least not among the aristocracy. Not where proper behavior is so regarded, and ladies are expected to yield to their husbands on all matters. I haven't a talent for yielding."

"Then don't marry among the aristocracy."

Until this moment, marrying a commoner wasn't something she'd even considered. "But wouldn't you be disappointed? It would be a feather in your cap—a son of the streets whose daughter marries nobility."

"I've never much fancied feathers." He gave her an understanding smile. "Marry a butcher, a baker, a candlestick maker. Don't marry at all. I don't care. Neither does your mother. All we've ever wanted was for you to be happy."

If she weren't so practical, she'd weep. For all his gruffness, there were times when he said things that below the surface were incredibly sentimental and sweet. "And if my happiness rests in doing something I ought not?"

"Like stealing my cigars?"

Her eyes widened. "You knew?"

"I can count inventory."

"Could have been my brothers."

He gave her a stern look. "They've never been as daring as you."

That was true enough, but then they'd never wrapped their father around their little finger either. She could get away with a good deal more, and they were smart enough to recognize it. "All right then, I've been caught. But back to my original concern, about doing something I ought not."

"Your mother ought not to have married me." He picked up his newspaper, shook it out, buried his nose in it. "That didn't turn out so badly."

Which she supposed was his way of saying he'd stand behind her no matter what sort of trouble she got herself into.

"WHAT the bloody hell do you mean that my financial situation is in dire straits?" Ashe bellowed as he tore his gaze from the ledger of dancing numbers that his man of business had set before him.

"It's the investments, Your Grace. As you can see, based on what I've outlined there, they are not doing as well as we'd hoped."

What he had outlined was nothing but a jumble of

sums. Ashe had never been able to tame figures, which had resulted in countless knuckle rappings from the tutor the marquess had hired. The man hadn't minded teaching one boy, but four was beyond his patience. In the beginning, Ashe had blamed the man for his inability to educate him on how to master ciphering. He'd suffered through the same struggles at Harrow until he'd eventually mastered cheating in order to avoid the degrading set downs when he arrived at an incorrect answer. As he'd grown older, he'd realized the fault rested within him and not with his school-masters. He simply couldn't grasp mathematics. Latin yes. Quite easily. He excelled at penmanship. He was a voracious reader. He could recite facts on Britain's history, including naming every monarch. He could write a detailed account of journeys taken and not leave out a single incident. He could master foreign languages. He served as interpreter on their treks through foreign lands. If they came across a people whose language they'd never heard, it took him no time at all to figure it out so he could com-municate with them. But put a series of numbers in front of him, expect him to make sense of them, and it was as though his brain considered them to be little more than colorful balls to be juggled around.

It was the true reason he avoided card games. It was a complete nightmare when values associated with cards had to be tallied. But roulette? He didn't have to make sense of any numbers. He simply placed his wager in a square or on a line.

He shot out of the chair and began to pace. "How could this have happened? I pay you a princely sum for sound advice. You recommended those investments."

"You wanted large returns, which means taking greater risks. Surely, you analyzed the figures I provided."

The figure of a woman he could analyze to perfection. But ones, threes, eights, every blasted numeral that existed escaped his comprehension if he had to do more than simply look at them. Even then, they seemed to weave before his vision like the exotic dancers he'd seen in the East. Which was the reason that he'd always insisted Nesbitt provide verbal reports. Nesbitt, being a man who loved numbers and could wax on about them for hours, also provided the information in written form to back up his claims. Not that they did Ashe any good. Instead, he was forced to focus on every word Nesbitt uttered in order to make his decisions. He'd understood that the income provided by his three estates was dwindling, tenants moving to cities to work in factories, agriculture not being what it once was now that it was cheaper to import from America. Ashe had known he needed to diversify. Investing had seemed the way to go.

He should have sought counsel from Grey or Locksley. Grey was managing his estates quite well, while Locksley had taken over his father's duties sometime back. But he would have been mortified to acknowledge that he couldn't handle matters on his own. Pride. Damned pride.

He could climb a mountain, survive crossing a desert, guide a boat up the Nile. He was swift in a race, didn't back down from a fight, protected what was his. The estates were his. He was going to have to make matters right, do whatever was necessary to regain the upper hand.

He stopped pacing and faced the man sitting behind the desk. "We'll need to sell our shares in these companies posthaste."

"You won't get much for them. Might be best to let them sit, see if things turn around."

Never gamble what you can ill afford to lose. He knew that mantra well enough. The investments had sounded so damned promising when Nesbitt had spoken about them.

"You're not completely without funds, Your Grace. You'll just need to tighten the purse strings."

Choke them, more like. Ashe knew very well how costly it was to maintain his estates. They'd been profitable in his father's day, had provided enough income to cover costs. No longer. He couldn't afford any more investments, couldn't put any more money at risk. He needed a sure thing, a way to gain funds that guaranteed pure profit. And he needed it soon.

AFTER meeting with Nesbit, Ashe was restless. He'd considered going to the Dragons, but he didn't want to see any numbers tonight, not even at a roulette table. If he became any more tense, he was likely to snap. He needed something that brought him absolute unfettered joy—which left only two options: a woman or taking a photograph. So greedy bastard that he was, he'd come to the Nightingale in hopes of acquiring both.

Sipping scotch, considering the selections, he stood with a shoulder to the wall. He'd been studying the ladies for the better part of an hour now, and he couldn't settle on one who would suit his purposes. One was too tall. One too short. Another too plump. Too thin. Not proportioned pleasingly. Not particularly elegant with her movements.

What the bloody hell was wrong with him? He wasn't usually this particular. He enjoyed the challenge of taking imperfection and making it perfect. He was master of light and shadows, controlled them at his whim, commanded them.

He should forget the photograph, be content with the sex. Women had approached him, but his disinterest had been obvious and they'd quickly moved on. None of them suited. None of them—

It hit him with the force of a sledgehammer to his skull. He needed *her* to be at the Nightingale tonight. He couldn't say why. He only knew that it was true.

With or without the mask. He didn't care. He wanted Lady V.

He knew that with her, for a little while, he could forget his troubles. He could stop chastising himself for taking a misstep with his inheritance, his legacy, his stewardship. He'd tried to ensure that the estates didn't fall into disrepair, that the remaining tenants would have fewer worries, that he could maintain his staff—not so much for his needs but for theirs. Some had been seeing to the residences for years. To show his gratitude for their service, he'd intended to see them well-off when they retired. Then there was the matter of securing a wife, his heir, and other children. He didn't want his son to be the only child. He'd had eight years of loneliness, of no one with whom to play or scheme. He was not grateful for his parents' demise, he'd never be grateful for that, but he was glad to have acquired three brothers with whom he'd been able to be mischievous. Normally he would have turned to them with the disappointing news delivered by Nesbitt, but his pride wouldn't allow it.

He should have gone to the Dragons although she'd indicated she wouldn't be there tonight. He'd scoured through invitations but there had been none for this evening. So where was she? At the theater, maybe at a private affair. But he needed her here.

"Your Grace."

Reluctantly, he turned his head at the soft voice. A lady wearing a burgundy mask with black gemstones and feathers smiled at him. Reaching out, he touched her chin, hating that only a small square of skin around her mouth was visible. It seemed the masks were becoming larger and more elaborate.

Whoever created them must be making a fortune. "Darling."

He called them all darling, except for Lady V. Why had he asked for her name? How had he known from the instant he saw her that she would be different from all the others?

Burgundy trailed slender fingers up his arm. "I've been watching you for some time, have heard you are quite skilled at delivering pleasure." She ran her tongue around lips that didn't tempt him as Lady V's had. "So am I. We would make an excellent pairing."

He had no doubt. She was nearly as tall as he was, with a stoutness to her that would provide cushion. And her legs, long, so long, but they weren't the ones he wanted wrapped around his hips. "I'm waiting for someone."

He suspected he'd be waiting all night. She wouldn't return, and his reasons for being here would again go unfulfilled.

Her mouth flattened with displeasure. She wasn't going to be gracious about his rebuff. They seldom were. Yet he had little doubt that Lady V would be. She wouldn't make a fuss. She understood that some things weren't meant to be.

"I won't give you another chance to make love to me," Burgundy said, a hardness to her eyes that he might have never experienced had she approached him before he became aware of Lady V. He wouldn't have turned Burgundy away. Yet, at this moment, he could work up no enthusiasm at the notion of being with her, and it rather disgusted him to think that before, he would have been content with only the physical.

"My loss," he said quietly.

She jutted up her chin. "Indeed." Her movements weren't particularly graceful as she stormed away. Halfway across the room, she settled into a saunter, and, by the time she reached Rexton, she was all poise and confidence. She certainly wasn't one to allow the moss to grow beneath her feet.

Ashe took no offense. One purpose of the place was to allow for a variety of partners. He didn't want to contemplate that Lady V, had she a taste of carnal knowledge, might take on an assortment of lovers. Why couldn't he get the vixen off his mind? He should have gone to the Dragons—

His attention was snagged by an angelic vision in white gliding into the parlor as though her feet didn't touch the floor. Perfect height, perfect figure, perfect everything. He'd set his glass aside and was striding toward her before he realized what he was about. Somewhere in the back of his mind, while he'd longed for her to come, he'd hoped that she wouldn't, that she was smart enough to avoid this debauchery disguised as something acceptable. A place for those of like minds, a secretive circle that rebelled against Society's mores and rules of morality. Nothing here was sacred except for the privilege of doing as one pleased.

He'd always embraced the notion, considered it forward thinking, but he didn't want her to be part of it. Yet, he couldn't seem to squelch his gladness at her arrival. Unable to take his gaze from her, he fought not to wrap an arm around her and haul her up against him when he was close enough to inhale her verbena fragrance. Lips, the palest of pinks, curved up ever so slightly as he arrived at her side. "Lady V."

"Your Grace."

Her voice was still the smoky rasp that curled around and through him, settling somewhere deep in his soul, filling an emptiness he'd held for too long. That was the only aspect of her that gave him pause that he might have misidentified her, but she could fabricate the timbre. Smart woman that she was, she would have done so, hoping for a further means to keeping her visit here secret. When most men wouldn't have gone to the trouble to unravel their partner's identity. Mystery was a good part of the allure.

"I must confess to being surprised you returned," he said.

"It's not the first time since our encounter."

His gut clenched so tightly that he nearly doubled over. "Pardon?"

The smile again, only a little wider. "I was here last night."

"Were you now?"

"Yes, but only until around midnight."

Impossible. She'd been with him, dancing in his arms. Unless he *was* mistaken regarding her identity. He could ask around, but he didn't want to draw attention to her. It was also possible that she was being a clever girl, fabricating a story in an attempt to throw him off the scent. But if she was speaking true, if he were wrong—

She'd ignored his advice; she'd had a man between her thighs . . .

He had the sudden, irrational urge to flatten some random gent's nose, bust a jaw, blacken an eye. But he wanted her more than he wanted anything else in his life.

"I have a room," he said.

Not waiting for her to respond, he grabbed her hand and headed for the stairs.

MINERVA thought she should have objected to his forcefulness, his determination. Instead, she found herself rather flattered that he appeared so anxious to be alone with her.

She'd lied, of course. She hadn't come here last night, but she needed to squelch any suspicions he harbored that Lady V was Miss Dodger. His questioning at Greyling's had left her a bit more unsettled than she liked, especially after he danced with her at the Dragons. She knew she was playing a dangerous game here, that she would have been better served to stay away, but she wanted to give him his photograph and perhaps a little bit more.

As they traversed the stairs, her calm surprised her. The images he'd captured in Africa haunted her. The exquisite beauty behind them, the story they told. They were preserved for all eternity. While she had never considered herself vain—as she had nothing about which to harbor vanity—she rather liked the notion of being a mysterious woman viewed through the ages.

At the top of the stairs, they walked down the same hallway, his large hand clasped tightly around her smaller one. Before the night was done, he might touch her elsewhere, someplace more intimate. She hadn't determined yet if they would go that far. She'd come here intending merely to pose for him. Beyond that, she'd not yet decided.

She couldn't deny her attraction to him. Did he think less of the women who posed for him? Or did he admire them? How would he feel about her when all was said and done?

He led her to the same corner room, inserted the key, and opened the door. After stepping through the opening, she paused just beyond the threshold, giving him enough space to join her. The door clicked closed.

Without warning, she found her back pressed to it, the duke's mouth latched hungrily onto hers. She should have shoved him away. Instead, she wound her arms around his neck, and when he used his tongue to insist she part her lips, she did so without hesitation, welcoming the deepening of a kiss so hot and consuming that she could do little more than become lost in it. This was what she had always yearned for: the unbridled passion, the madness, the smoldering desire.

She was aware of him bracketing his hands firmly on either side of her waist, then gliding them quickly upward. Not stopping when he reached her arms, he continued sliding his hands along them, moving them from about him until they were raised over her head. With one strong hand, he shackled her wrists together, before plunging the other in her hair, cradling the back of her head, taking further possession of her mouth as though he were its master and commander, leaving no part of it unexplored.

She had an idle thought that she would love to travel the world with him, experience all the various facets of it as they boldly surveyed everything before them. Then her focus narrowed to the present, to him. She tasted the richness of scotch on his tongue. His sandalwood scent invaded her senses. She wanted the freedom to touch him, yet couldn't deny the pleasure in being pinned as she was, his large body flattening her breasts against his chest. He growled low and feral, a wild animal that had captured its prey and was now at liberty to toy with it, to taunt it, to make it grateful to have been caught.

He dragged his mouth over her chin, over her throat to the dip in the silk where her breasts lay in wait. "Who?" he demanded, his voice rough and raw with some emotion she couldn't quite identify.

Breathing harshly, she could barely speak. "Who what?"

"Last night. Who bedded you?"

If she didn't know better, she'd think she heard pure agony threaded through his words, as though he'd forced them out through gritted teeth. Why would he have such a visceral response? And yet she couldn't deny taking some delight in his possessiveness. "No one. I wasn't here for that purpose." The problem with a lie was that it constantly had to be rebuilt, lest the foundation of it crumble. Why was she even playing this game? Why couldn't she be completely honest with him? He had danced with her. Yet so had other men, and in the end, there had been naught but disappointment and hurt.

She fought so hard to ignore the pain of rejection, but she had been schooled enough times to know that it refused to be ignored—at some point it would rush in like a huge tidal wave and overwhelm.

His head came up sharply. She felt more than saw the intensity in his gaze. "Then why were you here?"

"I'd changed my mind about posing for you. It occurred to me that mayhap I did myself no great service by being so cowardly. If I couldn't agree to your simple request, how did I think I was going to climb between the sheets with a stranger?"

"You're not. You're only going beneath the covers with me."

Her first inclination was to object. She was too independent to be told what to do. But she had already decided that when the time came, he was the one she wanted. That he wanted her only sealed things. "You don't bed virgins," she reminded him.

"I've decided to make an exception. God help me. I've not been able to stop thinking about you." Then his mouth came down on hers again, hard and demanding, as though he were intent on devouring every inch of her.

Fool that she was, she gloried in being wanted. It didn't matter that everything he yearned for, all that he knew of her, was the surface, her body and limbs. At long last, a man wanted to take her to his bed. Desired her. Was mad to possess her.

It wasn't complete or perfect, deep or binding. But it was all heat and fire, urgency and need. She'd take it.

She wanted to wrap her arms around him, but he still held them in place, maintaining control, taking without quarter. When next he broke off the kiss, he was breathing as harshly as she.

"Remove the mask. Reveal yourself," he commanded.

Slowly, she shook her head. He wasn't completely in control after all. "No."

"Why?"

Because the illusion of perfection would be shattered, and you wouldn't want me anymore. "You can't know who I am. That's the magic of this place. That ladies are anonymous, so we don't have to fear public ruination or damage to our reputations."

"I want to know who you are."

She shook her head. "I can't do this if you do. I can't do any of it. I can't even pose for you."

"Do you fear that I'll judge you?"

"No." *I fear you'll change your mind.* "I'm just more comfortable behind the mask."

She counted the heartbeats, waiting for him to react, to say something, anything.

"Then keep it on," he said quietly, and his hand loosened from around her wrists as he stepped back.

She lowered her arms. "Are you angry?"

"Disappointed. But we all have our secrets; we all have the right to keep them."

"I can't imagine that you have any."

His lips twisted into a wry smile. "Then you are sadly lacking in imagination." He walked over to the table. "Scotch or brandy?"

"Brandy."

"You didn't strike me as a shy miss," he said as he poured the amber liquid into two snifters.

"What we're doing here . . . I fear feeling exposed, when all is said and done. I'm not quite comfortable with it, but I don't know that I can live with myself if I prove to be an absolute coward."

Returning to her, he handed her a snifter. Taking a sip, she relished the warmth swirling through her but the result wasn't nearly as heated or pleasant as his kiss.

"So tonight, you're only here to be photographed?" he asked.

"That's my present course. I simply don't know that I'm prepared to go further, which I realize brings into question my wisdom in coming here the first night, but desperation sometimes has us being unwise. I know it's frustrating—"

"I shall have my photograph." He tucked his finger beneath her chin, tilted her head up slightly, and kissed her, not with the fire he had earlier, but with banked embers. Drawing back, he held her gaze and gave her a devilish grin. "And maybe I'll have just a little bit more."

When he looked at her like that, he was impossible to resist. It was silly to deny the attraction, to put him off when she'd come here that first night fully expecting to lie with a man.

He gave a sharp nod toward the area behind her. "Now get on the bed."

And her stomach dropped to the floor.

Chapter 9

SHE had known, of course, that this was where she would end up, but now that the moment was upon her, it was a little unsettling. The bed suddenly loomed massive and a great distance away.

"Where do you want me exactly?" she asked, nearly forgetting to alter the timbre of her voice until it reflected the throatiness she required. She didn't like not being in control, yet she suspected tonight she would be merely a puppet, his puppet. The notion should have filled her with anger or dread. Should have had her informing him that she wasn't a pawn, but could leave anytime she wanted. He wouldn't force or bully her. She was relatively certain of that. He was simply a man who knew what he wanted. She found that aspect of him quite attractive.

He wrapped both his hands around hers that was holding the snifter. She wondered when her fingers had gone icy, was amazed by how quickly they warmed with his touch. She would like to have him wrapped around her in winter, when the snow fell.

"For now, simply sit on the foot of the bed." He relieved her of the brandy, turned to set the glass elsewhere, giving her a moment of privacy.

She crossed the short distance to the canopied bedstead and climbed onto the edge of the mattress. Once situated, with her legs dangling over the edge, she looked up, and her breath backed up into her lungs. With his eyes focused on her, Ashebury stood near the fireplace slowly unraveling his neckcloth, his jacket draped over the back of the sofa. He eased the length of linen away from his throat, set it aside, and went to work on the buttons of his waistcoat.

"I do my best work if I'm comfortable," he said, as though he read her discomfiture in the shifting of her body, as though she required an explanation. Not wanting to appear flustered, she refrained from asking how comfortable he intended to get. For goodness sakes, she'd walked unattended through rookeries and slums to assist the poor. She wasn't some mewling miss.

She was, however, growing increasingly warm as he shrugged off the waistcoat, then loosened a few buttons on his shirt until a small V formed to reveal a hint of his chest. His cuffs were next. He began rolling up his sleeves as he prowled toward her, his gaze never once straying from her. She had a wild notion that he intended to pounce on her, to flatten her onto the bed and devour her with his heated kisses, raining them over every inch of her.

He stopped only when his thighs rested lightly

against her knees. "I'm going to remove the pins from your hair."

"It'll tumble down."

A corner of his mouth hitched up in that sensual smile he had that nearly stopped her heart from beating. "That's the desired effect. I'll use it to conceal the mask."

"I can remove the pins." She lifted her hands and his closed around them, preventing them from reaching their destination.

"I'll do it." His tone held no room for compromise.

But the thought of his performing such an intimate service . . . what the devil was wrong with her? She'd originally come here expecting a man to engage in something far more intimate. It was ridiculous to be squeamish now.

"Yes, all right." She needed the words to at least pretend she had some say in the matter.

When he released her hands, she forced them to fall into her lap when she would have much preferred pressing them to his chest. While he was busy searching for her pins, his fingers barely skimming over her hair, she lowered her gaze to the V of skin that traveled from his throat downward. She didn't know a single man as bronzed as he was. He no doubt didn't wear so much as a shirt to shield him from the sun when he was traipsing through Africa or the Far East or anywhere else he dared to roam. She was half-tempted to press a kiss to that flesh, to feel its heat and silkiness against her lips, but before she could be so bold, she was aware of the pinging as her pins hit the floor.

She grabbed his wrist and his gaze slammed into hers. "Give them to me instead of tossing them aside; otherwise, we'll have to search for them so I can put up my hair when we're done."

"We'll find a ribbon to hold it back. I assume you're not heading to a party after you leave here."

"In the wee hours? Something reputable? Hardly likely."

"Then I don't see the problem. Except for the mask. Its ties are in the way."

"I'm not removing it."

"Then hold it in place."

She put her hands over it, splaying her fingers so she didn't lose sight of him. Gently, he tugged on the bow. The ties fell forward, the mask slipped ever so slightly. Without his warning, she'd have been re-vealed. It kindled something sharp and sweet inside her. He wasn't going to take what she was not yet ready to give. He went back to work on her pins. *Clink. Clink. Clink.* She felt the shifting of her coif-fure, then the weight of her hair tumbling down over her shoulders.

"Glorious," he murmured right before there was a tug on the mask's ribbons, and he was securing them.

Lowering her hands, she looked at him through the tiny holes upon which her eyelashes kept catch-ing. Maybe she should get rid of the blasted thing, but his eyes held such appreciation that for a moment she could find no words, take no actions. With two fingers, he was rubbing several strands together as though he'd never before touched a woman's hair.

"You could have discovered who I was," she said quietly.

His attention shifted from her hair to her eyes. "You want the anonymity. I can honor that request. God knows there were times in my life when I longed for it."

"When?"

"When I was younger. I wasn't always the brightest of pupils. When I couldn't arrive at the answer, I often wished no one knew who I was. I'll wager you were an exceptional student."

"Why would you think that?"

"You have intelligent, expressive eyes. You're always watching, observing, striving to calculate where we're going before we get there."

"You deduced all that in our short time together?"

"I'm a keen observer, Lady V. It's why I'm so skilled at what I do." The smoldering look in his eyes implied he was referring to a great deal beyond the photography. It included kisses, touches, and far more intimate encounters. "Before we're done here, I hope you have the opportunity to experience all my skills."

"You're not frightfully arrogant, are you? Both times I came here, you were a solitary figure against the wall. No ladies hovering about."

"Because most know I make the selection. And I only select each lady once."

"Yet you selected me twice."

"It seems where you're concerned, I'm making a good many exceptions. On the other hand, we've yet to complete my purpose or yours in being here. So perhaps it's simply an extension of our first encounter. Now lie back."

It was silly to want to talk with him more, to want to get to know him better. But Grace, blast her, was correct. How could she be intimate with a man who was more stranger than friend? While she had come here only to pose for him, now she was considering him posing for her, while she took liberties—

"A change of heart, Lady V?" he asked.

"No, I . . . a spurt of nerves, but they're gone now." She rolled down onto her back, looked up—

Jerked upright. "Oh, dear God, there's a mirror there!"

He laughed, a deep, rich, rumble that made her smile, made her glad she had the power to elicit that response even if it was at her expense.

"I suppose I should have warned you about that," he said.

"*Why* is it there?"

"Some people like to watch themselves while they're . . . *copulating*."

"Oh." She had planned originally to be bedded with her eyes closed tightly, but if she did that, she would miss the beauty of his form. Still, she didn't want to watch the actual coupling. She considered what she knew of the act. "Ladies, you mean. Ladies like to watch."

"Men as well."

"It seems that it might be rather difficult since you're on top."

"I'm not always on top."

"Are you not?"

"No. Sometimes I'm on bottom. On my side. I've been known to stand." He wrapped a large powerful hand around the bedpost. "Sometimes I kneel. There are all sorts of positions."

"Do you know them all?"

"I doubt that. But I know a good many. I can share them with you when you're ready."

She didn't know if she'd ever be ready for all that, but she was intrigued by the possibilities. She had envisioned them coming together only once but, as she was beginning to realize she might never have enough of his kisses, perhaps there were other facets to him of which she'd never have enough.

Suddenly, barely aware of him moving, she found herself cradled in his arms. "What are you doing?"

"I'm going to place you where I want you, before you lose your nerve. My subjects don't usually talk so much. It's better to just get on with it. I'm going to touch you, but you can stop me if you become uncomfortable with my attentions."

As he walked around the corner of the bed, she

felt delicate when she never had before in her life. Having inherited her father's features, she'd always felt unfeminine, almost boyish. It hadn't helped that she'd loved climbing trees and following after her brothers.

He set her down gently in the middle of the mattress as though she were fragile glass. With his hands coming to rest on her shoulder and hip, he rolled her slightly. "On your stomach but not all the way. Extend your left arm up. You can rest your head on it. Your right hand here, near your ribs to provide some support."

She did as he bade. Then, as he'd promised, he began arranging her hair over her face, over the mask that she was coming to detest. What if she removed it? What if he realized who she was? Would he still be willing to bed her, or would he be put off by the notion of being with a woman no man had ever loved? Quite unexpectedly, she desperately wanted him to be the one who deflowered her. On his feet, on his knees, on his side, below her, above her. She wanted to be his first virgin. Wanted him to be her first lover. Even if only for one night, she wanted him.

Through the curtain of her hair, she watched him move back to the foot of the bed. He folded his hands around her feet, and although it made absolutely no sense, they felt delicate as well. "Left leg straight, right leg bent slightly at the knee."

Holding her ankles, he guided her leg. "There. Perfect."

A word that had never been associated with her before. She rather liked it.

"I'm going to move the silk up now because I want the emphasis to be on your legs. Most of the rest of you will be in shadow. I'll stop if you tell me you're uncomfortable. But I hope you're daring enough to let me reach my destination. It'll be pleasing for us both."

That was a challenge if she ever heard one.

He moved the silk up with his wrists, his hands remaining curled around her legs as he glided them smoothly up over her calves, her knees—

A quick release to tug up the material caught beneath her legs. Then a continuation of the journey up her thighs, slowly, slowly, giving her time to protest. Only she wasn't going to. She was her father's daughter, a man branded as a thief in his youth who had taught her never to back down.

Ashebury's hands came to rest just below the curve of her buttocks. "Good girl," he murmured, with appreciation laced in his voice. "Brave girl."

The joy that spiraled through her at pleasing him was rather confounding. Making him happy made her happy.

He adjusted the cloth, angling it higher on one side. "Are you aware that you have a tiny heart-shaped birthmark on your hip?" He placed a reverent kiss there that branded her flesh, scored her soul.

"Don't move a muscle," he ordered. Then he was gone, and she nearly wept at his leaving.

ASHE was as hard as granite. His body didn't usually react when he was positioning a woman for the camera because he was so focused on the task, all his attention devoted to discerning how best to pose his subject to bring out the beauty of the human form. But with her it was different. Everything with her was different. He hadn't wanted to stop at her hip. When he'd revealed the tiny birthmark, he'd wanted to continue exploring her, to uncover all the hidden secrets of her body.

Barely able to walk, he took his position behind the camera, peered through the lens. Exquisite, perfection. That, too, was unusual. Normally, he had to reposition a woman a little here or a little there. But he'd had two days to fantasize about her, to consider every facet of what he would do with those legs if he ever again had a chance to photograph them. All he needed now was to adjust the lighting.

Arranging chairs and small tables, he moved lamps to the foreground, increased their illumination, smiled as he became master of the shadows. They went where he willed.

So many times he'd almost tested his theory regarding her identity, almost called her Miss Dodger. But he didn't want to make her uncomfortable, didn't want to lose this opportunity. Didn't want to lose her.

He was going to bed her. Maybe not tonight, but very soon. He didn't know when he'd become so certain of it, but he wasn't going to let any other man have her. Not here, not anywhere, not for her first time. With her boldness, her willingness to go un-flinchingly after what she wanted, she deserved bet-ter than a man who merely wanted to sate his lust. Although Ashe had to acknowledge that desire such as he'd never experienced was a motivating factor for him. He wanted what he had no right to possess.

She was a contradiction. A woman bold enough to come here for a bedding but reserved enough that she insisted on the secrecy, that even her lover not know who she was. Because she didn't trust him not to hurt her? Had someone hurt her? Other than the dimwit who had hoped his children didn't favor her? If she revealed his name, he might take measures to ensure the man never had children. He wasn't prone to violence, except when survival was at stake, but she had him acting not quite like himself.

Yet she trusted him enough to be with him, to let him place his hands on her, to not harm her. Another reason existed for her reticence to remove the mask. It was a mystery he would like to solve. Slowly, over time, with relished moments and pas-sionate kisses. She was fire beneath the reserve. He had the power to unleash it.

He could stand here all night just looking at her lying there. He wished he could capture all her true shades. The paleness of her skin, the rich auburn of her hair. The way the shadows caressed her as he longed to. The way the light revealed her as she deserved to be seen.

But only by him. He wanted no one else to see her as he had been given the chance to view her. He would never share with another soul the fine lines of her legs, the curve of her backside, the slope of her hip, the birthmark. No one else would ever know her as he did at this moment.

He stepped away from the camera. "You can relax. It's done."

She came up on an elbow, and he couldn't help thinking that there was the opportunity for another remarkable photograph—if only she'd remove the mask. "I didn't hear anything."

"It's the latest model. Quiet as a whisper," he lied. She wouldn't understand his motives for not taking the photo. He wasn't quite certain he understood them himself.

She began shoving herself up farther.

"Hold," he commanded.

She froze, and even the loathsome mask of silk and feathers couldn't hide the surprise in her eyes.

"I'm not done with you yet," he said.

MINERVA fought for calm as one of his knees landed between her calves. Then the other. His hands came to rest on either side of her body, supporting him, his length barely touching her as he prowled toward her until his face was directly over hers. That was all she could see. His shadowed jaw, the intensity of his gaze, the hard line of his lips, parted ever so slightly. She couldn't see her reflection in the mirror above, couldn't see the looking glass at all. Her vision had narrowed down to only him.

To this man who made her feel things she'd thought herself incapable of feeling. To this man who could make her feel appreciated while at the same time bringing home what she might have possessed if she were the sort of woman a man could fall in love with. To know what it might have felt like . . . to have known only the hollow shell of it . . . well, it was better than having never known, better than nothing at all.

He lowered his mouth, claiming hers, keeping himself suspended so that all she felt was a light brush of his chest against her breasts. Her nipples puckered painfully, strained against the cloth. She wanted to press him to her. Instead, she buried her fingers in his thick dark hair as he plundered. Surrender was such sweet victory.

To be desired like this was heady beyond all imagining. All her reservations regarding coming here drifted away. He was no longer a stranger. She knew he smelled of sandalwood. Knew the rasp of his bristly jaw against her chin in the hours just past midnight when he'd gone so long without shaving. She knew the deep rumble of his laugh, the way he could make her skin tingle with awareness with only his gaze focused on her as he stood a few feet away from her. She knew he marveled at beauty and wanted to capture it. When she was with him, she knew what it was to have a man's undivided attention.

He lifted his mouth from hers. "Remove the mask."

The request was a whisper, dark and full of promises. But she couldn't risk the spell being broken. "No."

He pressed his lips to the underside of her chin. How could the skin there be so sensitive?

"In that case, I won't take your maidenhead, but I will gift you with pleasure as a means to express my appreciation to you for posing for me."

He trailed his hot mouth down her throat, over her collarbone, then along the fall of silk that led to the swells of her breasts. Giving her a heavy-lidded, sensual gaze that caused her toes to curl, he smiled as though he fully understood how easily he could unravel her. Over the silk, he closed his mouth around her turgid nipple, lathing his tongue over it, dampening the cloth, causing sensations of pure delight to cascade through her. Then he caught the tiny peak between his teeth, and with the gentlest of bites, he had her hips coming up off the bed, reaching for him, searching for the hard ridge straining against his trousers.

"Not yet," he insisted. "Not yet."

Slowly, provocatively he glided down her body, providing only enough pressure to drive her mad, to alert her that she needed more, that release was dependent upon more. Finally, standing at the foot of the bed, he wrapped his arms around her hips and dragged her to the edge of the mattress. He lowered himself. "Now, you'll learn what happens when I'm on my knees."

His gaze holding hers, he placed her legs over his shoulders, eased the silk up until he bared what she had always kept most private. She gave no thought at all to objecting. When a man looked at woman as though she were his moon and stars, how could she protest? When a man's eyes promised pleasure beyond her wildest dreams—

Turning his head, he pressed a featherlike kiss to the inside of one thigh, just above her knee. It felt so marvelous, so debauched. He gave attention to the other thigh, only a little higher up. This time, his tongue created a little circle of dew on her skin. An incredible sensation of wonder traveled from her tightening breasts to her curling toes. Back and forth he went, like someone climbing a ladder, taking her to heaven. When he reached the top, the juncture between leg and body, he locked his smoldering gaze onto hers. He held it for a heartbeat, two.

Then he lowered his mouth to the heart of her womanhood. Oh, dear Lord. Looking up at the mirror's reflection, she saw herself spread before him like some feast, his dark head nestled between her thighs, his fingers pressing into her hips as he took and gave and caused the most exquisite intense sensations to course through her. It was all so decadent, all so magnificent.

His tongue swirled, his teeth nipped at her bud as they had her nipple. The heat of him scored her even as it delighted. He suckled, bit, laved, and applied pressure when she needed it, where she needed it. As though he were one with her, as though he could feel what she felt. But he could not possibly be feeling this. She didn't know how anyone survived feeling this.

Pleasure coiled inside her, coiled so tightly that she thought she would break. And then she did. She shattered into shards of pleasure so rich, so remarkable that she thought surely this was death. Her cries echoed around her, her back arched, her body trembled. Breathing harshly, she was barely aware of him sliding up the bed, taking her in his arms, turning her into his chest, holding her tightly while her world slowly came back together.

"If we're going to continue with this," he said after a time, "the feathers need to go. They tickle my nose."

With a soft laugh, she pushed herself up, took in the sight of him sprawled over the bed like some giant lazy cat. Reaching up, he wrapped strands of her silken hair around his finger, studied them. Could the shade give her away? It wasn't uncommon. It was just hair.

"I want you to pose for me again."

"Now?"

Releasing his hold on her hair, he shoved himself off the bed. "No, another night."

Rebuttoning his shirt as he went, he walked to the sofa. There he slipped on his waistcoat, secured its buttons. He draped the strip of linen around his neck and began the process of creating an intricate knot.

Sliding from the bed, she padded over and brushed his hands aside. "I'll do it."

"An untouched woman skilled in tying a gentleman's neckcloth?"

"I'm not certain I still qualify as untouched," she said, finding it difficult to concentrate on her task with his nearness, his scent overwhelming her. "But I have a brother who is constantly in need of tidying."

"How many brothers do you have?"

Without considering consequences, she'd spoken to a man with whom she felt incredibly comfortable. Danger rested with that thought. She had to be so careful not to give him too many clues regarding her identity. Her reputation, her family's could be ruined. "Only one worth mentioning at the moment."

Cradling her cheek, he tilted her face up. "You'll trust me with your body but not your identity."

"I dared to come here because I believed it could remain a secret."

"Nothing ever remains a secret forever."

Her chest tightened with the thought of how disappointed her parents would be if they ever learned she'd come here. How mortified she would be by the public acknowledgment of her desperation. She was half sister to a duke. She wouldn't embarrass him for the world. "This must," she stated with finality, touching her fingers to the secured knot at his throat to press home her point.

"I want you . . . desperately. But I want all of you revealed." Turning away, he snatched up his jacket, drew it on. "You'll find me here tomorrow night if you've any interest in taking things between us further. But the mask comes off."

"I don't—"

He pressed his finger to her lips. "Don't answer now. Sleep on it. Then tomorrow night, at the witching hour, with either your presence or your absence I'll have your answer."

The remainder of tonight to think on it, to dream of it. "Well, then, we shall see."

"So we shall. I'll have my driver return you to your residence."

He knew she wasn't being taken to her residence, but she couldn't let on that she was cross with him because it was Minerva he'd claimed to see at the Dragons that night, not Lady V. Dear God, but keeping the two of them separate was going to prove challenging. But after tonight, she thought it might well be worth it.

ASHE stood in the street and watched as his carriage carted her away to the Twin Dragons. He considered grabbing a hansom and arriving there shortly after her. She once again wore green. He would find the gown and the woman inside it. If she were Miss Minerva Dodger, he'd have his answer. If she weren't, he'd know who she was. In either case, he could prolong their time together. She intrigued him. He wanted her to return here, for them to finish what they had begun.

Would she hate him for uncovering the truth of her? That was a possibility. And so he remained where he was.

Chapter 10

*L*ATE the following morning, Ashe was sitting at his breakfast table reading the *Times* when Edward wandered in looking like death warmed over in spite of the fact that he was properly dressed. His eyes were sunken, his pallor a bit gray.

"I need some black coffee," he muttered as he dropped into a chair.

A footman neared with a silver pot in hand and filled the cup at Edward's place.

"Bring me some toast," Edward ordered before looking at Ashe. "That's about all I can handle this morning."

"Too much drinking last night?" Ashe asked.

Edward brought the cup to his mouth, inhaled the dark aroma, sipped. "Among other things. So who was the white swan?"

Ashe came alert. "Pardon?"

"I arrived at the Nightingale just as you were fairly dragging a lady up the stairs. White silk, white mask. You seemed quite possessive of her. Or were you merely obsessed?"

Damnation. In his haste to be with her, he'd nearly forgotten that other men would be watching, other men might want a chance at her. They wouldn't force her, but they might attempt to entice her. "Believe it or not, I don't know who she is." He suspected, but he couldn't say with complete certainty. And in either case, she wanted no one to know, and he was going to honor that request.

"That's not like you. You can usually charm the mask right off them."

When they were younger, they had often boasted of their conquests, but Ashe had no need of doing that now. He had his own secrets when it came to the Nightingale. "The lady isn't the first unwilling to share her identity."

"It's rather unsporting of them, though, when they take that stand. I like to know whose wife I'm bedding."

"As you are well aware, and we've previously discussed, not all the women there are wives."

Edward perked up, his interest obvious. "Is your swan not?"

"I wouldn't know."

"Widow or spinster?"

"Again, I wouldn't know."

"Wild beneath the covers, or does she just lie there?"

Wild. Unfettered. He'd ached to be inside her when she became lost in the throes of rapture, imagined her muscles undulating around him, sucking him dry. "None of your concern."

"Aren't you protective? Seems odd to care if you don't know who she is."

"Women go there expecting the gents to hold their tongues. I merely adhere to the unwritten rule."

"Is she adventuresome?"

"I'm not discussing her or our time together."

"Maybe you failed at it. Maybe you couldn't get it up."

Took him a good half hour after she left to get it down. "Why the interest?"

"I was wondering if maybe I should keep an eye out for her, maybe seek to have a turn with her."

Ashe was aware of the newspaper crumpling in his hands. "If you so much as get within three feet of her, I shall lay you flat."

Edward arched a brow. "Sounds as though she's special indeed. I don't recall your ever being so possessive."

He never had been before. He didn't know why he was now. Perhaps because he had yet to experience her completely, hadn't yet ridden her, been enveloped by the heat of her womanly warmth. Shaking out his paper, Ashe wanted to get them off the discussion of Lady V. "I'm letting the lease on this residence go."

"What? Wait. Whatever for?"

"It's ridiculous to spend money on this place when my parents' residence sits unused." It was the last place he'd seen his parents. He'd visited there only once since reaching his majority. The walls still echoed his screams. But he could no longer afford indulging in excess expenditures. "I'll be moving out within the next few days. If you want to see about taking over the lease, you're welcome to purchase whatever furniture I have on hand here." His furnishing a second residence, in hindsight, had not been a wise use of funds, but he'd had such high hopes that his investments would at least triple his initial outlay.

"My brother provides me with a generous allowance but not that generous. And his devil of a wife is advocating that he become stingy. Still, I could probably spring for the lease." He glanced around. "It is a rather nice place. Could I arrange to buy the furniture over time?"

Ashe turned his attention to the article he was reading. "Why don't you determine which pieces you'd really like to have, and I'll sell the rest elsewhere?"

"Is everything all right?"

"Couldn't be better."

"Ashe."

He lowered his paper to see Edward's earnest gaze focused on him. For all the adventures, good-natured bickering, and jolly times they'd shared, they'd also been family from the moment they'd been deposited at the Marquess of Marsden's estate. While it was extremely difficult and mortifying to admit, he forced out the words. "I may have mucked up my coffers."

"Speak to Grey or even Locke. They're flush. I'm sure they could see their way clear to help you."

"I'm not going to take money from them."

"A loan. You can pay them back at your leisure."

"Nothing damages a friendship more than borrowing from a friend. Besides, I got myself into this without help. I can get myself out."

"How are you going to manage that?"

"I'm going to marry."

MINERVA arrived at Grace's shortly after breakfast. After greeting her half brother, she asked Grace to take a turn about the garden with her. Lovingdon merely smiled at her. "You ladies and your secrets." Then he returned his attention to whatever business was cluttering his desk.

Waiting until they were near the roses, Minerva confessed in a low voice, "I may have done something very foolish."

"Oh dear God." Taking her arm, Grace pulled her behind a trellis and studied her as though her actions were imprinted on her forehead. "Tell me."

Minerva took a deep breath. "I gave Ashebury leave to photograph my bare ankles."

"You bared your ankles to him?" Grace asked, doubt in her voice as though she'd misheard.

Minerva nodded. "And maybe my calves."

Grace's eyes widened considerably. "You're not sure?"

"Of course I'm sure. So yes, my calves definitely." She grimaced. "My thighs. The very edge of my bum."

"Minerva, are you mad?" Grace whispered harshly. "You allowed him to photograph these things? How did this even come about?"

"I returned to the Nightingale last night."

Grace gave her a pointed look. "So he was the one, that first night."

Minerva sighed. "He was. And he likes—" She shook her head. "I'm not supposed to talk about what happens there."

"You know your secrets are safe with me."

"Yes, but these are his."

Grace looked up at the sky, the trees, as though searching for patience. "I'll hold his as well."

He might never forgive her if he found out that she had told someone. On the other hand, she wasn't the first he'd taken to a room, so other ladies knew. She trusted Grace with her life, with all her secrets. "He likes to take photographs of ladies who join him in a bedchamber."

Grace's mouth opened. She snapped it shut. Her brows furrowed. "That seems lewd and unseemly."

"I thought so, too, the first night. I didn't do it then, but when I saw his photographs from Africa . . . I couldn't stop thinking about them. They weren't like the photographs we had taken when we were children and just stood there. Last night . . . Oh, Grace, he took such care, was so respectful. I could see in his eyes, the concentration on his face that it was so important to him. And he assured me I was tastefully displayed."

"Tastefully displayed? I'm not certain that's very reassuring as I'm not sure how one who is bared can be displayed tastefully."

"There were shadows, so many shadows that I felt . . . well, almost covered. If anyone were to see the photograph, they wouldn't know it was me."

"Are you certain?"

"I was masked. Although I do have a little birthmark. I thought nothing of it at the time, but now—I don't think he'll show anyone."

"Who all knows about the birthmark?"

"My mother certainly. My father probably. There is a slight chance that my brothers might know, but unlikely. I can remember us bathing together as children, but they wouldn't have noticed. Surely."

"But still. Where is he planning to display these things?"

"He's not. They are only for him. That's not my concern."

Grace took her hands, squeezed them in reassurance. "Then what is?"

"I think he suspects I might be Lady V."

Grace blinked, frowned. "Who is Lady V?"

Minerva's bark of laughter echoed around them.

"Um, that would be me. I had to give him some name that first night so I thought Lady Virgin."

Grace smiled. "Lady Virgin? Truly? Minerva, you are too bold by half."

"Not so bold. I'm still a virgin." She laced her fingers together, squeezed them. "He's offered to deflower me tonight."

Grace's smile withered, and concern was reflected in her eyes. "Are you going to do it?"

"He knows what he's about. I think he would make a remarkable lover. But I'm not quite comfortable with his knowing it's me. He's intrigued by the mystery of me. He'd be disappointed in the reality."

"But if he suspects . . . Honestly, Minerva, you can't think to keep something like this a complete secret. You're wearing a little mask."

"It's actually rather large, leaves very little visible."

"But he's going to see"—Grace looked down at her toes, carried her gaze back up to her eyes—"everything."

"Can't one make love in the dark?"

"Well, yes, I suppose so, but don't you want to see him?" She pressed her hand to her mouth. "What am I saying? I don't want to encourage you. I wish I'd never given you the address."

"Where did you get it anyway?"

"My brother. I'm fairly certain Rexton meets his mistress there. You saw him, didn't you?"

"I can't say."

Grace made a moue of displeasure. "All these secrets. I don't think any good is going to come of all this."

"Will you still love me if I go through with it?"

"Of course, but if he suspects, why not confirm the truth of your identity and see how things go?"

"I don't expect you to understand the beating that one's esteem takes after six years of watching others fall in love or make good matches that aren't based solely on their dowry. I want a man who looks at me the way my father looks at my mother, the way Lovingdon looks at you. As though no one else was as important, was as treasured. My brother would die for you."

"He almost did. But in the end, he lived for me, and that's so much better, Minerva. Do you like Ashebury?"

"Very much."

"I've never known you to be a shrinking violet. If you want him, go after him." She smiled brightly. "That's how I got Lovingdon. I'd wager money on you."

"I wouldn't wager much. The odds are against me. He could have anyone. But at least I know he fancies my legs."

*A*SHE stood on the top step staring at the dark mahogany door that opened into his parents' residence. It was silly to refer to it as such. They'd not crossed the threshold in twenty years.

With a sigh, he unlocked the door, released the

latch, and gave the wood a hard shove. The hinges creaked and moaned as the widening gap revealed the entryway. Stepping over the threshold, Ashe closed the door behind him, sealing himself in with the memories.

Dust motes danced through the soft light filtering in through the mullioned windows on either side of the door. The air sat heavy, reeking of must and disuse. The silence was thick, a residence abandoned, unloved, unwanted.

It had been his mother's pride and joy, a symbol of his father's wealth and station. Even at eight, Ashe had understood the statement made by this exquisite building. Now every piece of furniture was shrouded in white, giving things a ghostly appearance.

His footsteps echoed over the black marble as he approached the stairs. As though he needed the support, when he stopped, he wrapped his hand around the newel post and stared at the sixth step up, the one upon which he'd been standing when he'd seen his parents for the last time, the one from which he'd shouted that he hated them and hoped they never came back.

The pain of remembrance was a sharp jab at the bottom of his breastbone. He imagined he could still hear the hateful words echoing through the entryway, bouncing off the walls and frescoed ceiling. Only they'd followed his parents out, circling about them. Sadness had been in his mother's blue eyes when she glanced back over her shoulder, before his father ushered her out. What had his mother thought of him at that moment? Probably what he now thought of himself.

Pampered heir, spoiled brat, despicable child.

Those had certainly been his nanny's words as she'd dragged him back to the day nursery.

He should sell the house, everything in it. Only that course felt like defeat. He was a man now, strong enough to face the past, to deal with it, to move on. This place represented part of his heritage, his history.

He should be grateful that everything he didn't want to remember had occurred here rather than at the ancestral estate. Although it seemed odd now to think of them as being in London in November. His scoff disturbed the silence. What did it matter after all these years?

It didn't. With a length to his stride and a quickness to his pace as though he could escape the demons of recollection and regret, he strode into the parlor and was greeted by white sheets covered in a fine layer of dust. It was here in the afternoons that he would be presented to his mother so he could tell her about his day. His time in the park, his riding lessons, his tutoring curriculum. He could still hear the tutor's proclamation that he was not a bright lad, see the disappointment in his mother's eyes. But he was bright enough to know that the numbers didn't behave. When he tried to explain how they played tricks, she would give her attention to the birds fluttering about beyond the window. So he learned to hold his tongue in order not to disillusion her, not to lose her affection.

She would be sorely dissatisfied with him now, in his inability to properly oversee what had been placed in his keeping. So would his father. What he remembered most about the previous duke was his stiffness, the manner in which he could walk while hardly moving any portion of his body, the way he would arch a brow in censure. Ashe had always dreaded when the brow went up. It was usually followed with the words, "Find me a switch."

He remembered the bite of it against his bare backside and upper legs. Still, for all the coldness and rigidity of his parents, he'd felt unmoored when word came that they were dead. He'd screamed, and wept, and promised to be good if only they'd come back.

But the best behavior in the world couldn't undo what had been done.

As much as he fought it, his mind traveled to the last time he'd been in this room, standing vigil over his parents' coffin. So little of them remained that they'd been encased together. Or so he'd been told. He'd sat stoic and silent while mourners paid their last respects. Too young, too numb to truly understand everything that transpired, all the ramifications, he'd been left an orphan, alone in the world, with no close family. Those who had introduced themselves as relatives were unfamiliar. He'd never again seen a single one of them after the burial. No one checked up on him to ensure he was well cared for. No one penned a letter to see how he was getting on. No one inquired as to his health, his safety, his well-being. No one gave a bloody damn.

The morose thoughts threatened to consume him. It was the reason that he'd not taken up residence here. It wasn't a place of happy memories. Yes, he should sell it.

But he knew he wouldn't.

$\mathcal{I}$T was a lovely day for a stroll through the park. Minerva was grateful that when Lord John Simpson, brother to the Duke of Kittingham, had called on her, he had suggested they go out. It was a lovelier way to spend the time than sitting in the parlor, where her thoughts bombarded her with doubts. She hadn't yet decided what to do about meeting Ashebury tonight. If she weren't drawn to him, she would have no decision to make, but after last night, she found she wanted to experience all that he had to offer. While he might have suspicions regarding her identity, he didn't know for certain. She rather liked his not knowing for certain.

"—you see."

She glanced over at her strolling companion, who had seen all of nineteen years. He was fair-haired and tall, his side whiskers little more than peach fuzz. "I'm sorry. What did you say?"

He gave her an indulgent smile. "My brother and

I have never gotten along. He's mean-spirited, spiteful. Rather nasty, to be honest about it. He's going to cut off my allowance when I reach my majority, which leaves me in a bit of a bother."

"I can see where it would. But it's quite acceptable for second sons to become members of the clergy."

He grimaced. "The trouble there is that you have to always ask after people's problems."

"But I'm certain it must be extremely rewarding to provide comfort."

He shook his head. "Not really my cup of tea."

"Perhaps you could join a regiment."

"Dreadful amount of work, marching about, taking orders."

"Better than being forced to live on the street."

His steps came a halt and he faced her. "I was hoping you would do me the honor of marrying me."

She bit back a bubble of laughter. "I'm considerably older than you."

"As I'm aware, but it would get you off the shelf."

"I don't really have a problem being on the shelf. As a matter of fact, I'm rather liking the independence it affords me."

His eyes brightened. "I wouldn't take that away from you. It would be a marriage in name only. As the spare, I don't require an heir. So you would have no wifely duties."

"I have none now."

"But now all of London knows you don't. When we're married, it would be our little secret."

Her offers were getting more ridiculous. She needed to take out an advert in the *Times*, announcing that she was not in the market for a husband. "You gain my dowry. I'm at a loss as to what I gain."

"You won't be a spinster. You'll be *my lady*. And you'll have my protection."

"I have protection now."

"Your father isn't going to live forever."

"In his absence, I have brothers who will step in, plus I have a strong left hook."

He blinked. "You would engage in fisticuffs yourself?"

"If need be, yes."

With a sigh, he slumped his shoulders. "Is there nothing I can offer that would make marriage to me attractive?"

"Love."

He looked positively defeated. "I love another girl."

"Marry her."

"Her dowry is a pittance. I was going to use yours to give her everything I can't."

"We should probably stop talking now before I introduce you to my left fist."

He gave her a crooked smile. "I mucked things up."

He looked so young, and she felt remarkably old. "Consider the army, my lord. It'll give you backbone." Turning on her heel, she began the long trek home.

It was several minutes before he loped up to join

her. "You won't tell anyone about my offer will you?"

"Absolutely not."

"Thank you, Miss Dodger." They walked in silence for a while before he said, "What if I can't make a go of it on my own?"

"I have faith in you, my lord. It won't be easy, but if you really love the girl, you'll find a way. One that doesn't involve someone else's dowry."

As they carried on toward her home, she wondered how her life had come to this. Last night had contained no disappointments. It had been only joy and pleasure.

She wanted another night with Ashebury—on her terms.

"You rang for me, Your Grace?"

Standing at the window in his library, sipping his scotch, Ashe watched as twilight crept over the gardens. He was going to miss the quiet, miss not slamming into memories every time he turned a corner. For hours, he'd roamed the familiar hallways of his youth, remembering a few times worth savoring. His mother spritzing him with her perfume, tickling him until he laughed and begged her to stop. His father tying thread around Ashe's first loose tooth, securing one end of it to a doorknob, then slamming the door closed, jerking out the tooth in the process. Patting Ashe on the shoulder. "Good lad. You'll do well as a duke."

And Ashe never again telling his father when he felt a tooth beginning to wobble. Then no longer having the opportunity to tell him.

"We're taking up residence at Ashebury Place. Have the servants begin preparing it for our arrival. I should like to be moved in within the week."

"Very good, sir. We'll have to take on additional staff."

Because Ashebury Place was twice the size of this house. "We'll make do with what we have for now."

"As you wish."

It wasn't what he wished. Truth be told, he probably needed to let some of the staff go. But he couldn't bring himself to turn them out when their only crime was having an employer who had fallen on hard times.

"Will there be anything else, Your Grace?"

"No, that's all for now, Wilson."

"Very good, sir." Wilson left as quietly as he'd entered.

Ashe pressed his fist to the window, leaned his forehead against it. He didn't want to keep reliving the memories that had visited him today, but it was as though he were trapped in a barrel that was rolling down a hill. For the first time that day, he smiled. At Havisham, they'd once taken turns climbing into a barrel and being rolled about, so he was very familiar with the sensation. He'd taken pride in being the only one not to cast up his breakfast.

The thought about his pride brought him to his

photos, which brought him immense satisfaction. Following that thought was an image of Lady V lying across the bed with legs revealed, waiting for him to part them, to bury himself between them.

He needed her tonight. He desperately hoped she'd be there.

Chapter 11

SHE was three minutes late, one hundred and eighty seconds past the last gong that marked the witching hour, and he'd already found a replacement for her. With her heart clamoring and bitter disappointment settling into her breast, she stood transfixed in the doorway leading into the parlor of the Nightingale Club and watched as Ashebury nodded and smiled at a woman wearing a deep purple mask and elegant evening gown. It barely occurred to her to wonder why the lurid female wasn't dressed in the simple attire of every other lady in the room.

Instead, she was more concerned with why she thought she'd meant something to him, why she'd given any credence to his invitation, to the pleasure he'd brought her, to the exceptions he'd claimed to make where she was concerned. Lies spouted from his luscious, deceiving mouth like that of every other man who had ever deemed to give her attention. When she was out of sight, she was out of mind. She. Lady V.

She castigated herself. Had she really thought that a woman who visited a place like this was going to be revered and hold a man's affections for more than the time it took to bed her?

Then he was striding toward her, his smile broadening, and it occurred to her that it had never been for the woman in purple. That it had been for her the second she'd stepped through the doorway, and he saw her.

She had been three minutes late. It wasn't even a minute later, and he was at her side.

"Seems you're not wanting for a partner this evening," she said, hating the churlishness in her voice, striving not to reveal the full extent of her irritation and disappointment by shaking off the large, warm hand that he had curled over her shoulder, offering the touch she had planned to welcome with every aspect of her being.

His smile dimmed slightly, his gaze held hers commandingly, not allowing her to look away. "Lady Eliza is the proprietor. She was reassuring me that everything I asked for had been seen to."

"What did you ask for?"

He glided that cupped hand along her arm, took her hand, and lifted her fingers to his mouth. She was aware of the warmth of his breath, the softness of his lips. "Do you want me to ruin the surprise I planned for you?"

The tightness in her chest unfurled like a rose blossoming at first light. "What if I hadn't come?"

"I'd have left here a broken man."

A corner of her mouth curled up. "I doubt that."

"Well, perhaps not broken, but very disappointed. Shall we go up?"

The time had come. While her nerves threatened to jump about, she took a deep breath to calm them. She would not—could not—back out again. She'd made her decision to come here, to meet him tonight, because she wanted to be in his arms. He was the one, the one she yearned for, the one she wanted to take her more deeply into the realm of pleasure. She trusted him. He could have taken advantage before, could have pressured her, could have been angry when she changed her mind. But all along, he'd been patient, understanding, gentle—even though he'd told her that he liked it rough and hard. The kiss against the door had no doubt been a sampling.

It hadn't frightened her then, the thought of it didn't frighten her now. She wanted to be with him. For tonight, she relished the fantasy that he yearned to be with her.

She nodded. Wrapping his arm around her back, he turned her for the stairs, then brought her in closer against his side as they ascended them. When they reached the top, he escorted her along a different hallway, at the end of which was another set of stairs. He guided her up them. At the top was only one door.

She was shimmering with anticipation as he unlocked it, shoved it open. This time, after she passed over the threshold, she wasn't surprised when the door slammed in her wake and she found her back against it, her hands shackled over her head, his mouth hungrily and greedily devouring hers. This time she welcomed him without hesitation, without reservation.

"You were late," he snarled.

She laughed. "All of three minutes."

She'd almost not come. She'd climbed into the carriage, climbed out of it. Back in. Then she'd had the driver drop her off a few blocks from the Nightingale, sent him on his way, and prayed he'd say nothing to her father. But why would he? He didn't know her final destination or the mischief she was getting into.

"Each one was an eternity of agony," Ashebury ground out.

The joy spiraling through her only increased when he latched his mouth back onto hers. He wanted her, yearned for her, desired her. He made her feel beautiful and elegant. He made her feel as though she mattered to him.

"Take off the mask," he demanded, his mouth hot against her throat.

"No." Tonight was fantasy, the dreams of a homely girl who had never known the heat of passion, who had never been made to feel desired. Who had thought she'd be destined for a cold marriage until she'd decided she'd rather hold her head up high as a spinster than bow before a man who couldn't love her.

Leaning back slightly, he peered through the small openings of the mask into her eyes, bracketed his hands on either side of her throat, skimmed his thumbs along her chin. "After all we've shared thus far, why won't you reveal yourself to me?"

"Because it will change everything."

"Could change everything for the better."

"I don't think so. I'll become self-conscious, uncomfortable. Probably won't go through with it. But I want very much to be with you." She cradled his jaw. "Still, I need the mystery."

Placing his hand over hers, he held it in place while he turned his head slightly and pressed a kiss to its center. "How will you explain your touched state on your wedding night?"

"I'm not going to marry."

His eyes held hers. "What if you have an offer?"

"I don't trust any man to be sincere when he says he wants me. None has ever claimed to love me." She lowered her hand to his lapel, squeezed her fingers around it. "Don't say those words to me tonight. I don't need them. I want honesty between us."

"Says the woman in the gilded mask."

"There's no dishonesty in not revealing who I am when it is the mark of this place. Didn't you accept these conditions with other women?"

"But none of them intrigue me as you do. Yet if the choice is to accept your terms or not have you

. . . I'll accept your terms." He released her, stepped away. "Now, let's enjoy what Lady Eliza prepared for us."

She looked more closely at the room then, realized it was larger than the other. Thick red velvet hung from the canopy of the bed in stark contrast to the white satin sheets that glistened in the candlelight like a shimmering pool of decadence. Within the sitting area, a fire burned low on the hearth. Near the window was a cloth-covered table set with a light repast and a bottle of wine. Ashebury was pouring the burgundy liquid into two goblets.

Wandering over, she said, "I'm not certain I can eat."

He peered at her. "If not now, later. You need to keep up your strength. We have all night."

She almost told him that she needed to be home before her parents were up, and her father was an early riser. But she would worry about working her way through that gauntlet later. After taking the goblet he offered, she sipped the wine, smiled. "Very nice."

"I'm glad you like it."

She glanced around. "Why this room?"

"It's used only by the most elite, for special occasions. It doesn't seem quite as tawdry. It's isolated, which I thought might make you less self-conscious should you have a need to scream in pleasure."

After last night, she suspected he could very easily make her scream. She took another sip, licked her lips, watched as his eyes darkened. "You didn't set up your camera."

"I'm not here for photographs tonight."

"Did the one you take of me turn out?"

"It is without doubt my best work."

"I hoped you might bring it, show it to me."

He slowly shook his head. "I'll never share it with anyone, not even you."

"That hardly seems fair. Perhaps I'll have you teach me how to use a camera, and I'll take a photo of you."

He picked up a strawberry, placed it lightly against her lips. "I'll be happy to add that to the list of things I intend to teach you."

Taking a bite of the strawberry, she enjoyed the succulent sweetness, watched as he finished off the fruit. Everything was going so slowly, more slowly than she'd anticipated. "I thought we'd get right to it."

"I told you that first night that a slow seduction increases the anticipation and ultimately the pleasure."

"The slow seduction began two visits ago, wouldn't you say?"

The sensual smile he bestowed on her hinted at his devilish nature. "There is only one first time, V."

Her mouth was suddenly dry. "I see you've decided to go informal. Should I call you A?"

"Ashe. Would you rather I call you something else? Sweetheart, perhaps?"

"I don't want any false endearments."

"If I utter them, trust me, they will not be false. I don't play games. When I take a woman to my bed, I'm quite serious about it." Setting his glass aside, he took a step nearer to her, drilled his gaze into hers. "And your mask will come off. If you want me to do naughty things with you, it will come off." He trailed his finger along her skin, just below the lower curve of the mask. "I'm going to remove your clothing, and then I'm going to extinguish the candles, draw the curtains around the bed, so there is naught but darkness within it. You'll slip inside, remove the mask. When you're ready, I'll join you." He leaned nearer, whispered, "And when we're both ready, I'll slip inside you."

She quivered with need as the images bombarded her. Slow seduction indeed. She finished off her wine, hoping it would calm her racing heart.

"But first," he said, straightening, "I have something for you to wear so you won't feel quite so exposed." After reaching inside his jacket, he unfurled his hand to reveal a small chain of golden links with delicate golden tassels dangling between them.

"What a gorgeous bracelet!" She studied him. "You can't be meaning to give it to me."

"Not a bracelet exactly." He knelt, patted his thigh, looked up at her. "It goes around the ankle. I purchased it during a trip to India. I wasn't sure why I felt the need to own it, but I know it belongs with you."

"Honestly, I can't take a gift such as that."

"In a very short while, I'm going to take something from you. I should give you something in return." He patted his thigh again. "Come on. You know you want it, and it'll be our secret. You can wear it, and no one will see it beneath your skirts."

She remembered his saying that she should be a little bit in love with the first person she coupled with. Was he striving to ensure that she was? Because she was certainly falling for him. She placed the goblet on the table, her hand on his shoulder for balance, and her foot on his firm thigh, giving her toes the freedom to curl and uncurl at the familiar feel of him. He secured the gold around her ankle. She didn't think it had ever looked so delicate.

"Most gentlemen would probably give a bracelet or necklace or earbobs," she said.

"I am not most gentlemen." He unfolded that magnificent, well-toned body of his. "And you certainly are not most ladies." With his eyes on her, he slipped a finger from each hand beneath the straps of the loosely flowing gown and began to move them aside.

Her breathing hitched. The moment for which she'd long waited was upon her. She wondered if she should have been frightened or nervous. If she would have been on her wedding night. But she was merely overflowing with eagerness and anticipation.

The cloth lowered a fraction, his gaze dipped down, came back up to hers. Held. Waited.

"It's going to slither to the floor," he said eventually. "Then I'm going to pick you up and carry you to the bed."

"Not before I remove your clothing," she said, a little more confidently than she felt.

His smile warmed, his eyes glinted with pleasure. "And here I always thought virgins were shy."

"I'm not when I know what I want. And I want you."

With a feral groan, he released the straps, cupped her face, and claimed her mouth while the silk fluttered to the floor. She should have felt exposed, but she didn't. His arms came around her, pressing her against his chest while his mouth plundered. Rough and fast he'd once told her, and she suspected he'd been curbing his desires for fear of frightening her. But she had no qualms, no misgivings, no doubts. She needed this man as badly as she needed her next breath.

Breaking off the kiss, he lifted her and began striding toward the bed.

"Your clothing," she admonished.

"I need to get you nearer to the bed while I still have the strength. You weaken me."

Laughing, she cupped his strong jaw. He must have shaved immediately before coming here as she felt no stubble. She wouldn't have minded it, but she was pleased he'd gone to the trouble. He smelled of soap and freshly applied sandalwood. He'd taken as much care as she had preparing for this encounter.

Setting her on her feet, he gave her body a slow perusal. "You're exquisite."

Such a simple statement, but it made her feel flawless, beloved, appreciated. In a figure eight, he traced a finger around her breasts. They tightened, seemed to strain toward him.

"Take down your hair," he commanded.

"I thought you enjoyed unpinning it."

"I want to watch your breasts lift up when you raise your arms. The darkness will prevent me from seeing so much. Indulge me now."

She'd not considered that. Everything she wouldn't see. "Isn't this usually done in the dark?"

His eyes grew languid as he took them on a journey over the length of her. "Not always. Sometimes the darkness can add to the sensuality of the act. Sometimes the light can make it just as provocative. Depends what you desire. I'm the master of both."

She would accuse him of being boastful, but she'd seen the truth of his words in his photographs. Swallowing hard, she raised her arms, watched as his nostrils flared, his lips parted slightly, his eyes glittered with yearning. As she searched out the pins, she nearly regretted that she required the darkness, that he required the removal of the mask. But she wanted it gone as much as he did. She didn't want it hampering them.

She dropped the pins to the floor without ceremony. When she felt the weight of the strands shifting, the mask loosening, she turned her back on him in case the mask slipped too far before she could catch it. She heard his sharp intake of breath as her hair tumbled to her backside. Securing the mask, keeping her hands in place, she spun back around to face him.

"I thought I knew what you looked like," he said. "Based on the flow of the silk you wore. I was wrong. You're far lovelier than I imagined."

She didn't know what to say to that, to his compliments, to his praise. Slowly, she lowered her arms, feeling powerful and in control because she wasn't self-conscious with his perusal.

"What are you waiting for?" he asked.

"Pardon."

"My clothing. Didn't you claim you were going to rip it from my body?"

"What would you wear home if I did that?" she asked, slipping her hands beneath the opening of his jacket, flattening them against his chest, taking immense satisfaction in his sharp intake of breath. She eased her hands up, gliding them over his shoulders, down his arms, neither of them reaching for the jacket when it tumbled to the floor.

She began unbuttoning his waistcoat with fingers she didn't expect to be so steady.

"No nerves," he said. So he'd noticed.

Lifting her gaze to his, she gave him what she hoped was a saucy smile. "I want this."

"It's taking too long." While she unknotted his cravat, he began working on the buttons of his shirt.

Then he drew everything over his head, exposing a finely shaped torso.

Her fingers did tremble now as she touched the horrid, ragged scar on his left shoulder. "Mr. Alcott didn't exaggerate."

"Pardon?"

She jerked her gaze up to his, saw the question there. Without thinking, she'd made a mistake, might have revealed herself had she said more. "I was at Lady Greyling's when she welcomed you all back. I heard his tales, saw your photographs. They were the reason I changed my mind about posing for you."

"We didn't speak there. I would have remembered. Your voice is quite distinctive."

She released a slow breath of relief. "I'm a wallflower at events such as that."

"More's the pity. And it seems my scars have dampened the mood. Climb on the bed. I'll see to the rest."

"I don't find them hideous. They're a symbol of courage."

"More arrogance than courage. When captured by their beauty, I find it easy to forget that jungle creatures are wild." He held her chin, kissed her. "I'm anxious to discover how wild a creature you might be. Get on the bed."

Not so wild since she hesitated at the thought of removing his trousers. She gave a curt nod. As she clambered onto the satin sheets, aware of the tinkling of chains at her ankle, he began going around the bedstead, loosening the ties. The heavy velvet swung effortlessly into place, slowly enclosing her in the darkness.

Sitting there, she drew her legs up to her chest, wrapped her arms around them and listened to the muffled tread of his footsteps as he went around the room, no doubt extinguishing candle flames. She heard the thud of a boot dropping, then another. Straining her ears, she listened to the rasp of cloth as he shucked his trousers, but suddenly all was silent, all was quiet.

"Is the mask gone?"

She startled at the deepness of his voice, just on the other side of curtain. "Are your trousers?"

"They are."

She could have sworn she heard a hint of laughter in her voice.

"Come on, V, I'm dying to ravish you."

Taking a deep breath, she reached back and loosened the ribbons that held her disguise in place. Stretching out on her knees, she set it in a corner at the foot of the bed. Surely it would be safe there.

"I'm ready," she said softly.

The darkness parted to reveal deep shadows. She barely made out the form of a large man. The bed moaned as he climbed onto the mattress, the drapes closing behind him.

Snaking an arm around her, he drew her flush against him, flesh to flesh, from shoulder to toes, the heated length of him pressed hard against her belly. Unerringly, his mouth captured hers, and he plundered.

SHE'D almost given herself away. He'd almost told her that he knew who she was. But for whatever reason, she needed the secrecy, didn't trust him with the truth. Although at that moment, rakehell that he was, he cared only that she trusted him with her body.

Ashe intended to ensure she had no regrets on that score.

He cursed the blasted darkness. He'd wanted to do more than lightly trail a finger over her skin when she was bared to him, but he'd known that if he cupped a perfectly formed breast, pinched a pale pink nipple, buried his fingers in the curls between her thighs that he'd have not been able to hold himself in check. That he would have tossed her on the bed and had his way with her then and there.

But he'd wanted the damnable mask gone.

So now there was nothing to interfere with his enjoying her completely. Thrusting his hand into her thick, curling hair, he held her head in place while he thoroughly kissed every nook and cranny of her mouth. She tasted of wine and strawberry, decadence and desire. And she didn't hold back. She was exploring his mouth with equal measure, her fingers digging into his shoulders, his back. She was a match for any man, and some faulted her for it.

More the fools were they. Her enthusiasm was unrivaled, her eagerness incomparable. And he'd almost turned her away for being a virgin.

More the fool would he have been.

But then he'd spoken to her at Greyling's, been intrigued. A woman who knew her own mind, a woman of daring and courage and candor. Well, perhaps not all candor. She wouldn't reveal her identity. As much as he wished she would, he understood her hesitation. What was happening between them now would be frowned upon by polite Society. While she claimed she wouldn't marry, if her visits to the Nightingale were discovered, marriage would absolutely no longer be an option. She would be an outcast, not even welcomed into ballrooms or parlors.

So he didn't blame her for her caution. He would hold her secrets. All of them. Each one that he was uncovering.

The softness of her skin as he dragged his hand along her spine. The round firmness of her bottom as he cupped and squeezed it. The way her breast filled his palm as he cradled it. The sensitivity of the area just below her ear as he kissed it. Her sweet moan as she pressed her body more firmly into his. The hard peak of her nipple as his tongue circled it before he closed his mouth around it. The echo of her sighs, the feel of her sole rubbing his calf. The hot dew that coated his fingers as he tested her readiness.

Bracketing his hands on either side of her ribs, he buried his face between the pliant mounds of her bosom. He hated the thought of causing her any discomfort.

She threaded her fingers through his hair. "Ashe?"

"Are you certain you'll have no regrets?"

"I'll only regret if you stop." He heard her swallow. "I want you inside me."

In spite of the darkness, he squeezed his eyes tight and groaned low. Her words hardened him further. He'd already sheathed himself. He kissed the inside of one breast, then the other. "Then prepare yourself, sweetheart. I'm about to drive you mad."

About to? He'd already accomplished that feat. Every inch of her that he'd touched yearned to be touched again, every nerve ending was straining for what she knew he could deliver, for the pleasure that had rocketed through her before. She luxuriated in touching him, the areas she could reach, caressing her fingers over the flexing and bunching muscles.

With his mouth and fingers, he taunted. He kissed, he suckled, he nipped. Until she was writhing beneath him, until she was striving to meld her body with his, until she felt the push of his hardness against her heated opening. She stilled.

"Don't tense," he commanded, withdrawing. "Don't think of what's coming, just think of what is."

She nodded, realized he couldn't see the movement. Bringing up her legs, she wrapped them around his hips, heard the clink of tassels bumping together. "All right. But I'm ready for you. I know I am."

"I know you are, too, but there's no hurry."

"I thought you liked it rough and hard. Or was it rough and fast?"

"We'll have an opportunity for that later. We have lots of time."

"I don't want to disappoint you."

He slid up her, took her lobe between his teeth, and she moaned low.

"You're in my arms," he whispered hoarsely. "How could I be disappointed?"

She embraced him tightly. He'd said there were no falsehoods in his bed, and yet the words were hard to believe even though he uttered them with such conviction. Why couldn't she have had this without a mask and shadows?

And what a silly woman she was to lament what she hadn't possessed and not enjoy what she presently did. She had it now: his devotion, his desire. It didn't matter that it would only be for tonight. The memory would carry her through to her dotage.

She became aware of the pressure again, the slow easing in slightly, easing out. His mouth on hers, drawing her away from everything except the glory of it. She thought of the fortune hunters. Would they have been this patient? Would they have taken their time? Or would they have simply pounded into her in order to proclaim duty met?

He rose above her, his hips undulating, each movement taking him deeper. She felt herself stretching to accommodate him, the discomfort so minimal as to barely be noticeable. His breathing became harsher, his arms trembling slightly. She ran her hands over his chest, aware of the taut muscles, the strain.

A final hard thrust that went deeper than any of the others. He stilled. Beneath her fingers, she felt some of the tenseness ease. He took her mouth in a hard quick kiss.

"You didn't cry out."

She squeezed her legs against his hips. "It wasn't so bad."

"High praise indeed for my talents."

She blew out a puff of laughter, reached up, and bracketed his face between her hands. "I love the way it feels to have you buried inside me."

His growl resounded around them; she felt it quivering in his throat. "I absolutely adore your forthrightness."

Then his mouth was on hers again, and he began pumping his hips between her thighs, hard and fast. Sensations that had been hovering erupted into a burst of awareness and pleasure. Everything within her coiled and tightened.

He broke off the kiss, his movements quickening, and she became lost in the rapture, vaguely aware of screaming his name as a cataclysm engulfed her. He groaned, low, feral, and deep with a final thrust and a shuddering of his body. Taking quick breaths, he pressed his forehead to hers.

"Not fair," she panted lethargically. "You didn't scream out my name."

"Because you stole my breath."

Rolling off her onto his back, he brought her up close against his side, nestling her face in the crook of his shoulder, draping her leg over his thigh. She thought she should say something more, thank him. But she seemed capable of only drifting off to sleep.

SHE didn't know how long she slept, but she awoke to his arm still around her, his free hand toying with strands of her hair. She wished she didn't require the darkness, but she wanted nothing to ruin what had just passed between them.

"Was it all you expected?" he asked.

"How did you know I was awake?"

"Your eyelashes fluttered against my chest." He tucked her hair behind her ear. "Well?"

"More so. It doesn't seem right that women can't experience it outside of marriage."

"Obviously, there are women who do."

"But if they are caught, there are repercussions." She eased up, placed her chin on his chest, and narrowed her eyes, trying to discern his silhouette. "For someone with an aversion to virgins, you certainly handled matters well."

"Do you hurt?"

"I'm a little sore. Nothing I can't live with. But

how did you know the best way to ease things for me?"

"I have a friend who doesn't share my aversion. I asked him about his experiences."

She stiffened.

"Relax. I didn't tell him why, and he was drunk. He won't remember the conversation."

Edward Alcott, no doubt.

"If you're hungry, I'll bring some food over," he said.

"No, I should probably be going home now. My father is an early riser."

"Are you done with me, then? Or would you like another night?"

Disappointment laced his voice. Moving up until she was half-draped over him, she laid her palm against his jaw. It was bristled now. "I never thought I could be so comfortable being completely naked with a man."

"You're not completely naked."

Lifting her foot, she gave it a little shake, letting the tinkling of gold echo around them. "I don't know that it's wise to see you again. There is a risk I'll get caught. It was always only supposed to be one night."

He latched onto her hair, drew her down for a kiss. "And if I want more?"

There was more than the risk of getting caught. There was the risk of getting with child. "You told me that you only select a lady once."

"As I said, I make exceptions for you. Besides, you're not a fool. You know no other man can satisfy you as I do."

She cradled his roughened jaw. "You are so arrogant. You have spoiled me for other men. I won't be with other men." But she couldn't continue in this vein either.

"We don't have to meet here. We could meet at my residence. It's more private. But I want to know who you are."

She shook her head. "I can't."

"Send me a missive if you change your mind. You know where to find me."

"Are you angry?"

"Disappointed; although perhaps it serves me right that you should only want me for a night. I never considered how the ladies I selected felt afterward, knowing our time was done. I rather regret being such a bastard." Rising, he placed a quick kiss against her lips. "Don the mask, sweetheart, let's get you home."

Then he was gone, slipping out between the part in the draperies. She contemplated for all of three seconds following him out, leaving the mask behind. But in the end, she snatched it up and secured it.

He traveled with her in the coach this time, his arm around her as she nestled against his side. They didn't speak. She wasn't certain there was anything else to say.

When the coach pulled up to the Twin Dragons, he didn't react. She decided to take advantage. Moving up slightly, waiting for the footman to open the door, she looked back over her shoulder. "You don't seem at all surprised by our destination. You had the driver tell you the address."

"I gave you my word I wouldn't."

"Then why aren't you questioning it now?"

"Because I instructed him to bring me to the address that you'd given him. My vow remained intact."

The door opened.

"I see you're as clever with your mind as you are with your fingers." As she stepped out, his laughter followed her, making her smile. Halfway up the steps, she removed the mask. As she neared the door, she was so tempted to look back, but she knew he was watching, could feel his gaze on her as clearly as though it was a caress. She almost returned to him.

Instead, she carried on through the opened door, knowing that after tonight, everything would change.

Chapter 12

Minerva awoke slightly sore but not as much as she'd expected. Because Ashe had taken his time to prepare her for receiving him. He'd been a considerate lover, perfect for a woman experiencing her first time with a man. What she'd thought would be her only time. But now she knew the foolishness of that belief. Why give up pleasure when she enjoyed experiencing it?

However, she wanted to be wise about it. And she certainly didn't want to continue to worry about his realizing who she was. It was one thing to wear the mask in the Nightingale parlor. But when they were alone in a bedchamber, she needed to find the courage to toss it aside. Once he knew who she was, they could meet at his residence as he'd suggested. She'd never planned for the Nightingale Club to become part of her life. She had merely wanted it to serve as an introduction to pleasure.

It had certainly done that. With a smile, she rang for her maid.

She needed to determine how she was going to handle matters from here on out and to devise the best way to tell him who she was. Obviously, he'd enjoyed being with her. She'd not been a disappointment, which made her feel all warm and giddy, lost in the memories of him. If she were honest, she might have fallen just a little bit in love with him.

Just as he'd advised her that first night. Be a little bit in love with the person.

She wondered if it was possible that last night he'd fallen a little bit in love with Lady V. The giddiness dissipated, the disappointment settled in. She wanted him to fall a little bit in love with Minerva Dodger.

She was leading two lives, and if they should ever come crashing together, nothing would save her. Not her father's money, her family's position, her half brother's standing in Society. Her greatest fear was that she would simply drag them all into the gutter with her.

Ashe was no stranger to balls, but he'd never attended one searching for a wife. He came to flirt, to give attention, to gain attention, to have a jolly good time. A dance here, a game of cards or billiards there, a visit with a few gents, conversation about inconsequential things with many ladies—young, aged, and in between.

As one of the hellions, he was catered to. People were fascinated by their past, their travels, their adventures. As soon as they were announced and descended the stairs into the Lovingdon ballroom, he and Edward were unlikely to have any time alone. So while others were introduced, they stood slightly off to the side, looking out over London's finest.

Although Miss Dodger had told him that she wasn't going to be at many balls this Season, Ashe was fairly certain that she would be at this one. Her close friendship with the Duchess of Lovingdon would ensure it.

"If you never want to worry about your finances again, you should marry the Dodger girl," Edward said quietly enough that no one else would hear.

The comment irritated. Perhaps because Ashe could still feel the press of her against his mouth, could still feel her quivering in his arms. "Do you even know her name?"

"What does it matter? I know the amount of her dowry. It's substantial. Well worth overlooking her imperfections."

"And what would those be exactly?"

Edward gave him a sharp look, no doubt because his question had come out closely resembling a snarl.

"A father who would kill you slowly and painfully without compunction at the mere whisper of her unhappiness. Plus she's not particularly demure, has a tendency to speak her mind, and discusses subjects that should remain a man's domain."

Something that felt very much like jealousy pierced his chest. "When did you speak with her?"

"Oh here and there, over the years. At Julia's little

party the other night. Had the audacity to question the veracity of my tale."

"Can hardly blame her. You embellished it."

"The story overall was true. The details may have skirted the edge of what actually happened. Still, it was rather rude of her to imply I was a liar."

"She is forthright."

"She is that. Did you know she wrote a book? *A Lady's Guide to Ferreting Out Fortune Hunters.* Has made it deuced impossible for a man to court a woman without putting in a great deal of effort, from what I understand. I've heard a good many gents complain about it. You should probably read it. On the other hand, if I were you, I'd steer clear of her. She'd deduce your motives in a blink. Far too sharp to make a good wife. Besides, she's not the prettiest fish in the pond. Although I suppose in the dark, what would it matter?"

It was only because his hand was beginning to ache that Ashe realized sometime during this conversation, he'd balled his hand into a fist. He very much wanted to smash it against Edward's nose. "There are times, Edward, when you're an arse."

"Now you sound like my sister-in-law. Speaking of which, there she is. Dear God, I suppose I'll have to dance with her, just to be polite and not give the impression that I wish she would drop off the face of the earth."

"She's pleasant enough. I don't understand why you don't like her."

"She took my brother from me." As though uncomfortable with his words, Edward shifted his stance, averted his gaze. "We should get down there. I'm in need of some good scotch."

When there was a break in the line, Ashe and Edward were announced and began their descent into what Ashe fervently hoped would not be hell.

SHE'D been torn between hoping he'd be here and wishing he wouldn't, but when he was announced, a delightful shiver of gladness coursed through her, and she quickly chastised herself for her reaction. It was ridiculous to think he'd give her any attention this evening. He didn't know she was the woman he'd held in his arms the night before. Not that it would have mattered if he had known. They'd both been there for an unfettered encounter, nothing more. Certainly not anything that would extend their time together beyond the Nightingale, nothing that would cause them to seek each other out in public. Even though her eyes seemed not to have gotten the message and refused to stop staring at him.

Ladies swarmed to his side, dangling their dance cards in his face. His smile was broad, and he looked to be enjoying himself, touching a chin here, a cheek there, flattering the ladies with his attention. She tried not to be jealous. Tried not to be hurt or take offense. But she was having very little luck at accomplishing her goal. He was only hers at

the Nightingale. Beyond that, he belonged to all of
London.

She'd been enjoying herself as well until his arrival distracted her. Standing with her half brother
and two other gents she considered family, she'd
been discussing the merits of investing in a cattle
venture in Texas.

"I like the idea of it," Lord Langdon said, "but
I'm not too keen on investing blindly. I think someone should go over there and have a look at it."

Drake Darling grinned. "Would you even have a
clue regarding what you're looking at?"

"I didn't say I should go." Langdon gave her a
pointed look.

She laughed. "Me? You want me to go?"

"Makes sense," Lovingdon said. "You're the best
at analyzing things, and you've already put together
a summary outlining the advantages to doing this.
Besides, I've heard that there aren't many women
there."

She knew he spoke with the best of intentions,
but still, the words stung. "So I might find a husband among desperate men? Is that what you're in-
sinuating?"

"That's not what I meant."

"Well, it certainly sounded like it."

"I don't know why you're offended," Darling
said. "Based on the Americans I've encountered, the
men like their women headstrong and determined."

"You're not helping matters. If being unattached

is a requirement to testing the waters, then Langdon can bloody well go."

"Go where?" a familiar voice asked, and her chest tightened at Ashebury's unexpected arrival at her side. Her face warmed at the harshness of her language. When she was with these gents, she didn't always act the lady. They could bring out the worst in her. She didn't know why she didn't want Ashebury to witness her behavior, why she felt this ridiculous need to make a good impression. Perhaps because it struck her that she yearned for his attentions away from the Nightingale. She wanted him to find Miss Minerva Dodger as intriguing as he found Lady V.

Ashebury was gorgeous tonight, absolutely gorgeous in his black swallow-tailed coat and waistcoat. His shirt pristine white. His neckcloth knotted to perfection, and she couldn't help but recall how intimate it had felt when she had taken care of it for him. He was freshly shaven, but she preferred the shadow of stubble along his jaw. It made him appear more dangerous, more alluring, more disrespectable. Until that moment, she didn't realize that she rather liked the unpolished edge of a man.

"Forgive my intrusion," he said. "I was rude to eavesdrop, but traveling is one of my passions. Even if I'm doing it vicariously through someone else. Where are you considering journeying?"

Everyone seemed to be waiting for her to speak, but how could she with him so near, breathing the same air as she, the heat from his body reaching for her? And that mouth, smiling ever so slightly, that beautifully formed, perfect mouth that had touched her in the most intimate of places until she screamed. Heat crawled up her face, threatened to consume every inch of her. She had to remind herself that he didn't know she was Lady V. He didn't know that she was the one he had suckled, and nipped, and stroked. Oh, dear God, it was a ghastly mistake to be here. But she couldn't retreat and maintain any dignity.

Lovingdon cleared his throat. "We were considering the possibility of investing in cattle in Texas. Minerva has put together some numbers that indicate we could make a substantial return."

Oh, yes, by all means inform him how skilled I am with facts and figures because men find that ability so appealing in a woman.

"But we're thinking someone should go over to assess the situation more completely," Langdon said. "We were arguing the merits—"

"We weren't arguing," Minerva cut in, because again men found argumentative women so appealing. She was beginning to have a clue regarding why she was a spinster. This lot was not helping her cause. Not that she was looking for a husband any longer, but she had an insane need to impress Ashebury. "We were *discussing.*"

Ashebury's lips curled up, and she thought of them against her skin, lingering, exploring, gliding over her flesh. Thought of him demonstrating so very well what a man could accomplish when on his knees. Not a position of surrender but one designed to conquer. Thought of the weight of him above her as he took complete possession. She'd never been one to swoon, but at that moment, she was finding it increasingly difficult to draw in air. Her maid must have cinched her corset too tight.

"Discussing then," Langdon conceded. "Whether Minerva or I should go."

"You," Ashebury said sharply and succinctly. "Miss Dodger is far too delicate—"

"I'm not too delicate." Another reason she was a spinster reared its ugly head. She didn't like being viewed as incapable or prone to swooning. She thought it ridiculous that ladies held gatherings to practice fainting. A woman should be capable of standing on her own two feet. She tended to point that out at the most inopportune moments, such as this one.

Ashebury arched a brow. "My apologies, but you seemed upset by the notion of going. I must have misconstrued what I heard."

"Not upset. Irritated. I don't want to go, but it's not because I don't think I could handle myself." Maybe she should put the shovel away now, as she'd dug a rather large hole. "Perhaps we ought to change topic as I'm sure Ashebury has no interest in our business ventures." And ladies of quality didn't discuss business ventures.

"I prefer Ashe," he said, his gaze never leaving her. "And while I am fascinated by the topic, I'm more interested in a dance with Miss Dodger. I was wondering if there might be a space for me on your dance card."

Several spaces remained unclaimed. That hadn't been the case during her first few Seasons, when men had been lining up for a chance at her dowry. But as they'd learned she had no tolerance for fortune hunters, the dances claimed had become fewer. "I'm certain I can fit you in, but after the attention you were receiving from the other ladies, I'm surprised you have an open dance."

"You noticed that, did you?"

"It was a little difficult to miss. So which dances are you available?"

"All of them."

She was very much aware of her half brother snapping to attention, his gaze darting between her and Ashe. She could hardly blame him. His answer wasn't at all what she'd expected. For a moment, she was giddy, but then her practical nature kicked in, and along with it her suspicions regarding his interest. As far as she knew, he wasn't in debt. "I'm free the next dance."

"Then I shall just wait here, shall I? With your brother serving as chaperone?"

"Actually, I think all these gents were about to go search for their dance partners." She gave them each a stern look. "Weren't you?"

After bidding her and the duke farewell, they wandered away, leaving her alone with Ashe, or as alone as one could be in a crowded ballroom. The Duke and Duchess of Lovingdon were one of the most popular and beloved couples in Great Britain. No one declined their invitations.

"Why not commit to any other dances?" she asked Ashe.

"I enjoyed our dance at the Twin Dragons the other night. I wanted to ensure I had another opportunity to circle about the room with you in my arms. I'll fill in a few dance cards once we're done. Otherwise, tongues might wag."

"They'll probably wag anyway."

"Probably."

"Why have I your attention of a sudden?"

"You're quite blunt."

"It's one of my many faults."

"I don't recall describing it as a fault."

"Other men have."

"I think we established previously that some men are arses."

She couldn't help but grin. "Yes, I believe we did."

It was easy to enjoy his presence when she wasn't burdened with the desire for a marriage proposal. She could be herself although perhaps it was more that he didn't seem to sit in judgment, so she felt freer. Or perhaps it was just that they'd already shared an intimacy that had revealed their true selves. Not that he was aware of that, but she was.

It affected the way she looked at him, the comfort she felt with him. He'd kissed her birthmark, kissed her in ways and places that she'd never considered that a man might.

"I'm given to understand that you've written a book on identifying fortune hunters," he said.

"It was more of a collaboration between myself and the Duchess of Lovingdon based on her husband hunt."

"What of your hunt?"

"I'm not on the hunt."

"But you were."

She considered . . . "I don't think so. Not really. Not for a husband, anyway. Some ladies want a husband over love. I want love over a husband. I'm not convinced it's something you can hunt for. I think it just happens. If you're lucky."

"Have you ever been in love?"

She might have told him the question was too personal, but he'd shared his story of love. Not that he knew he'd shared with her. But where was the harm in answering? "No. Quite possibly I analyze too much. Right now, I'm not quite sure why I have your attention."

"You don't trust men." He said it as a statement rather than a question.

"I don't trust their motives."

The music drifted into a silence that seemed incredibly loud as she waited for him to provide some explanation other than he'd enjoyed a dance with her. Why had he come after her in the first place that night? Why was he standing here now?

"Then I shall have to work doubly hard to ensure you trust mine," he finally said, as the strains of a waltz started up, and he offered her his arm.

"What is your motive?"

"I've told you. I like you."

"No, you said you enjoyed dancing with me. Those are vastly different things."

"You're quite literal."

"Unfortunately, I am, yes."

"Then let's return to my original answer and grant me the pleasure of a dance."

She hesitated for all of two blinks before placing her hand on his arm and allowing him to lead her onto the dance area. Why did she have an insatiable need to understand his presence? She was attracted to him, and once again, she would be in the circle of his arms. Why couldn't she be content with that for now?

He wasn't one to give a lady attention for overly long. She should enjoy it while she had it.

$\mathcal{D}$ID he like her? He certainly liked her legs, the way passion burned within her, the echo of her cries at the moment of climax. He enjoyed dancing with her, watching the way she carried her own in a conversation or poorly disguised confrontation. He appreciated the way she studied his photographs. If he were going to marry for money, it wouldn't be a hardship to take her to wife. It came with the added advantage of having the luxury of bedding her— without a blasted mask, without absolute darkness.

But did he *like her*?

Dammit all, she deserved someone who did. He could make that claim because he did enjoy her company, but he also knew that she wanted to be more than liked. She wanted to be loved.

Every woman is worthy of love and should accept no less from a man she agrees to marry.

The opening words to her blasted book. He had known about it before Edward mentioned it, had in fact gone round to a shop and secured a copy once he made the decision to pursue her. He'd felt somewhat guilty when he'd announced he was available for all the dances. If he hadn't read *The Lady's Guide*—it wasn't overly long; apparently fortune hunters could be identified in short order—he'd have signed his name to several of the dance cards bumping his nose earlier and given her the scraps. Only according to her, "a lady deserved more than scraps from any gentleman who was in serious pursuit."

If she weren't willing to reveal her identity at the Nightingale, it seemed only fair that he not reveal his true purpose here: to fill his coffers. She'd taken advantage of him in the shadows—not that he was complaining. He was taking advantage of her in the light. Although knowing what an incredibly carnal creature she was, he knew she would gain a great deal as his wife: He could satisfy her in bed as no other man could, as no other man possibly wanted. He might not love her, but within his arms, she would never find herself lacking for attention. And she would find herself in his arms a good bit of the time.

This evening she wore a lilac gown trimmed in deep purple that brought out the warmth in her brown, almost black eyes. Her arms were bare, except for the ridiculously long gloves that went past her elbows. Why did Society have such an aversion to the display of skin? Well, not all displays. It was perfectly acceptable to tease a man with a showing of cleavage. His body tightened as he remembered the feel of her nipple in his mouth. Other thoughts began to line up like good little soldiers determined to take him through every minute that she'd been in bed with him, and if that happened, he'd barely be able to stagger off the dance floor.

"What was the reason?" he asked.

Her eyebrows drew together ever so slightly. "Pardon?"

"Your reason for not wanting to go to Texas. What was it?"

Her lips flattened, her nostrils pinched together. "It's not that I didn't want to go. But I didn't want to travel there for the reason that my brother suggested I should."

She licked those lips that he suddenly had an insane urge to kiss. "Women are scarce," she continued. "He thought I would have better luck finding a husband. I know he means well—"

"It was insulting, to think you can't compete."

Her head jerked back slightly as though she were surprised by his conclusion. "I wouldn't go so far as to say it was insulting. A bit hurtful perhaps. Mostly, it just irritates. I've had six Seasons and with each one, more well-meaning people are offering me advice on how to obtain love. Some of it is absolutely ridiculous."

"Such as?"

Her eyes twinkled. "Do you really want to know?"

Strangely, he did. "I might need it, as I'm getting up in years."

"Men needn't marry young. That's a burden foisted only on women as though, at a certain age, we curdle. *That* I find insulting, but you don't want to hear my rant on that subject I'm sure. As for what I can do in order to find love: hang a wishbone over the door to my bedchamber. Cook even provided the chicken bone when she offered that bit of tantalizing advice."

He smiled. "And it didn't work?"

She scowled at him. "I didn't hang it up. My lady's maid is always slipping a hand mirror beneath my pillow. Apparently, it will cause my true love to be reflected in my dreams. But he's there anyway, so I always remove it when I discover it."

There was that tightening in his gut again, that sense of jealousy he'd had earlier with Edward. "Who is he?" he heard himself asking, striving not to lock his back teeth together as he did.

She shook her head. "He's not any one person, but more of an ideal. Kind, generous, charming. Unrealistic. His breath is never foul, his body never odorous. His feet never stink."

Ashe chuckled. "Very much like the women in my dreams. They never nag, they're never ill-tempered, and all they want to do is . . . well, let's just say they're quite biddable."

A deep pink blush crept up her face, and he made note of its journey. If he were to ever see her with a mask again, he would now know the hue that might appear beneath it, how quickly it traveled, how it disappeared into her hair.

"I can't believe I told you all that," she said. "Spinsters are cautioned against drawing attention to their spinsterhood."

"You wear yours like a badge."

"I'm realistic." She gave him a gamine smile. "Well, except in my dreams."

It was with a measure of regret that he realized the music was fading, their dance was coming to an end. He enjoyed talking with her. She didn't bore him. "Take a turn about the garden with me."

She studied him as though she were searching for something. Was he moving too quickly? Was she going to deduce his motives?

"Yes, all right," she finally said. "I can see no harm in that."

If she didn't see the harm, then she didn't know men very well at all.

Chapter 13

As they wandered through her brother's elaborate gardens with its maze of paths, Minerva couldn't help but wonder if he'd figured her out. But if he had, wouldn't he announce it? Wouldn't he simply say, "Aha! I've deduced that you are Lady V!"

If he hadn't figured her out, then why were they here? Rich, powerful, devilishly handsome men did not escort her through gardens.

She wasn't accustomed to having a man's attention like this. Oh, she'd certainly gone on her share of walks, but they'd always left her in low spirits when her partner unwittingly—or in some cases wittingly—remarked on her "fetching" dowry as though he were seeking to court it rather than her. She didn't want that to happen here, didn't want him to tarnish her memories of last night.

"At the Dragons you mentioned a marriage proposal," he said. "Have you had many?"

"A few."

"None were to your liking?"

"I liked one of them rather a lot until he informed me that I was to make sure that I got with child quickly and produced a son. He would not tolerate any daughters. After he had his spare, we would be done."

"Done?"

Because she had liked him, his words had been particularly hard to hear. "Yes. After that, I was free to take a lover, as he intended to keep his mistress. He didn't care for me or my feelings on the matter in the least."

"He should have at least pretended."

His words gave her pause. Was *he* pretending? When they were at the Nightingale, what passed between them seemed more honest than what she usually encountered with men. "I prefer the honesty. I wrote my guide because some men are ever so good at pretending, but it's very difficult to hold on to that pretense for a lifetime. When it fades away, a lady might find herself surprised by what she's left with."

"Well, I can certainly understand your caution."

"I'm a spinster by choice because I refuse to be burdened with a man who doesn't love me. I'm fortunate to be blessed with parents who don't believe my singular purpose in life is to be a wife."

"Is that why you seek out opportunities like cattle ventures?"

She laughed lightly, striving to play down her talents. "I have a head for business and numbers. Too many in the aristocracy fail to comprehend there is a change in the wind. The gents within my intimate circle do understand, and they appreciate my business acumen. Unfortunately, some men are threatened by it. And I fear it makes me a dreadfully dull strolling partner."

"On the contrary. You fascinate me, Miss Dodger."

She tamped down the joy his words brought. Other men had taught her to be vigilant, not to take compliments at face value. Yet she believed him, wanted to desperately. More than that, she wanted him to kiss her. She wanted the intimacy they'd shared, but how could she acquire that without revealing she was Lady V?

Perhaps he sensed her yearning. He began leading her off the path. A harsh clearing of a throat stopped him in his tracks. He glanced over his shoulder. "Is that your brother and his wife walking toward us?"

Minerva looked back, sighed. "Yes, he's a bit protective of my reputation. He doesn't want me to be forced into marriage because a gent behaved badly."

"Have some behaved badly?"

His question surprised her, even more so the tone of it, as though he was angered by the thought. "One did rip my bodice, thinking if it appeared I was compromised, we'd have a hasty trip to the altar."

"Dear God, you can't be serious."

"I'm afraid I am. The next time I saw him, he was quite bruised and battered. I'm not certain who meted out the punishment: my father or one of my brothers. Lovingdon has been a hovering hen ever since." Turning slightly, she called back, "I'm fine."

"Grace was in need of some air," Lovingdon said, as they neared.

"I'm sure she was," Minerva muttered.

The couple stopped, and she was very much aware of Lovingdon sizing up Ashebury. "Should probably avoid the shadows," her brother said. "Might find yourself slamming into a fist."

"I have no plans to compromise your sister," Ashebury said, and Minerva wondered at her disappointment. Nor did the irony escape her—he'd already compromised her. He just didn't know it.

"Plans can sometimes go awry," Lovingdon said flatly.

"For God's sake, Lovingdon," Minerva snapped. "Nothing is going to happen that I don't want to happen."

"What exactly do you want to happen?" he asked sharply.

"Sweetheart," Grace said, flattening her palm against his chest. "We should probably return to our guests right about now."

"Not until I have an answer."

"It's truly not any of our business." He looked at his wife as though she'd gone mad. She cradled his cheek. "She's old enough to know her own mind. Now come along."

Glaring at Ashebury, he gave a long, slow nod.

"Yes, all right." Then he tilted his head at Minerva. "Remember what I taught you."

"Enjoy the gardens," Grace said before urging her husband back toward the residence.

"That was interesting," Ashe said.

"I'm sorry. He can be a bit much sometimes."

"It's not a problem. If I had a sister, I would probably want to look after her as well."

She couldn't help but think that his sister would be a very fortunate girl. "Shall we carry on?" she asked.

"What did he teach you?"

The heat of embarrassment rushed up her cheeks. "How to double a man over with my knee."

His eyes widened. "I see. Not trusting men seems to be common in your family."

"Again, it's not that we don't trust men. We question their motives."

"Quite right." He offered his arm, and she took it. They'd taken merely three steps when he said, "You didn't answer his question."

"Which question was that?"

"What exactly do you want to happen?"

IT was too soon. He knew that. If he didn't take into account their time at the Nightingale, it was too soon. But that lay between them, whether or not she admitted it. The remnants of last night lingered, sharpened the senses, made him more aware of her than he might have been otherwise. He couldn't help but believe that she was experiencing the same desires, the same needs.

He waited, when all he really wanted was to usher her into the shadows and kiss her senseless. Give her a reminder of why she should return to the Nightingale, what would be waiting for her there with him. She glanced around as though searching for an answer.

"It's not that difficult a question," he said.

She looked past him, and only then did he become aware of the footsteps nearing. A couple, talking low, walked past them, took a path to the left.

"If we carry on in this direction," she said quietly, "we'll reach a small arched bridge that crosses a shallow fishpond. I would like to go there. I think you might find it of interest."

He offered his arm, welcomed the feel of her gloved fingers grasping it. As they began walking along, he was half-tempted to glance back over his shoulder to ensure that Lovingdon wasn't traipsing along behind them.

"I noticed you arrived with Mr. Alcott," she said as though having a need to fill in the silence stretching between them, and he wondered if she weren't quite comfortable with him. "I suppose you're aware that the lot of you are referred to as the hellions of Havisham."

A corner of his mouth lifted up. "We're familiar with the term being applied to us. Although Grey isn't the hellion he once was."

"And you?"

He didn't know why he felt as though she were giving him a test, but she was studying him as though his answer was of importance. "It's quite possible that I could find myself tamed in the near future. Are you of a mind to do some taming, Miss Dodger?"

She slowly shook her head. "I wouldn't want you tamed."

"I'm extremely glad to hear that."

"So where will your adventures take you next?" she asked, shifting their conversation in a different direction as though not quite comfortable with where it had been heading.

"To someplace rather boring I'm afraid. My parents' residence in Mayfair. I'm moving there in the next few days."

He was aware of her studying him, even though he wasn't quite able to bring himself to meet her gaze. He wondered how she might react if she knew the state of his affairs. A woman with a head for business who was putting together information on a cattle venture in another country would no doubt consider him an idiot for his inability to make sense of numbers. On the other hand, she would be able to make sense of what he could not—if he could swallow his pride. Which he couldn't. He'd choke on it first.

"I suppose it's none of my business, but why weren't you already living there?" she asked.

"I wasn't ready to face the memories. It was the last place I saw them alive." He did look at her then. Although there were only a few gas lamps lining the path, they provided enough light for him to see the sympathy reflected in her face. He couldn't recall ever talking about his parents with any other lady, yet he had done it with her twice now. Something about her implied that she was a safe haven.

"Hopefully, you have some good memories there to overshadow the bad ones," she said softly, her fingers digging into his arm as she gripped it more tightly, conveying an astonishing sense of comfort.

"Haven't given a good deal of thought to my time there before they died." Except for the memories that bombarded him after he crossed the threshold. They still clung to him. "Their deaths overshadowed everything else, but perhaps you're right. Once I've taken up residence again, I'll recall happier times." But he was ready to move away from his past and back into the present. "Have you traveled, Miss Dodger?"

"When I was younger, I visited Lovingdon's estate a few times, but as a rule, my father doesn't like to leave London, so I never really got into the habit of traveling. I can't imagine all the things you've seen."

"I have a good many photographs. You're welcome to see them, browse through them." He thought he felt her fingers flinch.

"Do you only take photographs when you're traveling?"

He almost gave her a devilish look. Was she going to play the innocent when she knew damned well the sort of photographs he took? But they were engaged in a game. He wasn't quite certain of the rules, but he suspected that she had some. "I photograph anything that brings me pleasure."

"Then you should like the bridge."

They'd reached it. Barely wide enough for the two of them to step on side by side. Stopping halfway across, she removed her hand from his arm and grabbed the railing.

"I like to come here and toss bread crumbs to the fish and the swans," she said quietly. "It's always peaceful. All the foliage, bushes, and hedges seem to block the sounds from the city."

He moved up until his body was almost touching hers—not quite, but almost. Caution was his ally. He didn't want to misread the situation, her reason for guiding him to this secluded bit of the gardens. "There's not as much light here," he said.

"No, there's not. I'm not sure why Lovingdon didn't illuminate this area better."

"I'm glad he didn't. I like shadows."

She turned her head slightly until she was looking at him. "They can hide a good many sins."

"You don't strike me as a sinner or someone who would have anything to hide."

"At one time or another, we're all sinners, we all have something to hide."

Her words were said softly, and yet they struck

home with a force that nearly toppled him off the bridge. She couldn't possibly know about his financial situation, that he was willing to do whatever necessary to rectify it. She was probably referring to the photographs he took at the Nightingale. While he'd never shown them to anyone, he knew that not all the ladies who posed as his models were discreet. But he didn't care if people knew he took them. A few gents had even asked to see them; they'd been disappointed to learn he didn't share.

He knew what she had to hide. Her visit to the Nightingale. But her hiding her identity caused problems in his pursuit of her. There was a chance he would slip, take a misstep. He couldn't have both Lady V and Minerva Dodger. He was going to have to settle on one. Minerva wouldn't want him if he had an affair with Lady V at the Nightingale. Even if she was the same woman, she wouldn't know he knew that. He needed her to trust him, completely and absolutely, if he was to have any chance of winning her over—either as a lover or a wife.

"What do you want to happen, Minerva?" he asked.

Her eyes widened slightly, her lips parted. "You're being a bit familiar using my given name."

"You've led me away from the house and into the shadows. What do you want to happen?" he repeated.

"Are you going to make me say it? Surely you can guess."

"You're the daughter of a wealthy, powerful man who wouldn't hesitate to drown me in that pond if he thought I took advantage. So, yes, I want to ensure there is no misunderstanding regarding what you want."

Silence eased in around them, thick and heavy, holding even the music and din from the ball at bay. A splash interrupted the quiet. A fish, perhaps. Or one of the swans. It wasn't important. All that mattered was that they were alone, in near darkness.

"I want you to kiss me," she said boldly.

She might as well have latched her mouth onto his. Desire ripped through him at her brazenness. And then, perhaps, because he didn't immediately take her into his arms, she wilted at the edges, the doubt began to creep into her expression, and he cursed every man who had ever made her feel less than she was, every man who had looked at her and seen only a stack of coins.

Reaching past her, he cupped his hand on her shoulder and turned her slightly until she was facing him squarely. "Good, because I've been dying to kiss you ever since you sent your brother and his friends on their way in the ballroom."

Then he settled his mouth over hers and took.

MINERVA could hardly countenance that in the darkness of her brother's garden she was being kissed with such fervor and passion, as though she was one for whom ships set sail, wars were fought, and kingdoms razed. She'd only ever brought one other man here, a gentleman she'd been quite fond of. She wouldn't go so far as to say she loved him, but she thought in time her affection for him would grow and deepen. While staring at the swans, he'd proposed that they marry.

No bended knee, no gazing into her eyes, no taking of her hand.

His tone had been similar to the one she used when selecting a blend of tea in a teashop. When she suggested they not rush into anything, he'd merely shrugged and walked off. A week later, she read of his engagement to another.

She knew that later she would analyze this moment and every moment that came before it. Six Seasons had taught her that a man's attentions came with a price, and when she was unwilling to pay it, they faded away as though they'd never been. But for now she shoved aside all the doubts that clamored for attention and locked them away. For now, she allowed herself to believe she was desired. That this man longed to be with her as much as she yearned to be with him.

She nearly cried out in disappointment when his mouth left hers, before sighing with wonder as he cradled her face and rained kisses over every inch of it as though he adored what she had never learned to appreciate. Returning his mouth to hers, he gave no quarter as he deepened the kiss, and she fell irrevocably into the fiery passion burning within her. He stoked the flames with so little effort.

Drawing back, he skimmed his thumbs over her cheekbones. His grin flashed white in the darkness. "Well, hello, Lady V."

MINERVA'S heart slammed against her ribs, her breath backed up in her lungs. She considered denying it, but how could she do it with any level of believability? What was she to say? *I haven't a clue regarding what you're referring to.* On the other hand, she was somewhat relieved to have it out in the open. "When did you know?"

With a finger, he slowly outlined where the mask had been, along her hairline, around her lower cheek, across her upper lip. "I suspected when we were talking at Lady Greyling's party. Your size and shape seemed right, but it was more the passion with which you spoke. Your voice gave me pause, and your clothing. Women's clothing can be so ghastly deceptive. But then I danced with you at the Dragons, and my certainty increased. Plus, there was the verbena."

He'd known that long and had continued to pursue her, to meet with her at the Nightingale? "It's not an unusual fragrance."

"However, perfume provides a subtle difference in bouquet based on the skin to which it is applied. But the kiss just now sealed it. Your taste, your boldness, the manner in which you kissed me back. I could no longer deny the truth of who you are."

"This changes nothing between us."

"It changes everything. Knowing what can be between us, you can't expect me to blithely walk away, especially when there can be so much more between us. And I know you like me immensely; otherwise, you'd have not asked me to kiss you. Nor would you have allowed me the liberties I took last night."

"Shh. You don't know who's lurking in the shadows." She'd pressed two fingers to his lips to gain his immediate silence. Now he took her hand, turned it over, and placed a kiss in the heart of her palm, before curling her fingers over it as though for safekeeping.

"You weren't too concerned with who might be lurking about when we were kissing," he said.

"A kiss is one thing. The other is something else entirely."

"They'll both get you to the altar just as quickly if a father finds out about either one."

"No. My father's finding out about the other will get you a casket."

He seemed unconcerned, and he'd yet to release his hold on her hand. "Not if I have honorable intentions where you're concerned," he said.

She stared at him. "Are you talking . . . marriage?"

"It is within the realm of possibility."

"Even knowing who I am?"

"Especially knowing who you are. You intrigue

me. A rose by any other name and all that nonsense. You're a woman who knows what she wants and goes after it. You're not some mewling miss whining in the corner, waiting for someone else to make her happy."

"Most gentlemen are put off because I don't mewl about or faint or pretend helplessness."

"I'm not most men."

He could not have spoken truer words. Part of her concern was that she feared she could very easily find herself falling in love with him, and she didn't think he was the sort to love. While she'd been fond of a couple of her suitors, she hadn't been madly in love with anyone. Did one have to love in order to be loved?

Stepping back, she leaned her hips against the railing of the bridge, finding it easier to think when he released her hand and his wonderful masculine scent wasn't wafting around her. "Why do you want to marry me?"

He stepped forward, and she was immediately aware of his nearness, his legs brushing her skirt, his chest nearly touching hers. It would involve little more than her inhaling deeply to close that space between them. "There is fire between us. We're good together."

She narrowed her eyes. "What is your financial situation?"

"Not every man is after your dowry," he said curtly.

"Then why are you in pursuit?"

"Was it not your cries echoing around me last night?"

"And when the fire of passion burns out?"

"It won't."

"You can't guarantee that." Moving away from him, she faced the darkest part of the gardens. Was the physical reason enough to marry? Could a relationship without love satisfy for a lifetime?

Coming up behind her, he placed his mouth on the nape of her neck. Such a simple touch that caused everything within her to melt.

"I want you more tonight than I wanted you last night," he said, his low voice sending a warm shiver over her skin.

"Why didn't you tell me last night that you knew who I was?"

"You seemed to need the anonymity. Perhaps it was part of your fantasy. I wanted to give you what you desired. But I want to court Minerva Dodger. I don't think she'd understand if I was having an affair with Lady V while courting her."

Why couldn't she trust his motives? Why couldn't she believe he truly wanted her? "Do you love me?"

"Do you love me?"

She spun around and found his mouth on hers before she could utter a word. The fire ignited almost instantaneously. She melted against him, winding her arms around his neck. Was this enough to keep them both happy for the remainder of their days?

He trailed his mouth along her throat. "Allow me to call on you tomorrow. Give me an opportunity to show you that you can be as happy with me in the light as you are in the shadows."

At such a simple request, she could do little more than nod. He eased away from her. "You were correct," he said quietly, seductively, skimming his finger along her lips. "I very much appreciate your brother's fishpond."

Her laughter bubbled out, making her feel younger than she'd felt in a good long while. "I'm not certain I've ever enjoyed it quite so much."

"That's good to know. I have a competitive streak. I don't want you giving yourself to anyone else."

She couldn't think of a single gentleman who could compete with him, but she wasn't going to tell him that. He didn't need any more confidence.

"We should return to the ballroom," he said, "before our absence is noticed, and tongues start to wag." He extended his arm.

She had a hundred questions, a thousand, but she didn't want the warm glow to dissipate.

When they reached the terrace, he stepped away from her. "We've been gone a rather long while. To protect your reputation, you should go in without me."

"Would you be here with me now if I wasn't the woman—" She glanced around, not certain how to ask her question without giving away too much in case someone were listening. "—you thought I was."

"But you are, so it's moot."

"You know what I'm asking. I don't think it's what you're answering."

He studied her for a moment. "I don't know. I do know that the woman I met that first night at the Nightingale intrigued me, and I was desperate to find out who she was. Talking with you at Lady Greyling's I found equally intriguing. That the ladies are one and the same is my good fortune."

"At least you're honest."

She thought that in the space of a single heartbeat, he flinched, looked guilty. Why did she have to look for things that probably weren't even there? Footsteps sounded as other couples neared.

"Thank you for the pleasure of your company, Miss Dodger. I look forward to tomorrow."

"Your Grace." She went up the steps and crossed into the ballroom. No one approached her, no one stopped her as she headed across the room and ascended the stairs. She carried on until she reached a doorway that led onto the balcony that overlooked the grand salon. Ashebury had entered sometime while she made her way here. He was now dancing with Lady Honoria. It hadn't taken long for him to give his attention elsewhere. She fought not to feel jealous. It was a ball, people danced.

She stayed where she was, watching as he danced with Lady Julia, then Lady Regina. She couldn't help wondering if he might have photographed them.

Suddenly aware of a powerful presence coming

through the doorway, she stiffened. Her brother rested his forearms on the railing.

"He's a womanizer," he said without preamble.

"And you weren't?" she asked, not bothering to hide her sarcasm or irritation with him for pointing out a fact of which she was already incredibly aware.

"I had my reasons."

"Perhaps he does as well." She turned to look at him. "Is it inconceivable that a man could desire me?"

"No, of course not. To be quite honest, I'm unclear as to why you're not yet married. And I'm not saying he doesn't desire you. I just don't believe he's the marrying sort."

"I'm not searching for the marrying sort."

He straightened so quickly, she heard his spine pop. With eyes narrowed, he was quite formidable. "What are you implying?"

"That I've had it with fortune hunters. That I'm done with being on the marriage block. I'm not here to find a husband. I'm here because Grace is my dear friend, you are my brother, and you always host a smashing party."

"Then why accept his attentions?"

"Why not? No longer having any plans to marry is quite a relief really, freeing actually. I don't have to care if a man finds me pleasing. I can speak my mind and know it won't make a bit of difference, that his opinion of me is inconsequential to bringing me joy."

"Have you told your father this?"

"He approves."

His jaw tightened because obviously he didn't. "And our mother?"

"She only wants my happiness." Or so her father had said, and she believed him. "It's silly really for a woman's goal in life to be obtaining a husband."

"What is your goal then?"

"Whatever I want it to be." No reason to upset him further by spelling it out. Pleasure.

A footstep sounded. Glancing over her shoulder, she saw Edward standing just in the doorway. He scowled. "Stop shooting daggers at me, Lovingdon. I've only come to collect a dance with your sister."

Lovingdon gave a nod, looked at her. "Remember what I taught you." Then he walked off.

She sighed before turning her attention to Edward. He was remarkably handsome tonight in his swallow-tailed jacket. He smiled at her.

"I'm hoping your next dance is open," he said.

"It just so happens that it is. Shall we be off?" She took a step for the doorway, and he placed his hand on her arm, staying her actions.

"Let's dance up here. It's less crowded."

"It'll draw attention."

"I like attention."

"Are you trying to make someone jealous?"

He lifted a shoulder in a careless shrug. "Wouldn't *you* like to?"

Swallowing hard, she squeezed her hands together. "I'm certain I don't know what you're trying to imply."

"I saw Ashe take you into the garden. I also know that the ladies aren't going to let him be, and he's too polite to turn them all away. Can't be fun watching him dance."

"They don't usually let you be."

"'Tis true. I have only the next dance." He held out his gloved hand. "So shall we?"

"I suppose there's no harm in it. Perhaps we'll start a new tradition."

The music for a waltz started up. She expected him to take advantage, to hold her more closely than necessary, but he kept the appropriate distance between them.

"He likes you," Edward said.

"Pardon?"

"Ashe. He likes you."

"Because he took me on a walk in the garden?"

"Because he looks at you as though you matter. I've seen him with a lot of women. We both tend to use them as distractions." He shook his head. "Won't go into that. He doesn't see you that way. He hasn't taken his eyes off you since we got here. Even now, he's watching."

She fought not to look out over the balcony to verify that he was.

"It might not look like he is, but he is aware of everything. It's the reason he's so dashed good at taking photographs."

"Have you posed for him?"

"On numerous occasions." He glanced around before leaning in, and whispering, "Once I posed nude."

She narrowed her eyes at him. "I think you're embellishing."

"Well, I was nude beneath my clothes."

She laughed. "You're awful."

He smiled broadly. "Well, I am that. And our dance has come to an end."

Only then was she aware of the strains floating away.

He took her hand, kissed the back of her knuckles. "Thank you for the waltz, Miss Dodger."

"Thank you, sir."

He released his hold, took a step away, turned back, his eyes somber. "He's a good man. Don't hold it against him because he's my friend."

Then he disappeared through the doorway before she could respond.

I TOLD you that if you got within three feet of her, I'd lay you flat," Ashe growled.

Edward pressed his booted foot to the bench seat opposite him as Ashe's coach rumbled through the streets. He was surprised his friend had waited so long to confront him. On the other hand, the close confines would make it easier for Ashe to pummel him. Ashe had two inches on him, dammit. "No, you warned me away from the white swan. So I assume Miss Dodger *is* the white swan. I thought as much. She's the right size."

"Edward—"

"Relax. I'm not going to say anything. But I take it she's the one you're planning to marry."

"If I can convince her that I'm not marrying her for her dowry."

"But you are."

Even in the darkness, he felt Ashe's gaze bore into him. "Oh, I see. Wouldn't it be better to be honest with her?"

"Every man who has ever approached her has wanted her dowry. She wants love."

"Can you give her that?"

Ashe sighed heavily. "I don't know. Having seen what love did to Marsden . . . How did Albert get past it?"

"Hell if I know. The thought of falling in love scares the bloody hell out of me. So I won't do it. You know me. I always take the coward's way."

"Which is the reason you killed a lion with a damned knife."

He shrugged. "My rifle jammed."

"By the by, I'm not comfortable with the way you tell that story. If Locke had been at Lady Greyling's, he'd not have allowed it."

"But he wasn't, now was he? So I could embellish to my heart's content because you like my stories. Besides, you stabbed him as well."

"You delivered the killing blow."

"We can't know that for sure."

Ashe chuckled low. "God, you were a madman. I'm surprised your screech didn't chase him off."

"I didn't *screech*. I bellowed. Like an ancient warrior."

"Like a madman."

"Well, when you're raised by one, what more can you expect?"

Silence settled in around them, broken only by the steady clopping of horses' hooves.

"Why did you dance with her?" Ashe asked quietly.

"I recalled Lady Hyacinth's words at the roulette table. I like dancing with spinsters. They're always so grateful for the attention."

"You're an arse, Edward."

Edward smiled. Yes, he was. But he was a relatively harmless one. As long as nothing threatened those he cared about.

Chapter 14

MINERVA had taken extra care in preparing for the day, choosing a pale pink dress that managed to draw out the red in her hair so it didn't appear quite so dark. Her maid put it in a soft style that left tendrils curling along her cheeks, highlighting her eyes. She wasn't conceited enough to think she looked pretty, but she considered herself more than passable.

Her nerves causing butterflies to alight in her stomach, she barely ate any breakfast, incredibly grateful that her father didn't comment on it. She wasn't accustomed to being anxious about a gentleman's calling. She'd had plenty. But none with whom she'd lain. She knew the firmness of his muscles, the warmth of his skin, the way he moved against her—

She feared something was wrong with her moral compass because she felt no shame at all for knowing all these details.

While the hours ticked by until it was an acceptable time for a gentleman to call, she sat in the morning room trying to read. After scanning the same sentence a hundred times, she finally closed the book and walked around the outer edge of the room. A light rain had begun to fall, so she couldn't go into the garden. She considered writing a letter to the *Times* on the need for more people to engage in charitable works, but she doubted she'd be able to concentrate enough to make it eloquent or convincing.

Her nerves were stretched taut when the butler finally entered and announced she had a caller. Still, she was taken aback by the joy—

"Lord Burleigh," Dixon continued, his words slamming into Minerva and halting her progress across the room.

"Lord Burleigh?" she repeated as though she'd taken leave of her senses. The man had never called on her before, had never danced with her. They'd spoken in passing, but he certainly hadn't indicated an interest.

"Yes, miss. I saw him to the parlor. Your mother is joining him there."

Perhaps she should take out an advert announcing that she was no longer in search of a husband. On the other hand, she would be foolish to discount the possibility that she might find love late in life. Of course, any man now might have to accept her scandalous behavior. Not that Ashebury seemed to have any problem with it. "All right then."

Lord Burleigh, whose physique suited his name,

jumped up from the sofa as soon as she entered the room. "Miss Dodger."

"My lord, how nice of you to call. I've rung for tea."

"I'll leave you two young people to visit," her mother said as she picked up her stitchery and moved to a distant corner of the room to give them a bit of privacy.

Minerva sat on the sofa. Lord Burleigh joined her, keeping a respectful distance. She tried to imagine Ashebury doing the same and found it quite impossible.

"It's a rather dreary day," Burleigh said.

"I like the rain."

"As do I. Many people don't. It's good for reflection."

"It is that."

"I enjoy the sound of droplets pattering against the pane."

"That was rather poetic phrasing. Are you a poet, my lord?"

His cheeks turned red. "I dabble."

"Bravo for you!"

He narrowed his eyes at her. "Are you mocking me, Miss Dodger?"

"No, absolutely not. I think all creative endeavors are to be applauded."

"Apologies. I'd heard—" He snapped his mouth closed, took out his pocket watch, glanced at the time, no doubt disappointed to discover not even two minutes had passed.

"You'd heard what precisely, my lord?"

Shaking his head, he stuffed his watch back into his pocket just as the tea arrived. Thank goodness. Minerva set about preparing him some.

"Three lumps of sugar," he said. "A dash of cream."

She handed him his cup, which he expertly balanced on his thigh.

"Mother?" she asked.

"No, thank you, darling." She barely looked up from her needlework. Minerva could never become so absorbed poking and pulling thread through cloth although she certainly envied those who were able to create such lovely tapestries.

After preparing her own tea, Minerva glanced over at Burleigh to find him studying her. She gave him what she hoped was an encouraging smile.

Drawing his brows together, he cleared his throat. "I saw you at the Lovingdon ball last night."

Her heart gave a little stutter. Hopefully he'd not seen her in the garden. "Oh?"

"I realized that we've never really gotten to know each other."

"I do wish you'd asked me for a dance."

"My size makes me somewhat clumsy in that regard."

"I suspect you're a bit hard on yourself, but in either case, I think we could have managed."

He blinked several times. "You're kind to say so."

"You say that as though you're surprised I'm kind."

He touched his teacup, released it. "I'd heard you were . . ." He cleared his throat.

"A termagant?"

Giving a little nod, he furrowed his brow, wrinkled his nose. "Difficult."

"And yet you've come to call."

"My father recently passed."

What had that to do with anything? "Yes, I heard. I should have offered my condolences when I greeted you."

"No need for that. He was up in years; had a good life. But I must see to my duties now. I'm in want of a wife, and so I thought to call on you."

"That's very kind of you."

"I'm a bit older, and so I don't have a lot of patience for the silliness of young girls."

This reasoning was one that she hadn't encountered before. While it was refreshing, she also found it a bit insulting. "So my age appeals to you?"

"You don't giggle."

"Not as a rule, no, although I have been known on occasion to laugh."

"Not loudly, I hope."

"Depends, I suppose." She thought she heard the door knocker. She'd welcome Lord Sheridan at this moment.

She glanced over as Dixon walked in, holding a

silver salver. He extended it toward her. Lifting the card, she read it and tried to tamp down her joy. "Please show in the Duke of Ashebury."

Minerva didn't miss the speculative look in her mother's eyes as she lifted her head from her work nor the disappointment in Burleigh's. Everyone rose as Ashebury strode in. He headed straight for her mother, took her hand, and kissed the back of it.

"Madam, how wonderful you look."

"Thank you, Your Grace. It's a pleasure to have you visit."

"The pleasure is all mine, I assure you." Turning, he zeroed his gaze in on Minerva, completely ignoring Burleigh, as he crossed over. She halfway hoped he'd brazenly take her hand as well, but he merely tipped his head to the side. "Miss Dodger."

"Your Grace."

He shifted his gaze slightly. "Burleigh."

"Ashebury."

"Hope I'm not interrupting."

"You are never an interruption," Minerva said. "Would you care for some tea?"

"I would love some. One lump of sugar, no cream. I lost an affinity for cream on my various journeys away from civilization. Quite impossible to transport."

Minerva took her seat, aware that Burleigh sat just a little nearer to her. Ashebury took the chair closest to her. "You must have missed having tea on your travels."

"On the contrary, a gentleman always takes tea with him, even into the wilds."

"I don't see how one could properly prepare tea in the wilds," Burleigh said.

"Oh, it can be done," Ashebury said. "You must read *The Art of Travel*, Burleigh. Fascinating. You'd be surprised what one can and is willing to do out of necessity." Taking the cup Minerva offered, he sipped the brew. "Darjeeling. Excellent."

"I'm not certain I've ever had a gentleman identify the type of tea before."

"I have a refined palate. I can distinguish the flavors of almost everything that carries a unique taste: wine, spirits, tea." His eyes darkening, he lowered his gaze to her lips, and she realized what he had left unsaid: a woman's kiss, her mouth.

Shifting in her seat, Minerva took a most unladylike swallow of her own tea. Silence began to ease around them. She noticed the teacup resting on Ashebury's firm thigh, thought how much more delicate it appeared there than it did on Burleigh's thigh. While Burleigh was broader than Ashebury, Ashebury seemed larger. Perhaps it was because his clothes fit so well, leaving no doubt that he didn't possess an ounce of fat. It could also be that she knew the feel of that thigh beneath her sole, knew that it provided a very secure place upon which a saucer could rest.

"What were you discussing before I interrupted?" Ashebury asked.

"The merits of age," Minerva said, hoping he wasn't aware of where her gaze or her thoughts had drifted.

"Of wine?"

"Of ladies."

"That seems rather inappropriate. The ladies I know are so secretive about their ages."

"We were discussing that older ladies don't giggle like silly younger ones," Burleigh said impatiently.

"What's wrong with giggling?" Ashebury asked.

"It's irritating. I don't want a wife who giggles. Miss Dodger is not prone to giggling."

Ashebury's gaze came to bear on her. "Is she not? I wager I could make her giggle."

"Why would you want to?" Burleigh asked.

"Why would you not?"

"As I mentioned, it's irritating."

"On the contrary, Burleigh, it's a joyous sound. A woman should giggle at least once a day." His gaze never left her.

She noticed a faint tinkling sound, Burleigh's teacup rattling slightly on the saucer, as he was growing agitated. He was her guest. She couldn't let Ashebury unsettle him so. "How does one make tea in the wilds?" she asked.

Ashebury gave her a slow smile, and she knew he was fully aware that she was attempting to defuse the situation. "A fire, a kettle, a teapot, and tea."

"The same way one makes tea in civilization," Burleigh said.

"A little variance here and there. We did end up giving our kettle, teapot, and some tea to a tribal chief. He was rather fascinated by the process. I'm not sure where he'll obtain tea once he's used up all that we left. Would you like to see a photograph of him?"

"No," Burleigh answered as Minerva said, "Yes."

"I cannot deny a lady her desires," Ashebury said, setting aside his cup before shifting his body from the chair to the edge of the sofa cushion.

Minerva slid over quickly to prevent his landing on her, which only served to nestle her up against Burleigh. She was acutely aware of the man stiffening, couldn't imagine Ashebury reacting in a similar manner. If he found a woman up against him, he would no doubt curl around her.

A small smile played over Ashebury's lips. The bugger was enjoying manipulating them, making Burleigh uncomfortable. She shouldn't find herself drawn to him when he was misbehaving so, and yet, she couldn't seem to work up any annoyance over it. Burleigh hadn't done anything wrong, but neither had he done anything right. She wasn't attracted to him. His suit of her would go nowhere. She should probably tell him. Later. When Ashebury was no longer here.

He slipped a large hand inside his jacket pocket, removed a packet tied with string, and placed it in her lap. "You may do the honors."

He was as close as Burleigh, if not closer, his thigh

resting against hers, their hips touching, and yet she didn't feel crowded on the right side. She couldn't say the same for her left. Was it because she'd been incredibly intimate with the man, because of what they'd shared? Or was it simply his way to be completely comfortable against the female form? Probably the latter. She didn't want to consider how many ladies he might have been this close to.

Pulling the ends of the bow, she released the string from the wrapper and set it on the low table before her. Then she slowly peeled back the paper. She was greeted with the sight of the chimpanzees. Soul mates, she'd bet her life on it. The pyramids were next, dwarfing the humans who stood around them. She was familiar with the structures, had seen other pictures, had always wanted to visit them. No longer on the husband hunt, she was free to go wherever she wanted. She could go touch them in person if she so desired. The next picture revealed some sort of stone shrine barely visible through the foliage. She had no idea what it might be, and yet it seemed so lonely, as though waiting to be of use again.

Moving that picture aside, she was greeted by a man with long white hair and what appeared to be white paint in various designs on his dark, wrinkled face. Grinning, he held in his hand a dainty teacup that seemed remarkably out of place.

"That's him," Ashebury said.

"He looks so happy."

"He bargained me out of my teacup," he said grumpily.

She looked at him. He was close, so very close, his shoulder nearly touching hers. "What did you get?"

"Two of his tribesmen to escort us farther into the jungle."

"What did they get?"

"The privilege of accompanying us, I suppose. They have no need for money. They're self-sufficient."

"They're savages," Burleigh said.

"What exactly is a savage, Burleigh? I've met quite a few within England's borders."

"You know what I mean. They're not civilized."

"Not like you and I, perhaps. They can't quote Shakespeare, but I assure you that they hardly qualify as savage. As far as we could tell they live a peaceful existence. Welcomed us." He winked at Minerva. "Drank tea with us. Doesn't get much more civilized than that."

Moving that photograph aside, she caught her breath at the sight of a woman dressed in her native clothing, what little there was of it. But it wasn't the bared breasts that held her attention. It was the woman's face: so proud, with such a noble bearing. No embarrassment, no shame. How could anyone be offended by this remarkable image? It was simply . . . life. And Ashe had managed to capture the essence and beauty of it.

He was right. The human form in all its natural wonder was exquisite.

Although Burleigh apparently didn't agree. He was making gasping sounds as though the tea he'd swallowed had taken a wrong turn. Snatching the photo from her fingers, he went to his feet. "You can't show photographs like this to a lady!" It was a wonder that his indignation didn't cause the chandelier above his head to shake.

"Why ever not?" Minerva asked.

"Madam, the duke is showing your daughter vulgar photographs."

Her mother looked up, her brow pinched tightly.

"It's a native woman, Mother. In her natural habitat."

"She's not wearing clothes," Burleigh said.

"Not garments as we wear," Ashbury said, "but I assure you that to her people, she was perfectly attired."

With grace and dignity, her mother rose and walked toward them. Ashebury shoved himself to his feet. Her mother held her hand out to Burleigh. He hesitated.

"Lord Burleigh." She snapped her fingers.

"It is not appropriate, madam."

"I shall determine what is appropriate and what is not."

He handed it to her.

Minerva had to respect her mother's aplomb. She might as well have been looking at a blank piece of paper for all the expression that crossed her face. "If the woman is not accustomed to wearing clothes, I don't see how we can call her vulgar for honoring her traditions."

"But Ashebury shouldn't be shoving them in your daughter's face."

"We're all adults here, my lord. Surely we can't be offended by life." Still, her mother returned the photograph to Ashebury. "I have seen women wearing less in paintings although they are not works I would display in my parlor."

"My apologies, madam, if I offended you," Ashebury said.

"I'm not offended, just making a point. Shall we return to our tea now?"

"I must be off," Burleigh said.

"I shall escort you out, my lord," her mother said.

"What of Ashebury?"

"I don't believe his time is yet up."

"You can't leave them alone."

"Oh, I'm certain nothing untoward will happen." She slipped her arm through Burleigh's. "How are you holding up, stepping into your father's shoes?" she asked, leading him from the room.

As soon as they were through the door, Minerva slapped her hand over her mouth, her shoulders shaking as she tried not to laugh out loud. Ashe sat beside her, leaned in until his breath feathered over her cheek. "Are you giggling?"

A sound that very much resembled a giggle escaped. She shoved on his shoulder. "You did that on purpose, making him uncomfortable with that photograph."

"Don't be daft. I didn't know he'd be here."

"Then why didn't you wait until he'd left to show it to me?"

His eyes were dancing with mischief. "Because as I was sitting there, it occurred to me that it might be fun to see his reaction. He's a rather somber sort. Is he courting you?"

"I'm not sure. This is the first time he's ever come to call."

"He'll bore you to tears." He cradled her face. "He'll kill your spirit. Don't let him call on you again."

"It's not your place to tell me who I can allow to call on me."

He swept his thumb over her lips. "You won't be happy with him."

She capitulated. "I'm not going to marry him, but neither do I want to embarrass him. He's just lost his father."

"You have a tender heart." He leaned in. "I like learning things about you, Minerva."

She wondered if he might kiss her. She wanted him to.

"Come to the Nightingale tonight," he said seductively. "We can continue to learn things about each other in a more intimate setting."

"I'm expected at the Dragons."

"Do what's not expected."

The challenge mirrored in his eyes almost had her agreeing to meet him, but she wanted more than the physical coupling. She yearned for a coming together that involved hearts and souls. "Too many questions would be asked if I didn't show."

"I trust you can handle them."

"I'd rather not."

"I'd make it worth your while."

Slowly she shook her head. "I've no doubt of that, but I need you to be a little in love with me."

Lightly he touched her cheek. "You're turning my words against me."

"I simply understand them better now." She glanced back, returned her gaze to his. "My mother will be returning at any moment now."

"Then we should return to the matter at hand," he conceded without rancor. "Did you like the photographs?"

She smiled softly. "I did, yes. They were extraordinary. Especially the one with the woman. I quite agree that we're all prudes if we focus on what she isn't wearing rather than on what she is: pride, elegance, and grace."

"I thought you would appreciate what I had hoped to capture. She reminds me very much of you."

At the compliment, heat warmed her face. "You have quite the imagination," she said.

"If you can convince your brother to allow me

to use the bridge in his garden as a setting, I can show you."

"I'm flattered, but I seldom pose for photos or paintings. I never like the way they turn out."

"You'll like mine."

She laughed. "I don't know if you're confident or arrogant."

He leaned in a little more until his breath was skimming over her cheek. "You know what I can do in the dark. Let me show you what I can do in the light."

She was struck with the image of him laying her out across the bridge, hovering over her, before using his mouth to take a delicious journey along her body to the juncture between her thighs, bringing her pleasure as the sunlight warmed her skin, and her cries—

A throat clearing had her jerking as though her thoughts were dancing around the room for all to see. With a decidedly wicked smile that implied he knew exactly where her imagination had been traveling, he slowly shoved himself to his feet. Tamping down her pounding heart, Minerva rose as well.

"I must take my leave," he said. "You're welcome to keep the photographs."

"I shall treasure them." And she would. She wouldn't be able to look at them without thinking of him and the intimacies they'd shared. Those intimacies were beginning to go beyond the physical to include shared moments that connected them in ways that she'd never been associated with anyone outside her circle of family and close friends.

"Then I've found them a good home," he said quietly before walking away. He stopped to have a word with her mother, then carried on through the doorway.

Sitting back down, Minerva picked up the photographs. Nothing he could have given her would have pleased her more. She rather suspected he knew that. He knew her better than any other man. Should she be comforted or wary by that thought?

Acutely aware of her mother settling on the cushion beside her, Minerva fought not to blush.

"What an interesting afternoon. When did Ashebury start taking an interest in you?" her mother asked.

"We spoke a little when I attended Lady Greyling's party. Our paths have crossed a few times since."

"You looked rather pleased when he walked through the door."

"I find his adventures interesting and his photographs . . . he's very talented."

Her mother took the top one—the chimpanzees which Minerva thought would forever remain her favorite—and studied it. "He has a good eye."

She thought her mother was talking about more than the picture. "How did you know, unequivocally, that Father loved you?"

Her mother's eyes softened with remembrance. "When I met your father, he cared only about acquiring wealth. His coffers were overflowing, yet he wanted more. It was all he valued. Then, one day, he was willing to give it all up for me."

She'd always known the basics of her parents' tale, but not the specifics. "I think that's the reason that I dislike fortune hunters. They have nothing to give up."

"Don't be so sure, sweeting. Everyone has something to sacrifice."

"I THINK Ashe is in a bit of bother financially," Edward said, sipping his brother's scotch, waiting for his turn at the billiards table.

Grey lifted his gaze from the colored balls he'd been studying. "Has he told you that?"

"Not the details, but he's moving into Ashebury Place. His situation must be dire for him to do that." While none of them knew precisely why Ashe had an aversion to the place, they knew it was associated with the death of his parents. He'd suffered through nightmares when they first moved to Havisham.

"He's got pride, Edward. I can't do something if he doesn't ask. If he wanted me to know, he'd tell me." He turned his attention back to the table.

"Well, that's the thing you see. He thought I might like to take over the lease on his residence, and I thought it was a jolly good idea. I know it's a bother for me to stay here when I'm in London."

"Not a bother."

"Your wife doesn't like it."

Grey straightened. "You're a sloppy drunk, and you boast about your conquests. She finds it unseemly."

"She doesn't have to listen."

His brother scowled at him. He capitulated. "All right. I'm aware I can quickly wear out my welcome. But I can't keep imposing on Ashe either, so I thought it was high time I had my own place. He suggested I purchase the furnishings there. Would save me from having to search for pieces, would give him a bit of capital. If you could see your way clear, that is, to providing the funds needed. It would be helping him out, don't you see?"

"And the lease?"

"I would probably need a slight bump in my allowance for that."

Grey smacked a ball, sent another down a hole. "What are you going to do with your life, Edward? It should have some purpose to it."

"It has a grand purpose. Pleasure."

"Which was well and good when we were twenty. But you've lived for more than a quarter of a century now. You need to take on some responsibilities."

"I'm the spare and a gentleman. I'm required to live a life of leisure. I believe it's written in the law somewhere. Perhaps even in the Magna Carta."

Grey chuckled. "God help me, I'm torn between insisting that you grow up and hoping you never do."

Edward took a step forward. "Go on a final adventure with me. Our last. Then I'll settle in and do something respectable and mad—run for Parliament perhaps."

"Good God, the country in your hands? That would be a nightmare." Tossing his cue stick onto the table, he lifted his glass, drank deep. "You're smart, though, smarter than you let on. You've a good head on your shoulders, and I think somewhere"—he poked Edward's chest—"deep inside, you long to do good. But you'll have to accomplish all this without us doing a final trip. I can't leave Julia, especially now, when she's so vulnerable."

Turning away, Edward drained his glass. "When you married, I didn't gain a sister by marriage, I lost a brother."

"I grew up. You need to do the same. I think your having your own place is a step in that direction. I'll fund it."

He spun back around. "Including the furnishings?"

"To help Ashe, yes."

"Jolly good. He'll be relieved, I'm sure."

"When's he moving?"

"He'll be out completely in the next day or so."

"I think you gentlemen have had enough time alone with your after-dinner port," Julia said, interrupting them, as she went to Grey, lifted up on her toes, and kissed his cheek. "I was growing lonely. Missed you."

"The arrival of the mistress of the house is my signal to depart," Edward murmured.

"You don't have to go," Grey said.

"I believe I do." He gave his sister by marriage a little salute. "And it was scotch actually, rather than port."

"I thought gentlemen always drank port after dinner."

"As you've pointed out on numerous occasions, I'm no gentleman. Your husband indulged me, as he is one. But now I must be off. Thank you for the lovely dinner."

"We're glad you could join us," she said.

Leaning in, he bussed a quick kiss over her cheek, and whispered, "You are a lousy liar."

"It's not that I don't like you, Edward, but you have such potential and opportunities. Yet you waste it all."

"Without my wastrel life to pick over, how would you entertain yourself?"

"Edward, you've gone too far," Grey snapped. "Julia has your best interest at heart. She and I are both concerned."

"As you should be. I'm happy, have a jolly good time wherever I go, and entertain those who seek out my company. But now I must be off to plan my next adventure. Good night."

He strode from the room with a purpose to his step. The woman irritated the very devil out of him, and he didn't know why. She wasn't a complete witch, but not once had she ever looked at him as though he were anything other than a blight on the family name and honor.

WITH relief, Julia watched her brother by marriage storm from the room. Things were always tense when he was around. It didn't help matters that he'd been the first man to ever kiss her—not that she'd ever confessed that to Albert. Devilishly handsome, upstanding Albert had been courting her. But it had been devilishly handsome, disreputable Edward who had approached her in a garden during a ball, planted his mouth on hers, and introduced her to the passion that could exist between a man and a woman. It was an honor that should have belonged to Albert, should have been his, and well Edward knew it. But he had thought it would be a lark to pretend to be Albert, to steal the kiss, and she'd never forgiven him. Or herself for how very much she'd enjoyed it.

It was only by being ever vigilant since that she was able to tell the brothers apart. Their looks were identical. It was only their mannerisms and behavior that distinguished them. Edward cared for nothing save his own pleasures while Albert put everyone before himself. It was one of the reasons she loved him so very much.

Her husband walked to the fireplace, rested a forearm against the edge of the mantel, and stared down at the empty hearth. She disliked Edward's visits because they always left Albert feeling as though he should do more for his brother.

She glided over to him, raised up on her toes, and whispered, "I wish you wouldn't torment yourself so. I wish he was gone."

He turned his head, smiled at her, rubbed the lobe of his right ear. "Sorry. My bad ear. Did you say something?"

Another thing that distinguished the brothers. Albert had lost his hearing in the right ear when he was five and Edward had shoved him into an icy pond. That he'd then jumped in to save him didn't alter the fact that he was responsible for the infection that damaged Albert's ear. Not that Albert saw it like that. He claimed they were simply rambunctious boys who allowed things to get a little out of hand, but Julia sometimes suspected that Edward was jealous of his older brother. Albert inherited everything, while Edward was merely the recipient of his brother's generous heart.

"Only that I love you," she said.

His grin grew. "You should always say that only to the left ear."

"I'm sorry that I can't make him like me," she lied. She couldn't care less if Edward liked her. Every time he went on his travels, she prayed fervently that he wouldn't return. Life was so much easier when he wasn't about.

Albert tucked loose strands of her hair behind her ear. "Edward can be trying at times. I think where you're concerned, though, he's jealous. I have a beautiful wife. And he is alone."

She gave him a teasing look. "Based upon all the women he talks about, I'm not certain you can accurately claim that he is alone."

"But none of them are good for him. Not the way you were good for me. Although he did say that if we took a trip together, he would grow up when we got back."

Her chest tightened. "Are you going?"

Slowly, he shook his head. "I won't leave you."

Swallowing her fears, the fears she'd always had regarding her good fortune in having such a wonderful man's love, the fears that their happiness could be ripped away, she said, "You can go if you want."

Cradling her jaw, he held her gaze. "I'm not going to leave you while you're with child."

"I'll be perfectly fine."

"If you were to lose the babe while I was away, do you think I'd ever forgive myself?"

"It wouldn't be your fault. Neither of us did anything that caused me to lose the other three. I hope this one is a boy. I want to give you your heir."

"I hope only that it's healthy and that you survive bringing it into the world." He drew her close, wrapped his arms tightly around her. "I don't want to lose you, Julia."

"You won't," she promised, even knowing that some promises weren't meant to be kept.

SITTING in his library, Ashe swirled the amber liquid in his glass, mesmerized by a vortex that seemed to resemble his life. He needed to marry a woman with a dowry. Minerva Dodger had the largest available. Why would he settle for less?

Plus he liked her, especially in the bedchamber. What they had shared revealed a passion that far surpassed anything he'd ever experienced.

He hadn't liked one bit walking into the Dodger parlor to find Burleigh sharing the sofa with Minerva. As a rule, he wasn't the jealous sort, but it appeared, where she was concerned, none of his rules were holding.

Tomorrow, preparations for moving into Ashebury Place would begin in earnest. Tonight he was in need of a distraction. It existed at a gaming hell, even if he didn't wager. And Minerva would be within the walls of the establishment. Getting up, he returned his glass to the sideboard, turned for the door.

"Ah, there you are," Edward said as he strolled in. "Have some jolly good news. I've spoken with Grey. Whatever items you want to leave here, I shall have the means to purchase."

Ashe released a grateful sigh. "That certainly makes things easier all the way around. I'll have my man of business tally up the costs."

"I thought you'd be pleased." He walked to the table, poured himself a scotch. "What shall we do tonight to celebrate?"

"I was about to head to the Dragons. You're welcome to join me."

Edward studied his scotch as though he were seeking an answer within its depths. "No, I'm more in the mood for something that involves women."

"Women are at the Dragons."

"Respectable women." He shook his head. "Not the sort I fancy."

Ashe felt somewhat of a dilemma, not wanting to abandon Edward after his generosity but very much wanting to see Minerva. His desire to be with her won out. "As I'm not in the mood for the sort of women you fancy, I'll leave you to them."

Edward grinned. "You're already starting to sound married. By the by, when you do move out, leave the spirits."

"If you want any staff to stay behind, just let me know how many."

"Leave as many as you like. I'll keep them on." As though his words were of no consequence, he tossed back his scotch.

But Ashe knew them for what they were: an attempt to ease his burden. "Edward, I appreciate everything you've done here."

His lips twisted up into a mockery of smile. "We orphans have to stick together."

"As much as I wish you hadn't lost your parents, I was always rather glad I didn't have to go to Havisham alone."

Edward reached for a decanter. "You're getting sentimental. It doesn't suit you. Go lose some money. You'll feel better."

Grateful that Edward was putting an end to what might have become an uncomfortable conversation, Ashe chuckled with relief. "And you . . . go find yourself a good woman for the night."

"Don't want a good one." He grinned devilishly and wiggled his eyebrows. "I want one who is very, very wicked."

But Ashe knew that sometimes they were one and the same. Minerva Dodger had taught him that.

Chapter 15

*F*EELING restless and on edge, Minerva stood within the shadowed balcony of the Twin Dragons and looked out over the gaming floor. Seeing Ashe this afternoon had left her longing to be in his arms. She'd considered sending him a missive inviting him to join her here. But she rather hoped that he might make an appearance without her invitation, which was the reason she was standing here rather than being where she was supposed to be. Others were waiting on her. She needed to go.

Taking her gaze on a final sweep of the floor, she felt her heart kick against her ribs at the sight of Ashe wandering slowly about the card tables before heading for the roulette wheel. Had he been looking for her? Why else would he bother to take a detour through that area rather than heading straight for the wheel?

She very nearly shouted at him, to gain his attention, to invite him to join her. But propriety required a bit more decorum. She headed for the gaming floor.

He was standing near the roulette table, watching, not yet playing. She liked that he wasn't the sort to dive right into gambling, that he took his time. Some of the members were rather rabid about it. The gentlemen who were had been included on her list: *Men I'll Never Marry.*

She knew she could never love someone for whom gambling was an obsession rather than a pleasant pastime.

"Your Grace."

He turned, his brilliant blue eyes warming. "Miss Dodger. I was hoping to find you here, but I didn't see you at the tables."

When had any man sounded so sincere when speaking with her? "I'm playing in a private room. Would you care to join us? I know cards isn't a game you prefer, but you don't have to play. You could watch."

He gave her a wicked smile. "I've never seen the appeal of being a voyeur. However, watching you could prove me wrong."

"I don't think I'd be that interesting. And you're right. It's incredibly boring to watch someone play. I don't even know why I made the suggestion."

"If the choice is standing here watching a wheel spin and my coins dwindle or watching you, I choose the later. Besides, I'm assuming this is the exclusive game in the inner sanctum that is whispered about, but few are allowed to experience."

She smiled brightly. "It is indeed."

"Then I would be more than delighted to accept your invitation."

"Who knows? You might even decide to play."

𝒯HE private rooms were legendary. He wasn't surprised Minerva possessed a key that granted her access to them, but it did allow him to understand why she might have instructed his driver to bring her here. With her mask hidden in the folds of her skirts, she could whisk through the gaming area and find solace in here. Even if he'd followed his driver that first night, she'd have been able to disappear before Ashe would have been able to catch a good glimpse of her unmasked.

Clever girl.

She led him up a set of stairs and down a darkened hallway. They passed a shadowed alcove. Grabbing her arm, he drew her back into it and latched his mouth onto hers. She didn't protest or object. Merely wound her arms around his neck, pressed her breasts against his chest, drove him mad with her eagerness.

Why were they playing this damned game when this existed between them? Why weren't they at his residence, in his bed? And why was it that he couldn't get enough of her? Was it because she was the one who established the rules, the one in charge, the one who dictated the terms of their arrangement?

What arrangement? He was trying to keep his

head, court her the way her blasted book said he was supposed to court her, but all he could think of was cupping her bare breast, kneading it, suckling on it. All he wanted was the freedom to glide his mouth along her bare legs, kiss her behind her knees, press his lips to her birthmark, tease and taunt her with his fingers and tongue. He wanted to be inside her, riding a wave of pleasure that was more intense than anything he'd ever experienced.

He dragged his mouth along her throat. "Come to my residence."

"I'm not half-tempted," she said on a sigh.

"Be all tempted."

With a soft laugh, she cradled his face. "Doesn't it frighten you? This mad attraction between us?"

"No. We should glory in it. It's not always like this."

"Is it not?"

He cupped her cheeks. "For me, it's never been this intense with any other woman. Marry me, Minerva. We'll have this every night."

He heard her small gasp of surprise. "I don't know that it's enough to carry us through a lifetime."

"But what a ride we'll have until it burns out."

"So you think it'll burn out."

He cursed the disappointment he heard in her voice. Part of him thought it had to. Part of him couldn't imagine it. She wanted guarantees. He wanted to bed her again. But he wasn't going to lie to her.

"Do you love me?" she asked.

He bit back a frustrated sigh. "I care for you very much. Love . . . love is what made the Marquess of Marsden go mad. I know you yearn for it, but it is not all warmth and joy and happily-ever-after. This attraction we feel can carry us far."

"I just don't know if it'll carry us far enough."

He should give up on her. She wasn't the only woman with a dowry. But dammit all, he wanted her. Her stubbornness, her willingness to go after what she wanted, even her belief in love. He'd never known a woman as complex, complicated, or intriguing. A lifetime with her would ensure he was never bored.

He took her mouth once more, rough and hungrily, just one more taste, one more nibble, one more sweep of his tongue. When he broke off the kiss, she staggered. He steadied her, grinned. "We could have that every night. Consider it."

Taking her hand, he led her out into the hallway.

"You don't play fair," she said softly.

"This isn't a game."

"Is it not?"

It was the future of his estates, his legacy. He wished he could give her the love she wanted, she deserved. But he could ensure she didn't regret marrying him. "I want you," he said simply. "That's not going to change."

"How can you be sure?"

"Because I know my own mind."

"I want you to know your own heart."

He squeezed her hand, realizing only at that moment that he'd never released it. They weren't going to resolve this tonight, and he wanted to enjoy the time he was with her. Wanted her to enjoy the time she was with him. "I want to watch you play cards."

At the end of the hallway, she stopped at a door, knocked, and with a single word spoken, gained entry. He followed her into a room that he'd heard whispers about for as long as he'd been a member. The dark location offered sitting areas and tables lined with decanters.

Minerva escorted him through parted draperies into a chamber that was better lit. A large, round, baize-covered table was the focus, several people already sitting around it. Standing, the gentlemen narrowed their eyes suspiciously. The ladies remained as they were and gave him a more speculative look.

"I believe everyone knows everyone," Minerva said.

"Ashebury," Lovingdon said, and Ashe should have realized her half brother would be here. Lovingdon's wife was sitting beside him. The Duke and Duchess of Avendale were next. Lords Langdon and Rexton. Drake Darling.

"Lovingdon." Ashe bowed his head slightly. "Ladies. Gentlemen."

"We'll sit over here," Minerva said, taking his

hand and guiding him to an empty chair at the far end. By the time they reached it, a footman had added another.

Ashe assisted Minerva in taking her seat, then waited as the gentlemen finished sizing him up. It was several interminable minutes before Lovingdon gave a brisk nod, and the gents settled into their places.

"Ashe isn't going to play," Minerva said. "He's merely going to watch."

"Where's the fun in that?" Avendale asked.

"The fun is in watching you lose your money while I keep mine," Ashe said.

"Roulette is his game," Minerva explained, and he wondered at her need to defend him. After removing her gloves, she set them in her lap, placed her hands on top of the table.

He studied those slender pale fingers and recalled the feel of them wrapped around him. As discreetly as possible, beneath the table, he set his hand on her thigh, squeezing gently through layers of petticoats. Her eyes meeting his, he saw the pleasure in hers, watched as a small smile spread slowly—

"You may be only observing, Ashebury," Lovingdon said, "but I must insist your hands remain on top of the table."

Ashebury's jaw tightened. He was growing weary of the man's interfering with his seduction of Minerva—even if she was Lovingdon's sister, and he had an obligation to protect her.

"He's concerned with you cheating," the Duchess of Lovingdon said. "Or helping Minerva cheat."

He didn't remove his hand from her thigh. Instead, he squeezed again, before narrowing his eyes at her brother. "I'm finding it most difficult not to take offense. I do not cheat."

"Unfortunately, we do," Minerva said softly, her cheeks turning the most becoming shade of pink. "So hands must stay visible." Leaning over, she whispered near his ear, "Regretfully."

Regretfully indeed. Holding Lovingdon's gaze, Ashe set his left hand on the table, fingers splayed, placed his right forearm along the back of Minerva's chair and closed his fingers around her shoulder. She looked at him, looked at her brother. The tension mounted.

"I don't need help cheating," she finally announced. "I'm rather insulted that you would think I would. As long as hands are visible, I don't think they have to be on the table."

"As long as they're visible," Lovingdon affirmed, but he didn't sound very happy about it. Ashe wondered how happy the man was going to be when they became relations.

"Shall we begin?" Darling asked.

Murmurs of agreement filled the silence. Minerva rubbed her hands together, popped her knuckles. Ashe didn't know why he found the unladylike movement endearing and erotic.

Everyone tossed a chip into the center of the table. Darling began dealing the cards. Ashe was astounded by the stacks of chips resting in front of each person. He didn't resent them their wealth. He only wished he could emulate it. Although, if his plans came to fruition, he would very soon have an immense fortune himself.

As discreetly as possible, Minerva showed him her cards, gave him a gamine smile. Was she flirting with him or signaling that she was pleased with her hand? He tried to make sense of the numbers. In the best of times, it was difficult, but when she was quickly arranging the cards in some sort of order, it was impossible. Still, he smiled back, pretended to know what the bloody hell those dancing figures signified.

She discarded two of them. He hadn't a clue as to what she found offensive about them. He wondered if she would always be content with his watching, if a time would come when she would encourage, might even insist, that he play. Might think he was being rude or snobbish if he didn't.

When the round ended, she was the one who reached across the table and brought in all the chips. "Ah, five hundred pounds. Lucky me. You can help me stack them," she told him.

He could manage that. The various denominations were marked in different colors. He didn't have to add anything up. "How did you know how much?"

"I kept a tally as the chips went in."

In her head? She didn't even need to put it on paper? "Remarkable."

She scoffed. "Not really. I'm sure everyone at the table is doing the same."

Bloody hell. She was sharp. He would have to ensure that she never found out about his inability to conquer numbers. Otherwise, she might think him a complete ninny, and why would she ever want a man who couldn't keep up with her?

Darling gathered up the cards, began shuffling them with ease. "Say, Ashebury, I had a rather interesting conversation with Lord Sheridan recently. He demanded that I revoke your membership."

Every movement at the table stilled. Glasses lifted partway, people leaning in to say something to their spouse, wrists flicking to toss another chip toward the center of the table. Except for the shuffling of cards. Their rush of sound punctuated the otherwise hushed silence as all eyes came to bear on Ashe. Minerva's delicate brow furrowed, her dark eyes reflected concern.

"He said there was an altercation between you two," Darling continued, his hands never stopping the incessant shuffling.

"I'd hardly call it an altercation," Ashe said.

"He claims you tossed scotch onto him."

Sheridan's pride obviously prevented him from admitting that he'd also become intimately acquainted with Ashe's fist. "An accident, I assure you. I stumbled, and my scotch flew. I couldn't stop it from landing on him."

With a nod, Darling began dealing. "That was Thomas's account as well, which was the reason I didn't bother you with it earlier, but as you were here, I thought I would ask."

"Just clumsiness on my part."

"I never much liked Sheridan," Rexton said.

"I hope Lady Hyacinth does. I hear they are to marry," the Duchess of Lovingdon said.

"That came about rather quickly. How did he manage it?" Minerva asked.

"A compromising encounter in a garden, from what I understand. Better her than you, I say."

"Did he call on you?" Lovingdon asked.

Minerva waved a hand, before picking up her cards and beginning to arrange them. "Several days ago. I feel for the girl. He wants only her dowry."

Even after the girl had insulted her, she could still work up sympathy for her. Ashe wasn't certain he'd be able to do the same, and yet he wasn't surprised by her feelings. She possessed a decency that he'd found lacking in many of the ladies with whom he'd flirted over the years.

"She'll be a countess," Langdon said.

"She'll be unhappy."

"I doubt it. From what I understand, she arranged to be discovered in the garden."

"Still, she has my sympathy, and I saw you swap out your card, Langdon."

"You weren't even looking at me."

She merely gave him a triumphant smile that caused Ashe's gut to tighten. He wanted that smile. He wanted all her smiles.

Langdon tossed down his cards, crossed his arms over his chest.

Minerva glanced over at Ashe, her lips still upturned, and it was all he could do not to lean in and plant a kiss on them. "We may cheat at cards, but we do own up to it when we're caught."

"It's a good thing I'm not playing then, as I don't know how to cheat."

"I could teach you if you like."

He'd rather she be the pupil for what he wanted to teach her—how much passion could flare between them. Still, he knew a man would be a fool to pass on her offer, but he couldn't accept without the risk of her discovering his shortcomings. So he decided to turn the conversation in a totally different vein. "Did you ask your brother about his garden?"

"What about my garden?" Lovingdon asked, in such a way that Ashe was left with the feeling that he either didn't like him or didn't trust him. Smarts obviously ran in the family.

"Ashe was wondering if he could use it to take a photograph . . . of me."

The last two words carried a self-conscious lilt. Ironic that she was uncomfortable posing for him fully clothed when she'd been willing to do so with silk hiked up to the edge of her hips. Recalling that he'd heard the duke had acquired his heir, he said, "To show my appreciation, I'd be willing to photograph your family."

"You saw the pictures from his trip to Africa," Minerva said. "You know how talented he is."

He studied Ashe as though searching for an ulterior motive. He shifted his gaze to his wife, who gave him a smile that seemed to communicate far more than any words ever could. "I suppose there's no harm in it," he finally groused, as though he thought there probably was harm in it. He simply couldn't figure it out.

"Lovely. When would you like to do it?" Minerva asked.

"If the weather is clear tomorrow, around ten if that's agreeable," Ashe said. "Morning sunlight is more forgiving."

"Forgiving of what?" Lovingdon asked.

"My meager talents. It creates a softer image, which I prefer over stark lines."

"How did you ever learn all this?" the Duchess of Lovingdon asked.

"Mostly trial and error, searching for perfection."

"I've never found perfection particularly interesting," the Duchess of Avendale said, looking at Ashe as though she'd just discovered he'd stepped into a pile of horse manure. She wasn't particularly pretty, and he wondered how, as a commoner, she'd managed to snag herself a duke. Of course, Minerva was a commoner as well, and she was going to nab a duke, but then, she was bringing with her a fortune. The Duchess of Avendale had brought only a criminal record.

"Perfection in my style, not my subject." Although in his private collection he was searching for perfection in lines, something to shove out the horrific images that had bombarded him as a child.

The duchess lifted a shoulder as though to say that perhaps his boots weren't so mucked up after all.

"Are we going to play cards?" Avendale asked.

"You can't play and talk?" Ashe challenged.

"Not the way we play," Minerva said. "We're all terribly serious about winning."

She also thoroughly enjoyed the game, that much was obvious. And he enjoyed every aspect of her. Proving to her that what he felt for her would be enough was more challenging than he'd anticipated. But he wasn't going to give up. He wanted her back in his bed permanently.

THE following morning Minerva fought not to be nervous. She kept reminding herself that this was Ashe and that she had posed for him wearing far less. He was setting up his camera on a tripod while she paced near the pond.

Before Ashe had arrived, she'd had a small spat with her brother because he'd wanted to stand watch. But she wanted to be alone with the duke without her brother interfering. Ashe had departed from the club last night before they'd finished their card game, so she hadn't had a private moment with him.

She stopped her pacing. "Why do you want to photograph me?"

He looked up from whatever it was he was adjusting. "You're not comfortable with your features."

"That's no secret. As I've told you before, I look like my father."

He gave her a small, provocative smile that warmed the depths of her heart. "Hardly."

He went back to work, she went back to pacing. Halted in her tracks. "Why did you toss your scotch on Sheridan?"

He straightened completely. "Because I don't like him."

"He wanted to marry me."

He studied her for a moment, but it appeared he was carrying on an inner debate. Finally, he met her gaze head-on. "He was bemoaning the fact that you had rejected his suit. I took exception to some things he was uttering. While he didn't admit it to Darling, before we were done, I hit him."

She couldn't help the wonderful sense of satisfaction that swamped her. "You were being my champion?"

With three long strides, he was standing before her, the crook of his finger tilting up her chin. "Did you think I wouldn't be?"

"Why would you be?"

He shook his head slightly. "How can you not understand how much I adore you? You're a combination of boldness and timidity that I find irresistible. Not to mention the passion that flares between us."

"Yet you haven't kissed me since you arrived."

"Opportunity has been lacking. I would kiss you now except that I suspect your brother is in an upstairs window watching us through a spyglass."

She smiled. "He does have a telescope."

"Make no mistake, Minerva, I spend a great deal of time thinking about kissing you, doing other things as well."

His eyes darkened with promise, and her stomach fairly dropped to the ground. He took her hand, cupped his other hand against her waist. "I need you here."

He guided her to a spot just shy of the bridge. "I want you to sit with your legs curled against your hips."

"I should get a blanket."

"No, you're a woman who doesn't care one whit about grass stains on her skirt." Providing her with support, he lowered her to the ground. He had no qualms about touching her, moving an arm here, a hand there, shifting her leg so the skirts flowed just so. She was enthralled watching his concentration. He was entirely focused on the task at hand, lost in the moment of creating something that meant so very much to him. She did hope that he wouldn't be disappointed with the results.

He cradled her chin between his thumb and forefinger, tilted her head to the side ever so slightly. "Now don't move," he ordered.

Then he covered her mouth with a kiss that was both sweet and profound, that in spite of its quickness managed to elicit pleasure in every corner of her being. When he drew back, mischief sparkled in his eyes. "Be a good girl and I'll have another one of those for you when we're done."

"Thought you were worried about my brother watching."

"From this angle, he can't discern the details of what I'm doing." He sobered. "You may have to be still for a while, though. I want the sun just so."

"I'll pretend I'm in church."

He skimmed his thumb over the round curve of her cheek. "I'd tell you that I think you're exquisite, but I don't think you'd believe me."

She stared at him.

"There," he said, with a grin. "Keep your lips relaxed and parted just like that."

And then he was gone.

𝒦NEELING—Ashe cared not one whit about grass stains on his trousers—he looked through the lens of the camera. Because of the angle he'd wanted, he'd used a short tripod. He believed photos could be so much more than people standing stiffly, staring into the camera. Photography was in its infancy, its potential yet to be explored fully. But he had no doubt that it was art, and the image before him only reinforced that belief.

Minerva wore an elegant yet simple wide-brimmed hat and a pale yellow gown with voluminous skirts. Her burnished hair and brows, deep brown eyes, and strawberry red lips stood out in stark contrast. She was slightly to the right of the bridge, so it and the pond behind her served as background. But the focus, the key element of the piece, was her. The morning shadows, the filtering sunlight were almost exactly where he needed them for maximum effect.

He loved this moment, when he was in absolute control, when he decided the outcome of his efforts. If only numbers came as naturally, when he looked at her he wouldn't have to see a dowry. With her acumen with figures, he knew that she could help him manage his estates, that she could help ensure he had a magnificent legacy to pass on. But that would require revealing the mess he was in presently—she would neither understand nor appreciate his predicament. With her aversion to fortune hunters, how could she view him as anything else?

"We're almost there," he called out.

She didn't move, didn't acknowledge him. Her control, her discipline amazed him.

The sun grew bolder, the shadows retreated only slightly. He captured the moment.

He stood, walked over to her, and extended his hand. She looked up at him.

"It's finished?"

"It is."

"That was relatively painless," she said, placing her hand in his.

He drew her up, latched his mouth onto hers, welcoming the taste and feel of her. She pushed back slightly.

"Lovingdon."

"Let him watch."

"I fear he'll do more than watch. He'll claim you compromised me and insist we marry."

"Would that be so bad?"

She furrowed her brow. "You mentioned marriage last night, but you can't be serious."

"I've never been more serious." He pressed his thumb to her lips. "Don't answer, but think on it."

"Why would you marry me?"

"Why would I not?"

"You can't answer a question with a question."

He snaked his arm around her waist, drew her up against him, and angled his mouth over hers. Why did she have to be so suspicious? Why did she have to question his motives? He cursed every man who had come before him so that his task now was all the more difficult. Then he cursed her brother because he *was* probably watching. Ashe didn't want to force her into marriage. He wanted to lure her into it. Drawing back, he gazed down into her languid eyes. "There's fire between us and no reason to think that another night together will extinguish it."

"For anything long-lasting, there has to be more than the passion."

"I've already told you that I adore you. I admire you. You fascinate me. So perhaps the fault is with me. You find me lacking."

Turning on his heel, he returned to his equipment to begin packing it up. The duchess did want a family photograph taken, but thank goodness, she wanted it done on another day, when the heir wasn't so cranky.

"Ashe?"

He glanced back at her.

"I don't find you lacking," she said. "I'm simply not accustomed to a man's desiring me. I had decided to accept my life as a spinster."

"Decisions can be changed." He picked up his equipment. "And I'm not one to give up, so get used to that as well. Walk me to the gate?"

With a nod, she fell into step beside him. "When will you show me the photo?"

"Soon."

"I might not want to see it. When I was eight, my mother had a portrait painted of me. When I saw it, I took a piece of coal and blackened out the face. I have the most unattractive nose."

"Sometimes, Minerva, we look at things and

see what we expect to see rather than what's really there. But when I look through the camera lens, I see the truth."

"The truth isn't always pretty," she said.

No, it wasn't. And there were truths about himself that he would never tell her.

Chapter 16

Ashe was standing in the foyer of Ashebury Place when he heard the gentle sneeze and spun around to find Minerva in the open doorway. It had been three days since he'd seen her, since he'd taken the photograph of her in the garden. While the servants were managing most of the move, he needed to oversee some areas. Spending much of his time here did not leave him in the most amicable of moods. But seeing her now, he realized his foolishness in withdrawing. The gladness that swamped him at her presence was a bit disconcerting, was far beyond anything he'd ever before experienced.

"My apologies," she said. "I was passing by on my way to the milliner when I saw all the activity going on here and recalled that you were moving in. I thought to stop by to see how you were doing with the memories."

The only memories revolving through his mind at the moment involved her: at the Nightingale, at the club, at the ball. He wanted to jerk her to him, claim her mouth, carry her up the stairs, and claim her body. Instead, he tamped down the beast ravaging through him, and lacquered on a veneer of civilization. "I'm afraid I'm not really set up for visitors yet."

"I don't mean to impose, but I hadn't seen you at the Dragons. I just wanted to ensure you were all right. I know how difficult all this must be." Sneezing again, she pressed a lace handkerchief to her nose.

"Sorry, the servants have been uncovering things for days now, disturbing twenty years of dust."

"Has it been that long?"

He nodded. "The house was closed up when I was taken to Havisham. A few years back, I came to check on it. Didn't make it past the foyer before realizing I wasn't ready to live here, so I leased a place."

"But now you are ready?"

Forced to be ready. The edge of poverty made a man do things he otherwise might not. Like marry. Although the notion of spending the remainder of his life with her almost made him glad to be reclaiming the house. "I think so, yes. The ghosts are a bit quieter now."

She glanced around. "From here, it looks to be quite grand."

"Would you like a tour?"

"I don't want to impose."

"No imposition. As I said, it's not quite ready, but

I could show you this level, so you can get a sense of it." *Since it is bound to become your home as well.*

"Yes, all right. I'd like that."

As he escorted her down one of the hallways, servants bustled out of their way. Seldom seen, they were usually more discreet in taking care of matters, but so much needed to be done here that they had no choice except to work an odd schedule. The rooms spoke for themselves: a sitting room, a private parlor, the breakfast dining room.

They stepped into the library. Servants were pulling down the sheeting that had protected the shelves.

"I think the number of books a person owns says a lot about them," she said, glancing around, apparently pleased to see so many leather-bound volumes.

"My father liked to collect books, but I don't recall him reading them."

"You were a child. You were probably in bed long before his reading time."

He'd never considered that. She wandered to a shelf, touched a spine. "My vision of my father when I was eight was very different from my vision of him now."

He walked over and leaned a shoulder against a shelf. "And how did you see him at eight?"

"So large. I had to crane my head back incredibly far to see him towering over me. He seemed scary, easily displeased. He was gone a good bit, managing the club. And he made my mother laugh. He never had a harsh word for her. The same couldn't be said of my brothers. He was quick to admonish them if they misbehaved. Not so quick to chide me."

"And now?"

She grinned. "He's rather a kitten."

Ashe laughed deeply, the sound vibrating around them. "I don't quite believe that. I think any man who made you unhappy would find himself floating in the Thames."

"He does have a reputation for being surly, doesn't he?"

"That's putting it mildly." Ashe didn't fear the man, but he did respect the power he wielded. He could easily destroy anyone who displeased him or brought sadness to his daughter.

He led her back into the hallway. "I would show you the gardens, but they're rather a jungle presently."

"Will it be difficult being back here?"

"Not as hard as I thought. I already have a pleasant memory to replace the not-so-pleasant ones—as you'd hoped I would. I'm glad you stopped by."

She faced him as they reached the entryway. "I know you're remarkably busy, but I wondered if you might be attending the Claybourne ball tomorrow night."

"Only if you promise me the first and last waltz."

She smiled with pleasure. "They're yours. I've missed seeing you."

"I'll make up for my absence to you tomorrow."

"I can hardly wait. Have a good day."

With that, she spun on her heel—and he thought he heard the barest tinkling of chimes. Standing in the doorway, he watched as she strolled down the path to a waiting carriage, watched as she was assisted inside by the footman, watched as it traveled out of sight. His plan involved seducing her, yet he couldn't help but feel that he was the one being seduced. Every time he saw her, he was charmed just a little bit more.

*I*T began with the explosion. The crash of engines, the splintering of wood, the eruption of fire.

It ended with the mangled bodies, strewn over the ground—

And Ashe sitting up in bed, breathing heavily, covered in sweat, tangled in sheets, feeling as though he would suffocate.

Years had passed since he'd had a nightmare as vivid, as horrific. He clambered out of bed, strode to a small table, poured himself a full glass of scotch, and downed it all in one long swallow. He should have expected this. It was his first night to sleep in the residence, his first night encased in the memories.

He walked to the window, gazed out on the darkness, fought to push out the gruesome images of blood and gore. He imagined tiny toes curled against his thigh, his hands folded around a shapely calf. His breathing calmed, his clammy skin began to cool.

He thought of Minerva stretched out on the bed, her face hidden by her mane of hair, the silk resting at her hips revealing the long length of her slender legs. The delicate ankles. He began to concentrate on the details: the heart-shaped birthmark, a tiny mole behind her knee. Everything a camera could capture. Her fragrance as passion took hold. Her taste. Everything that eluded the camera.

Her perfection, beauty conquered the demons of remorse and regret. He tried to recall other women posing for him, but she was all he saw. From the beginning, something about her was different. From the beginning, something about her had called to him. From the beginning, she had somehow managed to work her way into the fabric of his being.

He wanted her as his wife. It was time he stepped up his game.

Chapter 17

As Minerva traveled in the coach with Grace and Lovingdon—he'd been good enough to provide her with transportation this evening—she didn't think she'd been filled with this much anticipation when she attended her first ball. She was wearing her favorite white gown, elaborate pink silk roses stitched along the front that trailed down just past her hips to end at the short train. A layer of ruffles added a bit more elegance. Her hair was swept up off her neck, held up with strategically placed silk roses that matched those adorning her gown. For the first time in longer than she could remember, she'd brought an extra pair of slippers. Not that two dances would wear out the soles of the ones she was presently wearing, but if she began her evening with Ashe's attention, she might find herself dancing a bit more than usual.

Not that she wanted to dance with anyone else. If it wouldn't send a hundred tongues wagging, she'd dance every dance with him.

They said absence made the heart grow fonder. How much she'd missed him surprised her, had her considering the merits of marrying him. He was a duke, his lineage respected, his estates flourishing from what she'd been able to gather from her closest friends. He'd never once mentioned her dowry or his need for it. He traveled, he had adequate staff, he moved into another residence without much ado. He dressed well, his clothing the latest fashion, finely stitched by the best tailors. Not a single thread frayed or worn.

He didn't need her dowry. He wanted her. He didn't mind that she spoke her mind. Seemed to enjoy it actually. He made her smile and laugh and be glad that he was about. And the passion that flared between them—she missed it as well.

"You look particularly lovely this evening, Minerva," Grace said.

"Thank you."

"There's not a particular reason is there? A certain gentleman you're hoping to impress?"

She couldn't stop her smile from spreading across her face. "Maybe."

"I'd advise you to avoid going into the garden with him," Lovingdon said with a voice that brooked no disobedience, that signaled he was a man accustomed to giving orders.

"I'd advise you to mind your own business."

"Minerva, you are playing a very dangerous game."

She released a heavy sigh. "What is the very worst that could happen?"

"He could leave you with child."

His words were a blow, as though he knew exactly how far she had gone with this man. "I don't know why you think so ill of him."

"I saw him kiss you the morning he was taking your photograph in my garden."

"You had no right to spy, but be that as it may, are you telling me you never kissed Grace before you married?"

"What I did with Grace has no bearing on this matter."

"Why can't he want me for me?"

"I'm not saying he can't. Just be wise about it."

That was one of the problems with having a brother who had possessed a scandalous reputation before he settled into marriage. "I'm not a fool, Lovingdon, and I know that there is absolutely no reason for him to want me, to give attention—"

"That's not what I meant. It's just that he seems to be moving very quickly."

"Which I'm grateful for as I'm aging quickly." She bit her lower lip. "Trust me, dear brother, I do keep questioning. As it makes no sense whatsoever. He could have anyone. Why me? Is he in debt?"

"Not that I've heard." Her brother knew a great deal about a great many lords. "I can ask around if you like."

"No. I'm enjoying his attention. I won't do anything stupid." Although he would no doubt claim that she already had if he knew about her trips to the Nightingale.

"I think he's giving you attention because he's a smart man," Grace said. "And because he's enamored."

"You are a loyal friend, Grace," Minerva assured her.

"It's not that. I watched him the other night. Watched him watching you. In his eyes, I saw admiration, affection, warmth—anytime he looked at you. He paid little attention to the cards you were striving to share with him. All his focus was on you. I think he cares for you. I think that's why you have garnered his interest."

"But why this Season? It's not as though either of us has suddenly burst into the ballrooms. He's been in them for as long as I have."

"It has been my experience that when one faces death, one comes away from the encounter with not only a greater appreciation of life but an understanding that it's incredibly precarious. Perhaps that lion's pouncing on him made him realize it was time to put his affairs in order and settle down."

"I suppose you have a point."

"You enjoy his company, so simply bask in his attentions and be happy."

"I suppose I do seek out too many answers."

"Having been in your position of fending off fortune hunters, I know we tend to be suspicious, but when all is said and done, I believe we should trust our instincts. And how he makes us feel."

She smiled. "He makes me feel treasured."

"There you are then."

Grace made it sound so simple, so uncomplicated. Perhaps she had the right of it, and Minerva should simply embrace the moment and, if opportunity arose, embrace Ashe as well.

*H*E would have preferred not to have three women fluttering their fans in his face or whispering to him behind their hand when he first caught sight of Minerva, but he'd been fending off advances for the better part of half an hour now, and it was growing wearisome. He shouldn't have arrived as early as he had, but he wanted to ensure she didn't have too much time to capture anyone else's attention.

She looked ravishing tonight in her white and silk. He thought of her on other nights in white and silk. She didn't need the pink roses for embellishment. The sleekness of her lines enhanced the gown all on their own.

The broad smile she's been wearing when she first walked in dimmed a little when she saw him. He should have made excuses to this trio sooner. "If you ladies will excuse me . . ."

"You haven't signed our cards," Lady Honoria said.

"I'm afraid I've already reserved my dances for the night." Turning, he searched the crowd for dark

auburn hair and pink roses. Finally, he spotted her
on the dance floor performing a quadrille. Her partner . . . Edward. He stifled a groan. Hopefully, the
man was merely serving to keep other would-be
suitors away, but if his sister-by-marriage really was
advocating that Grey give him less of an allowance,
then he might have decided to go into the hunt for
a dowry. Edward wouldn't settle for a pittance. Of
them all, Edward was the spendthrift, the one who
found pleasure in simply handing over money.

Moving to the edge of the dance floor, Ashe let
his irritation float away as he watched Minerva,
the grace of her movements, the sparkle in her eyes.
He didn't resent that she was enjoying herself. He
merely wished she was with him.

He hated that he needed money. He hated that
she had so much. Always his debt and her dowry
would be between them. Even if she never learned
of his financial situation, he would know. The trick
was not to let it matter. But studying her, he feared
it would matter a great deal.

The song ended, and the couples began to scatter,
Edward leading Minerva off the floor to a distant
side. Ashe began wending his way around people,
trying not to get sucked into conversations. The
next dance was a waltz. He intended to have her in
his arms the moment that the first chord was struck.

IN spite of the concentration that the quadrille took,
Minerva had been very much aware of Ashe's gaze on

her for a good part of it. She didn't know why she'd thought he'd be standing off to the side like some wilting wallflower waiting for her to arrive. He'd always attracted the ladies, probably always would.

As Edward escorted her from the dance floor, she had to admit that she'd enjoyed his company, in spite of his irreverent comments regarding what some of the ladies were wearing. Or perhaps because of the comments. He didn't seem to take himself seriously, and yet she sensed that he was a man within whom still waters ran deep.

"Thank you for the dance," he said, delivering her to an area where girls were lined up as though they were on a bidding block. He lifted her hand to his lips, pressed a kiss against her knuckles. His eyes shifted slightly, and the humor reflected in them deepened. "Ashe."

Minerva spun around, not able to go nearly as far as she'd have liked because Edward still had hold of her hand and seemed determined not to release it. She gave it a little shake to gain her freedom, then smiled at Ashe. "Your Grace."

"Miss Dodger. I believe the upcoming waltz is mine."

It absolutely, most assuredly was.

"I enjoyed the dance, Miss Dodger," Edward said as though he hadn't already thanked her or was trying to convey some message to Ashe.

"Thank you, sir."

Then Ashe was taking her hand and leading her

onto the dance floor. They were positioned before the first tinkling of music reached across the salon.

"Why were you dancing with him?" Ashe asked as he swept her into the circle of dancers.

"He asked." She furrowed her brow. "He is more family to you than friend. Why are you upset?"

"Because I know him, and he's always up to no good."

"Are you jealous?"

He scowled, and she thought a lesser woman would be intimidated, might even swoon. She couldn't stop her smile from spreading. "I've never had a man be jealous where I was concerned. I'm very flattered."

"I don't like seeing you with other men."

"And yet I'm forced to see you with other women."

He groaned. "I wasn't enjoying their company. I was simply being a pleasing guest."

"Are you dancing with them?"

"No. Tonight I shall dance only with you."

Pleasure sluiced through her. He always knew the right thing to say to bring gladness to her heart. "Well, then, I suppose I can forgive you."

She so enjoyed being with him. She enjoyed the way he held her gaze, not looking around as other men had done. The way his eyes glinted with pleasure as though he found it pleasing to have her in his arms. The way he held her firmly and a little too closely to be entirely proper. The way he made her not care.

All too soon, the music faded and they were left standing in the middle of the dance floor.

"Take a turn about the garden with me," he said, not so much request as command, and maybe with a little desperation as though he couldn't bear the thought of not having another minute in her company.

With a small nod, she wrapped her fingers around the crook of his elbow. As he escorted her from the ballroom, she realized she'd never anticipated a visit to the garden with quite so much excitement. It was a little frightening to acknowledge that she would go anywhere he asked, to let him have such power over her when she'd never allowed any other man to have it. Yet he never made her feel as though she were not in control. With him, she had a sense of equality that she had never experienced with anyone outside of her family and closest of friends.

They stepped out onto the terrace where other couples were already mingling. The drone of their whispers reminded her of the Nightingale. Was what happened out here so very different? People striving to take their flirtation to a level that required shadows. Striving for the appearance of all being proper when she suspected—knew now— that a good deal of it wasn't proper. That some ladies were fortunate enough to be courted by a gentleman who wanted to do improper things with them.

Before Ashe, she'd not been that fortunate. Her

walks with gentlemen had been more about exercising her legs rather than exercising her fantasies.

"Claybourne doesn't have a pond," she said, as they took the steps down to a dimly lit path.

"Pity. But we'll make do." His free hand covered hers where it rested on his arm. Glove to glove when she longed for skin to skin. Before him, there had been no gentleman who made her wish that gloves had never been invented.

"Is there some gentleman who will be disappointed not to find you in the ballroom?" he asked.

"Langdon, but he'll make do."

"As close as you are, I'm surprised he didn't court you."

"One does not court one's sister."

"You're not related."

"Not by blood, but I've always thought of him as a brother. I assume he viewed me as a sister."

"Fortunate for me then."

She laughed. "As though the Duke of Ashebury could have competition among the mortals."

The gas lamps provided enough light for her to see his brow furrow. "What do you mean by that?"

She shrugged. "I don't know. From a distance, I always thought you rather godlike. You're handsome as the devil, have a smile that melts women's hearts, can act as improperly as you like, and are forgiven by Society in a trice."

His gaze on her intensified. "I'd like to act improperly with you." He glanced back over his shoulder.

"He's not there."

He looked at her. "Lovingdon," she clarified, knowing precisely who he was searching for. She'd never before been so in tune with someone else. It was a marvelous feeling to know what someone else was thinking. "I told him if he traipsed after us tonight, I'd bring him to his knees."

"I'm disappointed he's not there then. I should have liked to have seen you do that."

Before she could think of anything to say, he took her hand and tugged her off the lit path through a break in the hedgerows and farther back, where there wasn't any light at all. He spun her, and she was aware of her spine meeting the brick wall that enclosed Claybourne's gardens. Warm hands were suddenly cradling her face, and she had half a heartbeat to wonder when he'd removed his gloves before his mouth unerringly blanketed hers, and his tongue swept through it to claim and conquer. She didn't bother to subdue her sigh of pleasure as she scraped her fingers through his scalp, holding him near, her tongue parrying with his. She'd missed the taste of him, the feel of him. He was pressed against her, and she couldn't miss the presence of the hard bulge against her belly. He wanted her, desired her, and she regretted that they weren't at the Nightingale, so he could possess her completely.

"Damnation, but I want you," he rasped, taking her earlobe between his teeth, sending shivers of delight coursing along her nerve endings.

Then let's quit this place, she almost said. Lady V could have said that, and he'd have taken her away without a moment's hesitation. But Minerva Dodger had a reputation to protect, a father and brother who would not see her ruined.

"You drive me to distraction," he said as he trailed his mouth along her throat, lower, along the gentle swells of her breasts. "I want to taste, suckle, kiss every inch of you."

She gasped a sharp intake of breath as he cradled her breast, his thumb toying with her taut nipple. Heat swirled, consumed. She knew where all these sensations could lead, and her body strained toward him, wanting to take the journey he offered. With her hand behind his head, she brought him in close, nuzzled her nose against the soft skin below his jaw, inhaled the fragrance of him, heated with his own desires, his need for her.

It was a heady feeling to be this wanted.

She became aware of his hand traveling along her leg, her skirts rising, his low groan as his fingers slipped through her curls to her dew-moistened core. He growled low. "You're so ready for me. I would give my soul to possess you fully."

Do it, do it, do it, her mind screamed, but the lady she was supposed to be kept her lips sealed tightly. What would he think of a woman who opened herself up to him completely in a garden where anyone could stumble across them?

She was certain they weren't the only ones seeking out shadows for an illicit few moments, but she relished the fact that he was here with her now, that he was doing things he ought not to be doing, that even though she was fully clothed, he could make her body sing.

His hand cupped her intimately, his fingers stroked and teased, his mouth covered hers just as she began writhing against him, as sensations coursed through her, building to a crescendo—

She clutched him, holding on tightly as he ravished and plundered, as her body surrendered and shattered. With his mouth, he captured her scream, while his fingers gentled their movements, and his other arm snaked around her waist, holding her firmly against him, so her weakened knees didn't carry her to the ground. She clung to his shoulders, clung to him, trembling with the almost violent release.

How she longed to feel the weight of him buried inside her.

His mouth left hers, and he pressed his hot, damp lips to her temple. "Spare me this interminable torment. Marry me, Minerva. We can have this every night, every afternoon, every morning," he said, his voice rough, low.

Breathing rapidly, she leaned back slightly, trying to see him more clearly, but they were lost in the darkness. Still, she could feel his gaze homing in on her.

"I could speak to your father tomorrow evening," he said. "If you're agreeable."

A bubble of laughter escaped before she could

stop it. She pressed her fingers to her mouth as joy spiraled through her. "You keep talking of marriage, but I find it difficult to believe that you truly want me for an eternity."

"I shall spend the remainder of my life demonstrating that I do." He cupped her cheek. "You complete me."

She wanted to believe him. He'd given her no reason not to.

"I'm not like the others," he said quietly.

Pressing her face to his chest, she welcomed his arms coming around her, holding her near. No, he wasn't like the others. He'd never been. The fault was with her. She who was so confident in all matters save this one. He might not say that he loved her, but surely he did. Otherwise, he would have walked away long ago.

"Yes," she whispered nodding. Tilting her head back, she met his gaze. "Yes," she said more loudly. "Yes, I'll marry you."

He slashed his mouth over hers. She felt the joy cascading through him, through her. He wanted her. She was lovable. She was going to have her own happily-ever-after.

Chapter 18

*I*T was strange, but when Minerva awoke that morning, everything felt so much brighter, as though every color in the world had become richer.

Standing behind a curtain while an assistant helped her into her clothing after a fitting for a new gown, Minerva wondered if she should go ahead and talk with the seamstress about her wedding gown. She and Ashe hadn't discussed how quickly they would marry, but she didn't want to wait overly long. The end of the Season, perhaps. Certainly not the end of the year.

During the last dance, they'd spoken not a word. After their torrid encounter in the garden, after his stating he would speak with her father, what more was there to say? He'd made his claim, and while he'd not voiced the words *I love you*, he'd certainly made it clear that he held her in high esteem and affection.

He'd held her more closely during the waltz, he'd never once looked away. With his gaze, he communicated everything. He was offering her everything she'd ever dreamed of when gentlemen who barely gave her any attention danced with her. When they hinted that they were her last hope for a marriage and children. That she should be grateful for their attentions, just as they were for her dowry. No romantic notions of love but practicality had ruled the social scene for her.

Until Ashe. Until he looked at her as though she were more than coins. Until he looked at her—

"I simply think it's sad is all," a lady said coming into the fitting room. "She wore such a moony-eyed expression as they were dancing last night. I thought at any moment she was going to swoon right into his arms. I feel rather sorry for her, making such a fool of herself with him."

"I can't blame her," another woman said, and Minerva knew that voice. Lady Honoria. "He is the most dashing of the hellions."

Everything within Minerva turned to ice. She couldn't be talking about Ashe. While Minerva considered him dashing, she knew many ladies preferred the playfulness of Edward. Surely, she was referring to him, causing some lady to swoon.

"To be sure." She recognized the speaker now. Lady Hyacinth. "I simply find it ironic that she wrote a book on how to identify fortune hunters, and she has failed completely in identifying one and has been totally ensnared by someone who is after her dowry."

The assistant reached for the curtain. Minerva grabbed her arm, shook her head, held a finger to her lips.

"Are you quite sure he's after her fortune?"

"Quite. My brother has the same man of business as Ashebury. He'd stopped by to see Nesbit some time back and he overhead Ashebury shouting about his coffers being empty. Of course, my brother made a hasty retreat, not wanting to embarrass the duke when he emerged from Nesbit's office. But there you have it. Winslow even suggested that I set my cap for Ashebury, as my dowry is nothing to sneeze at. I tried, but it became obvious rather quickly that he needs a substantial amount more than what I can offer. Where is the assistant? I really must get on with this fitting."

Minerva released the woman's arm, gave her a nod. She slipped out between the slight gap in the curtains, while Minerva leaned back against the wall, barely able to draw in a breath. She'd dared to believe that he wanted *her.*

Perhaps she'd been partially influenced by how precious he'd made her feel at the Nightingale. She'd fallen a little bit in love with him there, carried the emotion with her when she left rather than leaving it behind as she should have done. She'd allowed it to blind her to the truth.

He might have been more polished and subtle about it, but he wanted from her what every other man only wanted: her dowry.

ℋE was sitting at his desk, papers strewn over the top of it, head bent, hair mussed as though he'd tunneled his fingers through it repeatedly. Standing in the doorway, Minerva thought he'd never looked more appealing, and a tight painful ball formed just behind her breastbone. She'd fallen in love with him, but he was as much a fabrication as Lady V.

She'd arrived at Ashebury Place and—with a secretive smile and a wink—she'd managed to convince the butler to allow her to surprise the duke with her arrival. Having been in this room before, she'd not required an escort. Her heart had been thundering so heavily that she was surprised he'd not heard her walking down the hallway. Then she'd laid eyes on him, and everything had settled into a dull ache.

"Your coffers are empty," she said quietly, but still he must have heard her because his head came up swiftly, and if ever there was a person who looked guilty, it was he.

Shoving back his chair, he rose to his full height, reached for his jacket draped over the back of the chair, and shrugged into it with one smooth movement. "Minerva, what a pleasant surprise. I wasn't expecting you."

Walking toward him, she was amazed that her legs retained the strength to propel her forward. "Your coffers are empty."

He arched a brow. "Is that a question?"

Stopping before the desk, she ran her gaze over

him, his perfect bone structure, his perfectly proportioned features. She'd wondered why he'd begun giving her attention, and he'd made her believe that her imperfections didn't matter. "Are your coffers empty?"

"Nearly so, yes. How did you learn of it?"

At least he hadn't lied, denied it. She'd give him that. "At my seamstress's of all places. Apparently someone heard from someone else . . . you know how it goes. There are no secrets among the aristocracy. Why didn't you tell me?"

"I didn't see that it made a difference."

She stared at him. "Not make a difference? How could it not? You need my dowry."

"Just because my coffers are bare does not mean I was in pursuit of your dowry."

She jutted up her chin. "Are you saying it wasn't a consideration?"

Somberly, he said, "No."

That simple word deflated her. She looked at the papers strewn over his desk, columns of numbers neatly laid out in contrast to the disarray in which the ledgers were arranged. She spied a blue corner peering out, a familiar blue. Snatching it up, at the sight of the painstakingly written *A Lady's Guide to Ferreting Out Fortune Hunters*, she was aware of her soul crumbling. The edges were worn, the spine cracked—the usual sign of a book well loved, well read. Well studied. She flipped through the pages. He'd even made notes in the margins.

She raised her eyes to his. "I thought I was providing information to the ladies. Instead, I provided you with the strategy on how not to get caught."

"This doesn't change anything, Minerva."

"It changes everything. You needn't bother to speak with my father this evening. I have no intention of marrying you now."

"I don't see why not."

"You deceived me."

"I'm certain there are things about yourself you've not told me."

"Nothing as bad as this. You wasted your inheritance. You traveled the world, sought out pleasures, while your estates languished. Did you think there would be no consequences to your unbridled spending, to your failure to take responsibility?"

"I'm taking responsibility now."

"It's too late. I will not marry a man I cannot respect, and I cannot respect a man who allows his financial situation to get to this state"—she swept her hand over the desk—"and then expects a lady's dowry to undo the damage." She was not a woman who cried, and yet she felt the sting of tears. "You should have been honest with me, Ashebury."

Turning on her heel, she headed for the doorway. She'd nearly reached it when his voice echoed around her, through her. Full of confidence, warning, and victory.

"I'm not certain you're in a position to deny me . . . Lady V."

ASHE was angry at the accusations she'd thrown out at him. What did she know of his struggles, of how he'd come to be in his position? Why did she discount his feelings for her just because he was in need of her dowry?

Spinning around, she glared at him. "Are you threatening me with blackmail? Do you really think I'm the sort to be intimidated by such poppycock? What passed between us doesn't change anything. I won't marry you."

He strode across the room, stopping only when he was near enough to smell the verbena. "I'm certain your father will feel very differently when he learns that I deflowered you."

"It will be your word against mine."

If she didn't look at him with such loathing in the depths of her brown eyes, he might have let her go, but she'd stung his pride. "Truly? Because all of London knows about the heart-shaped birthmark at the bottom of your right hip? Even with your skirts on, I can lay my finger unerringly against it. What will he say then?"

"He won't force me to marry a man I have no desire to marry."

"And what will London say when they find out that the prim and proper Miss Dodger visited the Nightingale Club three times?"

"You won't divulge that. They'll kick you out. You'll never be welcomed there again."

"What need will I have for the Nightingale when I have a wife to satisfy all my baser needs?"

"You're mad if you think I'd welcome you into my bed."

"You're too sensual a creature to not welcome me, to deny yourself the pleasure I can bring you."

"Arrogant prig."

He gave her one of his more devilish smiles, designed to conquer a woman's heart. "Don't be a fool, Minerva. Yes, I need your dowry to set my financial matters to rights, but that doesn't mean that things can't be good between us. Things *are* good between us. The Nightingale proved that." Before she could react, he grabbed her, drew her in close, and slanted his mouth over hers, determined to remind her of the passion that flared so easily between them, to spark her desire, to—

The pain hit low, hard, sharp, and doubled him over. His knees slammed to the floor, the rest of him smashed against it, and he curled into a fetal position, fighting to catch his breath.

"I will not marry a man I cannot love," she stated flatly, "a man who does not love me."

Through his watering eyes, all he saw were her skirts and the heels of her shoes as she made her way out of his library, out of his life.

Chapter 19

SHE refused to cry. The stinging in her eyes was the result of London's wretched air, not her heart's breaking.

"I am going to take out an advert in the *Times* announcing that I will never marry and am no longer entertaining suitors."

After returning home, she'd joined her parents in the library. They stared at her following her announcement while she merely tossed back the scotch she'd poured for herself after entering the room.

"Has something happened?" her mother asked.

"I misjudged Ashebury's affections."

"How far did you misjudge them?" her father asked, eyes narrowed. She knew his anger wasn't directed at her.

"Far enough that he might think you will force me to marry him. But I will not, under any circumstances, marry him."

Her father stood. "Difficult to marry a dead man."

"Sit down, Father."

He narrowed his eyes further.

"Please."

He dropped down onto the sofa beside her mother, who placed her hand over his balled fist, resting on his thigh.

"I did something I ought not," Minerva said, "which I will not elaborate on. I don't regret it. I simply regret that I allowed my judgment to be impaired. I thought he wanted me, but as it turns out, he needs my dowry. I can see now that whenever I asked after his finances, he didn't give me a direct answer. So I was a fool."

"You weren't a fool," her mother said kindly. "He's very charming. It's understandable that you would like him and trust him. It's also understandable that being raised as he was, he might not fully comprehend love."

Minerva shook her head. "Don't make excuses for his behavior. All of London makes excuses for the hellions. None of us has a perfect life. We make the best of it."

"What's not perfect in yours?" her father asked.

"No man loves me."

"I love you."

The air was getting worse. The damn tears were threatening. "I shall be content with that."

"Taking out an advert seems a bit excessive," her mother said.

"I don't want any gentleman callers."

"I shall inform the staff."

"I especially don't want to see Ashebury."

"You won't," her father said.

"Neither do I want him dead."

"Bruised?"

She couldn't help it. She released a light laugh. "No, although I do believe I left him bruised."

"Left hook?"

"No. A little trick Lovingdon taught me. He'd be proud. I would tell him about it, but then he'd threaten to kill Ashebury, and I can't hold you both at bay."

"Perhaps you and I should go on holiday somewhere," her mother said.

"I have something else in mind. I'll share once I've worked out the details. But rest assured, I'm not going to mope about here. I intend to take steps to ensure that I never again cross paths with Ashebury or any other fortune hunter."

THE winds shrieking over the moors buffeted the coach as it turned onto the long drive leading to Havisham Hall. Ashe couldn't claim to have a sense of going home, but he did experience a bit of bittersweet nostalgia at the gloominess settling in that would soon cloak the moors in moon-shadowed darkness. Profound sadness had visited him here, but he'd also known some of his happier moments.

The Marquess of Marsden had not been a particularly attentive guardian, but neither had he neglected his charges. He would join them at meals, telling them tales of his youth, ones that included Ashe's father as well as the Earl of Greyling. Through Marsden, Ashe had been given insights into his father as he would have never envisioned him: a rabble-rouser, a student who struggled with his studies, a lad who enjoyed a good prank.

Sometimes, when the wind was quiet, Ashe would catch a glimpse of the man the marquess had been before he lost his wife in childbirth, before he stopped all the clocks at the precise moment of her death. To love a woman such as that—Ashe didn't know if it would be a blessing or a curse.

The coach drew to a stop in front of the manor house that no longer seemed as large and foreboding as it had to his eight-year-old self. He knew the rooms, the hallways, the shadowed corners as well as he knew his own hand. No one emerged to greet him, but then he wasn't a guest. He was family of sorts. Comfortable here, he bounded up the steps and through the front door. Silence greeted him. The clocks still didn't tick, didn't move forward, didn't mark time.

Candles flickered to light the way. He strode down the familiar hall, glancing in through doorways as he went, not surprised that he didn't find an occupied room until he reached the library. A single flame on a waxed taper set on the ebony desk revealed the bent head of Viscount Locksley as he made notations in a ledger. He glanced up, smiled.

"Ashe, what the devil? You should have let me know you were coming."

He shoved himself away from the desk and met Ashe halfway, shaking his hand, clapping him on the shoulder. "What brings you here?"

That discussion was for later. "How's your father?"

"Mad as ever." Turning away, Locke crossed over to the sideboard and splashed scotch into two glasses. He handed one to Ashe. "He's sleeping now. He'll enjoy seeing you tomorrow." He sat in a chair before a lazy fire, stretched out his legs. "Bored with London already? Planning our next adventure?"

Ashe took the chair opposite him. "Planning mine at least. I'm thinking perhaps it's time I married."

"Good God. What's brought this on?"

He wasn't ready to confess. "We're getting up in years."

"We're not even thirty."

"I'm closer than you are." By two years.

"But not there yet." With a blunt-tipped finger, he tapped his tumbler, considering, his green eyes penetrating. Locke had always been the watcher of the group, taking his time, considering all angles, knocking down façades. Perhaps because he'd been cursed with having to witness his father's gradual decline into madness.

Ashe supposed that was an advantage to not having his parents about. He didn't have to witness their aging and infirmity. Although their sudden departure had very nearly destroyed him. While he didn't want to trade places with Locke, he had no luck squelching that little spark of envy because Locke could at least still talk with his father.

"Who's the woman?" Locke asked solemnly.

"Miss Minerva Dodger."

Locke gave a low whistle. "You'll live like a prince off the money she brings into the marriage."

"She's more than coin."

A corner of Locke's mouth hitched up. "Is she? I don't recall you having much interest in her before. Has she suddenly transformed into a fetching skirt?"

"Why is everyone so consumed with looks? And why can they not see the beauty in her?"

Locke's smile grew, until it almost resembled one of childish wonder. "You're in love with her."

"What? No. She intrigues me is all. She's bold as brass and can stand toe to toe with any man. She states her mind. She doesn't back down. It's refreshing."

"Refreshing for now, she might be, but she'll grow stale over the years with her nag, nag, nagging. Bold women determined to speak their mind have a tendency to irritate after a while."

"Is that based on your extensive experience with women? When have you ever stayed with one for more than a night?" Ashe downed the remainder of his scotch, then rose to refill his glass. "More?"

"No, I have to finish going over the books tonight."

Ashe looked over his shoulder. "Everything all right?"

"With the estate? Absolutely. No troubles there."

Ashe reclaimed his seat. "How do you keep your finances in such good order?"

"It's not as though my father is a spendthrift. A butler, a cook, a housemaid, a footman to manage this monstrosity."

"Not all of it is managed."

"No, only the rooms in which we live. The others are left untouched. God knows we could probably plant seeds in the dust that's accumulated over the years and have a bountiful harvest."

"That'll change when you take a wife."

"I'll never marry. Madness is not a legacy to pass on."

"It'll end with your father. You're not mad."

"Maybe I'm simply better at covering it up." He sipped his scotch, once again studying Ashe. "You're not yet betrothed, so no exciting news there. I'm still trying to determine what prompted your visit."

"Wanted to ensure you were all right. You left rather abruptly when we got off the ship."

"We were gone longer than I'd planned. Needed to make sure all was in order here."

"Are you coming to London for what remains of the Season?"

"I don't think so." He stood. "I need to finish up. Shall we go riding tomorrow?"

"First thing. I'd like that."

"Good." He started walking toward the desk. "You can tell me then why you're really here."

*W*HY was he here? Ashe wasn't even certain he knew. The quietness in the house as he wandered about was eerie. The absence of the ticking of clocks making it more so. When he was a lad, he would sleep with his father's watch beneath the pillow just so there was something other then the winds howling about. He'd found the pocket watch resting on the table beside his father's bed. It was strange that it had been left behind, and sometimes Ashe wondered if his father had had a premonition about what would happen. But if he had, why hadn't he left himself and his duchess behind instead of just the watch?

He stepped into a long hallway, where only one door stood slightly ajar, a pale finger of light slicing along the floor. Even knowing he should turn back to avoid upsetting the old man, he carried forward and walked into the bedchamber that smelled of bergamot and lavender. He thought perhaps the marquess kept lavender sachets around the residence, because there were pockets of the scent in the air here and there. In the marchioness's bedchamber—which hadn't been touched since the night she died, other than to remove any evidence of her death—on the vanity had stood a bottle of lavender perfume. Ashe knew because he and the others had snuck into the room one night, even knowing it was forbidden. Grey and Edward had gotten into one of their usual shoving matches. When Grey had pushed Edward into the table, the bottle had toppled over onto the floor and broken into a thousand shards. The sound had brought Marsden into the bedchamber.

He'd been furious at their intrusion. It was the only time that he had ever punished them. In the library, he'd lined them up, made them drop their trousers and grab the back of their knees. He'd taken a switch to each of them, repeatedly, determinedly, and harshly. Until his arm grew tired, until he dropped into a chair, and wept. Huge, gut-wrenching sobs that had hurt Ashe more than the switch slapping against his backside.

After that, the door to his wife's bedchamber had been locked. Not that Ashe had any desire to return to it. He'd never again wanted to make the marquess weep with such soul-crushing despair.

But still, at nine, he'd offered the man no comfort. With the others he'd stood there, stared, and shifted his feet in discomfiture as the marquess grieved the loss of a fragrance. Not until he grew into manhood did he fully realize the man was grieving the loss of so much more.

"Ashe," the marquess rasped, as though his vocal cords had grown tired.

"My lord," he said, walking farther into the room until he reached the cushioned chair where Marsden sat in front of the window. He pressed his shoulder into the casement, welcoming the support, the sharp bite of the wood. The marquess's hair was stringy, unkempt, the white strands brushing his shoulders. White stubble dotted his jaw. He had no valet, but someone had shaved him recently. Probably Locke.

His dressing gown was threadbare and faded. Ashe wished he'd thought to bring the man a new one from London. Not that he would have worn it. He didn't like the unfamiliar.

"She's out there tonight, waiting for me," Marsden said, his fingers trailing over the small, framed painting resting in his lap. "Do you hear her?"

"Yes, my lord."

"I'll join her soon. When Locke is happy." He grinned slightly, his green eyes boring into Ashe. "When you are. When Greyling and Edward are. How are they?"

"They're well, my lord. In London."

"Why aren't you?"

Ashe looked out into the darkness. He thought he'd needed to see Locke. He was wrong. "You loved her very much."

"No."

Surprised by the answer, Ashe shifted his gaze back to the marquess, who was shaking his head.

"That does not even begin to describe what I felt for her. What I felt was . . . everything. When she was no more, everything was gone."

"In all my years here, you never told us about her. What was she like?"

A faraway look came into Marsden's eyes as though he were traveling back through the years. "She was the moon and stars. The sun and rain. I did not like her as much as I liked the way I was when I was with her. I was optimistic, invincible. Kinder, gentler. She brought out the best in me. Does she bring out the best in you?"

Ashe wrinkled his brow. "Who?"

"This woman you love."

He stared at the marquess. His eyes held knowledge, understanding. "I don't love her, but there is a woman, yes. She's sharp, clever, strong-minded. I need her dowry. I made rather a mess of my fortune." He pressed his shoulder harder into the sharp edge of the casement. "I can't make numbers work."

"Neither could your father."

Ashe straightened away from the window edge. "Pardon?"

Marsden chuckled low. "It was his secret. But he told me. Was fearful he wouldn't be able to manage his estates. So he would bring me his books, and I would provide him with the answers. I forgot that. All the years you were here, I never thought to tell you. Never paid any attention to your studies. Damnation," he whispered. "That's why he selected me. To be your guardian. I knew his secret. He thought I would guide you. Instead, I failed you."

"I wouldn't say that. If anything, it was my pride, not letting on that I was struggling. Relying too much on my man of business, when I wasn't completely open with him. I need to find someone I can trust to know everything." If he could convince Minerva to put *her* pride aside, she would make an excellent person to manage his accounts.

Marsden waved a finger. "Locke, he's your man."

Ashe wasn't convinced. Quite possibly what he needed was a woman.

THE horse's hooves thundering beneath him, Ashe rode hell-bent for leather over the moors, with Locke riding along beside him, his gelding keeping pace. Being out here brought forth memories of running wild, of spending days doing whatever he pleased, never worrying about estates, income, salaries, upkeep, expenses. Numbers, figures, tallies.

"Enough!" Locke yelled, bringing his horse to a halt.

Ashe drew his up short, circled about, and guided the black back to where Locke waited on a white. Heaving, the beasts' nostrils flared, created puffs of smoke in the early-morning gloom.

"Let's walk for a bit, shall we?" Locke asked, dismounting before Ashe had even given his answer. Locke might be merely a viscount and younger than Ashe, but this was his home, and he'd always reigned here, knowing that one day he would be master of it all. There was something to be said for growing up on the ancestral estate. It created an immense sense of appreciation, of understanding one's place and responsibilities. Those had come late to Ashe.

Probably to Grey as well. And never to Edward, as second son.

Holding the reins, he fell into step beside Locke, their long strides stirring the fog that lay low over the moors. Locke didn't harangue, it wasn't his way. Still, Ashe knew he was waiting for Ashe to speak first.

"I moved into Ashebury Place," he finally said.

"Put the ghosts to rest? That's good."

"It's more that I couldn't afford to pay the lease on the other place. Edward's taken it over." Reaching down, he plucked up a tall blade of grass for no other reason than it gave him a moment to collect his thoughts. "I'm in a bad way financially."

"Hence the decision to marry Miss Minerva Dodger."

Ashe gave a curt nod. "Unfortunately, she doesn't fancy fortune hunters and is rather put out with me at the moment for failing to acknowledge—or at least reveal to her—my impoverished state. She refuses to marry me even though . . ." He grabbed another sprig of grass.

"Even though?" Locke prodded.

"I compromised her."

Locke stopped walking, grabbed his arm, and spun him around. "On purpose?"

Ashe glowered. "Well, I certainly didn't accidentally fall into bed with her."

Locke sighed with annoyance. "You know what

I meant. Did you compromise her to force her into marriage?"

"No, I bedded her simply because I wanted to. I desired her as I have desired no other. Locke, she visited the Nightingale."

The viscount's green eyes widened, disbelief crossing his rugged features, but Ashe knew whatever was said here on the moors stayed on the moors. "Indeed?"

"That's where she first came to my attention as desirable. She had decided to accept spinsterhood and thought she had nothing to lose. She quite charmed me." He shook his head. "Charmed is too tame a word. She's bold, courageous, goes after what she wants. She's unlike any woman I've ever encountered. Why I failed to notice her before is beyond me. Why no man has taken her to wife simply demonstrates the foolhardiness of men. She is remarkable. So I began courting her through traditional means, within Society, at balls and such. She was agreeable to marrying me, and then she discovered I had no coins lining my coffers, and told me to go to the devil. My courtship was wasted."

"I don't see the dilemma," Locke said and began striding forward again. "You simply need to begin courting a woman who doesn't care that you want her for her dowry, one who is enamored of your title and good looks. Shouldn't take overly long for you to snag another fish."

"You're right. I just need to find another dowry. It's disappointing is all, after all the effort I put into the courtship and gaining her willingness." And they were very good together in bed. He didn't know if he'd ever been so well matched. He regretted that he wouldn't have that. Or her smiles or her humility. "I'm not usually one to give up on a hunt, but I don't know how I can make things right with her."

"What if she had no dowry?" Locke asked.

"Pardon?"

"Miss Minerva Dodger. What if she had no dowry? You wouldn't have gone after her, you wouldn't be disappointed. You'd have never known what you were missing."

"But I do know, that's the hell of it." He wanted to slam his fist into something, but there was nothing within miles except for his horse, which he would not abuse, and Locke, who wasn't deserving of a fist to the face. "I know how stubborn she can be. How magnanimous. I know she can tear a lady down if she set her mind to it, but she sets her mind to not doing it. She could win a fight in a boxing ring. She smells of verbena. She's brazen in the bedchamber. And she's smart. Incredibly smart. She devises investment opportunities. She thinks like a man, which common sense tells me should make her unattractive, but all it does is make me want her all the more."

"You've fallen in love with her."

"No, no. I just—" He spun around, paced three steps one way, three the other. It was just that he adored her. Every inch. From the top of her head, to the tips of her toes, inside and out. He adored the challenge of her. He adored the times when he was with her. He liked talking to her, listening to her opinions. He liked that she had opinions. He liked everything about her, even her stubborn belief that she deserved a man who loved her. He stopped pacing, removed his hat, and tunneled his fingers through his hair. "I may very well have, yes. But she's not going to believe it. I can pen love letters, write poems describing my feelings. She's not going to believe them. Not when no man before me has ever wanted anything other than the fortune that comes with her."

"Then I ask you again, what if she had no dowry?"

"If she has no dowry, then I remain an impoverished lord."

Locke met and held Ashe's gaze, his intense green eyes reflecting a myriad of questions, the possibilities of answers.

Ashe looked out over the moors. "But if I asked for her hand in marriage under those circumstances, she would have no choice except to believe, to understand, that I wanted *her*."

"Well, then, that seems simple enough, doesn't it? I'll race you home."

Locke mounted and was off, before Ashe completed deliberating all the consequences of what he was considering. With a laugh, he climbed into the saddle, urged his horse into a frenzied gallop, and sprinted after the man who fate had deemed would become one of his brothers.

Chapter 20

"Mr. Dodger."

"Ashebury." Off Jack Dodger's tongue, the name sounded like an insult. Not that Ashe blamed him. On the way back from Havisham, he'd given a lot of thought as to how to approach the former gambling-house owner. He'd been surprised that the butler had shown him into the man's library. He was grateful that Minerva, as of yet, didn't know he'd come to call. "You're a brave man to show up here after breaking my daughter's heart."

"It was not my intention to break her heart."

"Yet you did it all the same. I've killed men for less."

"Not recently I hope."

A corner of his mouth shifted up. Minerva had not inherited the shape of her mouth from her father. Perhaps her mother. Otherwise, it was all hers. "Whiskey?"

At least Ashe was assured he'd live long enough for a drink. "I'm a scotch man."

"I think I have some on hand."

Ashe watched as Dodger poured scotch into two tumblers. There was nothing delicate in his movements, nothing polished. Every inch of him spoke of a man who had begun his life in the streets. He might have risen above them, but they still clung to him.

He turned toward Ashe and extended a glass. "Have a seat."

"I prefer to stand."

"I prefer to sit." He dropped into the chair behind his desk, took a sip of his scotch, studied Ashe. "So why did you come?"

"To ask you to take away Minerva's dowry."

Arching a brow, Dodger slowly set his glass on the desk. "It's not often I misjudge a man's purpose in meeting with me. I must say your request has taken me by surprise. Why would I not honor my promise to provide her with a dowry?"

"Because it will always come between us. Because she will always doubt the reason I married her."

"I don't recall giving you permission to marry her."

"But you will because her happiness means everything to you."

"And you'll make her happy?"

"Ecstatically so. But she has been hounded by fortune hunters, and she believes it is her dowry that drew me to her."

"And it wasn't?"

"No."

"What was?"

Ashe wondered if, when he heard the answer, Jack Dodger would break his jaw or blacken his eye. He was likely to do both. "Her legs."

"And how is it that you happened to see her legs?"

"That's between her and me. Her legs drew me, but her boldness, her spunk, her cleverness, her character held me. She is quite simply the most remarkable woman I've ever known. I love her. Beyond all imagining, beyond any capacity that I thought I had to love. But she will always doubt my veracity if, when she gives me her hand, it holds a pouch of coins."

"Her dowry is much more than a pouch, boy."

"I'm well aware. It was a figure of speech."

"I've made inquiries. I know your financial situation. She'll do without."

"Never. I can sell a good many of the treasures that I amassed during my travels. They'll provide us with a tidy sum. Not as much as her dowry, but it gives us a start. Working together, we can build it into something grand for our children. I want her to be my partner. Equal."

"To come to you with nothing?"

"Dear God, how can you possibly believe there is any part of her that is equal to *nothing*?"

Ashe saw newfound respect and admiration enter Jack Dodger's dark eyes, eyes he'd passed on to his daughter, and he knew on this matter at least, he'd won.

MINERVA was sitting in the morning room scribbling down an array of notes when her parents entered.

"We'd like to have a word," her mother said.

"Now is an absolutely perfect time as I need to speak with you as well. I've given it a good deal of thought, and I've decided to go to Texas to look more closely into this cattle venture that I want to convince the fellows is worth investing in with me. I've worked it all out. I'll hire a companion and—"

"Minerva," her mother said, settling onto the sofa beside her while her father took a nearby chair. "Texas is so far away."

"I'm not moving there forever. I shall be home by Christmas. It's just that based on my numbers, it's a wonderful opportunity to branch out, to not be so dependent upon what we can earn here in Britain."

"You'll have to talk with your father about that. He's the one with the head for business."

She looked at the man lounging in the chair as though he hadn't a care in the world. Jack Dodger had never been one for formality. "Would you be interested in investing, Father?"

"Will it make money?"

"It should, yes. A good deal, as a matter of fact."

"I'll think about it, but first I need to speak with you about a decision I've made—with your mother's blessing."

She released a laugh that didn't sound quite like herself. "All right, but you both look so deadly serious. Has something happened?"

"In a manner of speaking, yes," her father said. "I've decided to rescind the offer of a dowry."

It felt as though he'd punched her. "Why?"

"Well, for one thing, you said you weren't going to marry, so it's not as though you need it."

"That's true enough. Don't suppose you'll see your way clear to loan me some money so I can invest in this cattle venture I'm so set on?"

He waved a hand. "If you want it, you can have it. I'm talking only about your dowry." Leaning forward, he planted his elbows on his thighs. "I may have done you a disservice by offering it, by making it so large. I'm afraid men haven't been able to see beyond it to you."

"We don't like the notion of your not marrying," her mother said. "Of being alone."

"I'm not alone. I have friends. And I have family. I don't need a husband to complete my life. So take the dowry. I have no problem with that. It's not as though a man will marry me without it. And I don't want to marry a man who"—she swallowed hard, the words difficult to say—"needs it."

"Like Ashebury?" her mother asked.

"Like any number of men," Minerva said impatiently. "As for Ashebury, I'm quite over him."

Smiling, her mother squeezed her hand. "I'm glad to hear that, as he's joining us for dinner this evening."

Traitor was her first thought, but she didn't voice it aloud. After all this was her mother, the woman who had brought her into the world. "You can't be serious."

"I thought it would be nice to hear about his travels to Africa."

Unbelievable. Minerva scoffed. "If you want to hear about Africa, invite one of the other hellions. But I see no reason to burden us with a deceiver such as Ashebury."

"Yet Ashebury is here, isn't he." It was a statement, not a question.

Minerva had heard through the grapevine that Ashebury had left the city. "You mean in London?"

"No, well, he's in the residence, so he's technically in London. He's waiting in your father's library."

Minerva leaped to her feet and glared at her father. "You let him in? You welcomed him? Knowing that I despise the man, that I find him despicable?"

"He brought his photographs," her mother said as though that made everything all right. Why were mothers—including hers—so willing to forgive the hellions all sorts of bad behavior?

"He will not be staying for dinner." In a rush, she pushed past her mother and headed for the door. "He will not!"

"I don't think she's as over him as she thought," she heard her father say. She seldom was out of sorts with her parents, but at that moment, she was furious. She was not only going to travel to Texas, she was going to move there.

Seething, she marched down the hallway. How

dare he show up here! In her home, in her sanctuary.

The library doorway was open. She swept through and staggered to a stop at the sight of him standing at the window. He looked awful, completely, absolutely awful. As though he'd gone without sleep, as though he'd lost weight.

Yet at the same time he somehow managed to look wonderful, completely, absolutely wonderful. Immaculately groomed, his clothing pressed to perfection, everything in order. And he smelled wonderful. Sandalwood mixed with his own unique scent. She had not stopped as soon as she should have because she was near enough that she was able to detect its presence, could see the crystal blue of his eyes, could see not a whisker. He'd shaved before he came over.

"So I understand you've been invited to dinner," she said tartly.

"It was kind of your mother to ask."

"I'm rescinding the invitation."

"I thought that you might."

"If you were any gentleman at all, you wouldn't have accepted it."

"Except that I wanted to see you more than I wanted to be a gentleman."

She slammed her eyes closed. "Don't." Opening her eyes, she glared at him. "Don't say all the right things that are designed to make a woman lose her head. They won't work on me, and they are a total waste. I've just been informed that my father has withdrawn my dowry, so you will need to search elsewhere for your funds."

"I know about the state of your dowry," he said quietly. "I asked him to take it away."

In confusion she shook her head. "Why would you do that?"

"Because as long as you had it, you wouldn't believe that it was possible that I wanted you more than I wanted the fortune."

"But you need the fortune."

"I need you more."

"You can't mean that. Your estates, your legacy—"

"Can go the devil." He grimaced, shook his head. "They won't. I'll make sure they don't. You were wrong when you said that I didn't care about my responsibilities, that I squandered my inheritance. The estates were not bringing in the income they once were, so I made some investments that, unfortunately, proved to be unwise." He walked to the desk, placed a slip of paper at its edge, picked up her father's pen, dipped in an inkwell, and held it toward her. "Write down three numbers, small ones, in a vertical line that I can tally."

"I don't see what this has to do with anything."

"Just do it. Please."

With an impatient sigh, she walked to the desk, snatched the pen from between his fingers, and redipped the pen in the inkwell. She looked at him askance. "You seem to have recovered from my knee's causing you to double over."

"I'm surprised you were able to maneuver so well."

"I'd left my petticoats at the dressmaker, so I had more room to maneuver. I was hoping for a chance to deliver a decisive blow."

"You're a bloodthirsty wench."

"You shouldn't be surprised. I told you that first night that I would take joy in killing a man who hurt me."

"So you did. Three numbers."

She did as he requested.

5
7
9

Putting a finger on the edge of the paper, he dragged it closer to himself and stared at it. Closed his eyes. Opened them. Squinted. "I can't tally them. In my head, all I see is chaos. I know they are numbers. I know they form a sum. But I can't understand them. And I can't explain why I have such trouble with them. Lord Marsden told me my father was the same way. Numbers made no sense to him. He trusted Marsden. I only found out a few days ago when I went to Havisham. I've been too proud to admit that I have this difficulty. So when my man of business gathered information on various investments, I had him explain the risks verbally, I listened to his recommendations, and I made what I thought were the best choices. What he considered an acceptable risk, had I been able to analyze the numbers, I might not have. When I returned to England, I discovered the investments were losing money and, with very little income at my disposal and a ghastly amount of upkeep needed on my estates, I had very little left in my coffers."

"How can you not understand numbers?"

"I'm at a loss, Minerva. Although I feel stupid, I'm not. I master other things. But numbers baffle me."

She sighed. "So you lost your fortune and decided you needed to marry a woman with a substantial dowry. And you pursued me."

"Not exactly. I met a woman at the Nightingale who intrigued me. Then I discovered her at a party and was further taken with her. The fact that she had a dowry hardly mattered. I wanted to get to know her. Then I fell in love with her. I didn't realize it until she walked out on me."

With his declaration, Minerva's heart slammed against her ribs. She had longed for a declaration of love, and yet she was hesitant to believe them. He'd studied her book. He knew the correct things to say. But she couldn't quite bring herself to toss them back into his face. Rather, she needed to remind him of the reality of the situation. "Except now she doesn't have a dowry."

He grinned. "But she knows how to invest. I have a little capital. Whether or not she marries me, I want her to help me rebuild my fortune."

"Perhaps we could stop talking about her as though she weren't in the room?"

His smile grew. "Will you help me figure out what I need to do to get back on my feet?"

"I suppose I could see my way clear to do that."

"When I have no need of a dowry, will you marry me?"

She cradled his jaw. "Ashe—"

"Tell me what I must do to convince you that I love you."

"I want to believe you. It just seems too incredible to me that someone like you could love me."

"Because you don't see yourself as I do. Here, I want to show you something." He reached into his pocket, withdrew a small rectangle, and handed it to her.

It was a photograph of a woman sitting near a pond. Her face revealed such strength, such character, such invincibility, and yet there was a vulnerability to her as well, a delicateness—

It took Minerva a moment to realize that it was her, the photo he'd taken of her beside Lovingdon's pond. "I'm actually quite pretty. How did you manage to make me look pretty?"

"You are pretty. You're more than pretty. But I used shadows and light to reveal what I see when I look at you. True beauty can't exist without both."

"What about the photo you took of me at the Nightingale?"

"I didn't take it."

"Why?"

"Because it was just for me. Sometimes, something is just so perfect . . . perfect isn't the right word. It's more than that. Transcendent. It feels as though it would be a sin to capture it. But whenever I think of charred remains or mangled bodies . . . I think of you, with your long legs and your small feet, stretched out on the bed waiting for me—it overpowers the images that have lived with me for so long. It makes them nothing. They fade away quietly, no longer screaming for attention because they won't get it, as I have something so much better. Or at least I did before I botched things up. I had you, Minerva. And I desperately want to have you again."

She, who never cried, was feeling those burning tears once again. "Ashe—"

"I can make do without a dowry. I can't make do without you. Even if you don't love *me*—"

"I do! I tried not to, but I can't stop thinking about you, missing you, wanting you. Yet I'm afraid that these feelings aren't real. The love we both claim. What if it's pretense, like Lady V?"

"She's not pretense. She's simply another part of you. Minerva, almost from the beginning, I knew who you were. Everything we had at the Nightingale, we'll continue to have. Everything we had outside the Nightingale, we'll continue to have. We'll have it all."

And she believed him. The truth was there in his eyes, in the way he smiled at her. "I love you, Ashe."

The look he gave her melted her heart. It was the sort of look for which she'd waited six Seasons. It was the sort of look that promised an eternity of happiness. "Although I'd rather marry sooner than later."

"How does the end of the month suit you?" he asked.

"People will think we were forced to marry."

"We were—because we couldn't stand to go a night longer without each other." He drew her in close. "Keep the knee down."

Before she could assure him, she would, he took her mouth and kissed her as only a man who was in love with her could.

Chapter 21

Miss Minerva Dodger's upcoming marriage to the Duke of Ashebury was the talk of London. Especially as it became evident whenever they were seen together that they were madly in love. Minerva, who usually hated the gossip rags, suddenly found herself enjoying them very much.

But more, she'd enjoyed preparing for her wedding. She wasn't at all nervous that it was almost time for her to head to the church. Rather, she studied her reflection in the cheval glass, loving the way that her gown of white Honiton lace and pearls molded to her body. Orange blossoms circled the crown of her veil, holding it in place. Wearing the gold anklet, she jangled just a tiny bit when she walked.

"You look beautiful, Minerva," Grace said as she adjusted the train.

"I do rather, don't I? I knew love was worth waiting for."

"I told you that you would find a man who loved you."

"I still have a difficult time believing it some-times."

"But you're happy."

"Immeasurably so."

A knock sounded on the door. Grace opened it, and Minerva's father walked in.

"Fathers need a moment with their daughters on their wedding day. I'll be waiting downstairs," Grace said before slipping out of the room.

"You're as beautiful as your mother," he said.

Minerva gave him a teasing smile. "I always thought I more closely resembled you."

"You have my dark eyes, but other than that, you are your mother."

"I have your head for business."

"But you have her backbone. Are you sure you want to marry him?"

"Very sure. I love him, and he's not going to like this, but I want my dowry back. I was so busy searching for someone to love me, to prove he loved me, that I didn't realize it was enough that I loved him. I don't want him to have to sell his treasures or be burdened unnecessarily because his investments didn't pan out. I know he loves me with or without my dowry, but more importantly, I love him. I want him to have the funds you promised."

"They're already in his bank account. It's your wedding present. I intended for you to find out in a few days when his man of business pays him a visit to give him a report on his finances."

In spite of the fact that she might wrinkle her gown, she wrapped her arms around her father's shoulders and hugged him tightly. "I love you so much."

"Always remember, Minerva, I was the man who loved you first."

"I know." The tears fell, and she didn't bother to stop them.

"Don't cry. I can't stand it when a woman cries."

With a laugh, she shoved away from him. "I know that as well."

He turned away, but not before she saw dampness in his eyes. "Let's get on with it," he said. "It's not every day I give my daughter away."

"You're not giving her away. She's still yours."

With a smile, he glanced back. "That she is. That she will always be." Reaching toward her, he lowered her veil over her face. "Lucky man, him and me."

Lucky girl, she thought, to have the love of two incredible men.

THE wedding was grand, more than Minerva had ever expected. The church was packed, the reception following well attended. Ashe had looked so handsome standing at the altar. The expression on his face as she neared—how had she ever thought that he didn't love her?

Now she waited in her bedchamber for him to come to her. The gaslights burned low, chasing away the shadows. She wore a silk nightdress, the gold around her ankle, and—

The door opened. Her breath caught at the sight of her husband in a silk dressing gown. He looked at her. Laughed.

"Oh, no, we're not having that."

She couldn't stop herself from smiling as he strode across the room. Reaching behind her head, he untied the ribbons and tossed the mask aside. "That's better," he murmured, just before taking possession of her mouth.

They'd managed to sneak in a handful of kisses during the past month, but she had wanted to wait for more until their wedding night. Now they would have all the time in the world to be in each other's arms. He peppered kisses over her face, along her throat. She sighed, whimpered.

"My wife," he murmured.

"Your wife."

He stepped back, untied the sash on his dressing gown, and shrugged out of it. Her breath caught at the sight of him, her mouth went dry. "I'm going to learn how to use your camera."

He grinned. "Not tonight."

He walked over to the bed, climbed onto it, and sat back against the headboard, his arms behind his head.

"What are you doing?"

"Take off the nightdress . . . slowly. I want to watch the light touch every inch of you."

"Do you?" she asked, as she sauntered nearer to the side of the bed. She was amazed she could be this comfortable with him on her wedding night. On the other hand, it wasn't as though she was a virgin. Very slowly, she released a button. Then another, another, watching as his eyes darkened into a smoldering haze, his body tightened, his breathing shortened. When the last button was released, she skimmed her finger along her torso between her breasts. His breath caught.

Oh, she liked having this power. She eased the cloth off one shoulder, slipped it off the other. The silk slowly glided down.

He growled, low and feral, before moving swiftly, capturing her, and rolling her onto the bed until she was on her back, and he was pressed against her side, raised up on an elbow, gazing down on her. "You have no idea how badly I've wanted to see you in light. When we go to the estate, I'm going to take you out to a field, where the sunlight can shine down on you, and I shall make wild, passionate love to you there."

"Outside?"

"We're going to make love everywhere: in the forests, in the rain, in every room, every building." He skimmed his hand along her side. "I love you, Minerva."

"I shall never tire of your saying that."

"Good. I intend to say it every day."

"I love you, Ashe. I can't believe how much. I didn't know it was possible to love this deeply."

He lowered his mouth to hers, and she allowed everything she felt for him to bubble up as passion consumed them in a conflagration that she feared might leave them both scorched. How was it that there could be so many various sensations coming together to create a marvelous journey into pleasure?

As they touched, kissed, stroked, caressed, the fire that had always been between them built, higher, wider, stronger. Their movements became frenzied, their needs overwhelming. When she thought she would go mad with wanting, he plunged into her, hard, deep. Her body closed around him, held him tightly.

Lifting himself above her, he gazed down on her, pumping into her with sure, steady, hard thrusts. Wrapping her legs around his hips, she dug her fingers into his buttocks, holding him close, urging him on. Every inch of her felt as though sparks were shooting from her. Their bodies became slick. Their moans and groans echoed around them.

The sensations built, tightened, then exploded. Fireworks burst behind her eyes as she cried out his name, heard him growl hers as he threw his head back with a final thrust.

Then he stilled. His breathing as harsh and heavy as hers. With a satisfied smile, he kissed the tip of her nose before rolling onto his side and bringing her flush against him.

"It's magnificent with light," she said breathlessly. "When I can see everything."

He chuckled low. "I should have a mirror installed above us for you."

She nipped at his nipple. "Maybe we'll just go to the Nightingale one night."

"If you like."

"Might be interesting."

"We'll go on the anniversary of your first visit."

She trailed her fingers along his chest. "Will you show me your private collection of photos sometime?"

"I burned them."

Rising on her elbow, she stared down on him. "Why?"

"Because I no longer needed them." He tucked her hair behind her ear. "They helped me deal with the images of carnage that I couldn't get out of my mind. I thought that if I could replace those images with perfect lines, I could conquer the nightmares. But it didn't work until you. As I told you, thoughts of you silence the horrors. So I had no need to keep the others."

"I should have liked to see them."

"I can re-create them with you as my model."

"If I pose for you, you must pose for me. Tit for tat."

Grinning, he threaded his fingers through her

hair, held her head. "My daring and wicked wife. Is it any wonder that I love you?"

Then he brought her down, captured her mouth, and plundered.

Wasn't love grand?

Epilogue

Several years later

STANDING on the sixth step of the stairs that led into the foyer, Ashe stared at the door through which he'd watched his parents leave. It was odd that the older he got, the more he missed them.

He wished they could see how he and Minerva had managed to turn their finances around with investments—and without touching the gift her father had given them for their wedding. It was merely held in reserve in case it was ever needed. Otherwise, since it wasn't part of the entailment, it would be divided among their children.

He wished they could have met Minerva, the rudder in his life. He had not thought it possible to love so thoroughly. There were times when the depth of his feelings for her scared the hell out of him. He'd hold her all the more tightly.

He wished they'd had an opportunity to know their grandchildren.

The patter of tiny feet echoed through the foyer as his son and daughter rushed to the front door, their mother following at a slower pace. She was once again with child.

"Papa, come on!" his burnished-hair daughter cried. "Grandfather promised to teach us how to pick pockets today."

Ashe scowled at Minerva. "Thought he was going to teach them how to avoid getting their pockets picked."

She shrugged a shoulder. "You know my father."

He started down the steps. "I suppose you'll teach them to cheat at cards."

"Lovingdon's son has already mastered it. We can't have our children at a disadvantage."

He slipped his arm around her. "How are you feeling?"

"Making progress. My breakfast stayed put."

"Come oonnn!" their son lamented. "Everyone will already be there."

All of Minerva's siblings and their families were meeting at her parents' residence to celebrate her parents' wedding anniversary.

"All right then," Ashe said. "Off we go."

The footman opened the door, and the children rushed out.

"Our children need to master patience," Ashe said, as he started to escort Minerva across the foyer.

"I prefer their enthusiasm."

"Then enthusiastic they shall be."

At the door, Ashe stopped and glanced back. Once the screams of his youth had haunted this place. But now all he heard was the laughter of his children, the joy in his wife's voice, and love.

Author's Note

ASHE suffered from a condition known as dyscalculia. It's similar to dyslexia, except that it involves the concept of numbers. I first learned of this condition many years ago when a friend's son was diagnosed with the condition. With the patient help of knowledgeable educators, he was able to learn how to work with numbers. This condition would not have been understood during Ashe's time.

As for the Nightingale Club, it is based on the Parrot Club, a house set up in the 1850s by three ladies who wanted a place to meet and share lovers. For this story, I took the liberty of expanding its purpose and its membership.